KITCHEN SURPRISE

Hayley crawled to her knees. What had she tripped over? She didn't know where the switch to the overhead lighting was, so she opened the oven door. The light inside came to life and illuminated a body sprawled out on the floor.

Hayley gasped.

It was a woman's body.

Hayley shook the left shoulder. "Karen, is that you? Are you okay?"

Then she remembered the wet and sticky substance on her hand.

Dear God. Please let it not be blood.

But it wasn't. It was milky and white. She smelled her palm. It was clam chowder.

Hayley placed her palm down on the stovetop and pulled herself up to her feet. The light from the oven was bright enough so that she could see the light switch next to the range. She reached over and snapped it on. A blinding light flooded the room and Hayley, squinting, stepped back away from the body.

She recognized Karen Applebaum instantly.

Even though the poor woman was facedown in a turquoise-colored porcelain bowl of New England clam chowder . . .

A Hayley Powell
Food & Cocktails Mystery

Death of a
Kitchen Diva

Lee Hollis

KENSINGTON PUBLISHING CORP.
http://www.kensingtonbooks.com

KENSINGTON BOOKS are published by

Kensington Publishing Corp.
119 West 40th Street
New York, NY 10018

All Kensington Titles, Imprints, and Distributed Lines are available at special quantity discounts for bulk purchases for sales promotions, premiums, fund-raising, and educational or institutional use.

Special book excerpts or customized printings can also be created to fit specific needs. For details, write or phone the office of the Kensington special sales manager: Kensington Publishing Corp., 119 West 40th Street, New York, NY 10018, attn: Special Sales Department, Phone: 1-800-221-2647.

Kensington and the K logo Reg. U.S. Pat & TM Off.

ISBN-13: 978-0-7582-6737-5
ISBN-10: 0-7582-6737-1

First Mass Market Printing: March 2012

10 9 8 7 6 5 4 3 2

Printed in the United States of America

Death of a
Kitchen Diva

Chapter 1

Hayley Powell stood at the stove in her tiny, cramped kitchen, which would embarrass any self-respecting chef, stirring her homemade mushroom Bolognese sauce with a wooden ladle, and wondering where the time had gone. It was three years to the day since her divorce was finalized. And the thought of dating again had never even crossed her mind. Until now.

Hayley had decided to take a chance and accept an invitation to dinner from a strapping six-foot-two, deep-voiced hunk of man who had been pursuing her. She had been dragging her heels, making up excuses like she wasn't emotionally ready, or work was too busy, or there was something going on with one of her kids. She had basically exhausted her supply of reasons to avoid going out with him.

So when her admirer kept pushing the issue, she finally gave up, threw her hands up in the air, and uttered that one dreaded word. "Yes."

And then she immediately agonized over it.

Why did she have to say something so stupid as "Yes"? Especially when "No" was so much easier. If she had just said "No," right now she would be curled up on her couch, petting Leroy, her dirty white Shih Tzu with a pronounced underbite, and sipping a Lemon Drop Martini, while settling in for a cheesy yet addictive Lifetime TV movie starring Jennifer Love Hewitt.

She turned the heat up on the burner and reached for a package of pasta shells to pour into another pot of boiling water, when the sauce bubbled up and splashed on her dress. Hayley stared numbly at the dripping stain for a moment. She refused to let this minor catastrophe get the best of her. No, Hayley thought to herself, she was going to remain calm and collected and solve this.

Think, Hayley, think. Club soda. There had to be some club soda in the fridge to blot out the stain. She crossed the kitchen and opened the refrigerator door just as her thirteen-year-old son, Dustin, strolled by, swigging down the last of the club soda and tossing the empty bottle into the recycle bin out on the porch of their small two-story house on a quiet neighborhood street.

"When's dinner? I'm starving," Dustin said, his eyes drooping as he scratched his blond hair, before wandering back into the living room to finish watching a rerun of *Family Guy*.

"Five minutes," Hayley said, desperately rearranging the items in the fridge to get a good look at everything, her hopes fading that she would find another bottle of club soda.

It was time to try something else. She hurried into the laundry room, only to find a giant pile of clothes on the washer, stacked so high her son's Superman T-shirt on top nearly touched the ceiling. She hadn't done a load in almost a week so finding another outfit that didn't smell like dirty socks and was not covered in dog hair was completely out of the question. Maybe she should cancel the date until she could get it cleaned.

Yes. That's what she would do.

Hayley looked up at the clock above the washer/dryer. It was already a quarter to seven. Her date was due to arrive in fifteen minutes. How rude would that be, canceling at the last minute? He'd just have to understand.

"Mom! Have you seen yourself in the mirror?" Hayley's fifteen-year-old daughter, Gemma, said as she burst through the front door just as Hayley hurried out of the laundry room.

"Is the stain that noticeable?"

Gemma glanced at the front of her mother's dress. "Yes. But I'm talking about your makeup. Did you let Jessica at the salon do your face again? You know she makes you look like a two-dollar hooker."

Gemma, still in her soccer uniform, her long blond hair pulled back in a ponytail, followed her mother into the kitchen and set her knapsack down on the counter. She opened it and pulled out a hand mirror and shoved it into Hayley's hand.

Hayley didn't want to see the damage. She knew it was going to be bad. But it was like coming upon a car wreck. You just can't help but look.

"Jesus wept!" Hayley cried. Her face was so caked with makeup she looked like something from Madame Tussaud's Wax Museum. The mascara was so dark it appeared she hadn't slept in weeks. And the Strawberry Frost lipstick Jessica had raved about made her lips look so big and fat, her date would probably be accused of punching her in the mouth before they were even seated at the restaurant.

"You're right, I can't go out looking like this." Suddenly the sauce stain on her dress seemed like an afterthought as she grabbed a dishrag from the counter and started furiously wiping the gunk off her face.

Gemma, who was fit and statuesque and already taller than her mother, steered her toward the staircase. "I'll finish making dinner. You go find something in my closet to wear."

"Your closet? I can't go out looking like a Gossip Girl," Hayley wailed.

Hayley hadn't gotten up three steps when a commercial came on the TV and Dustin, who never ever took his eyes off the television, happened to glance out the window.

"Somebody just pulled into the driveway," he said, then picked up the remote and started channel surfing.

"No, this isn't happening. He's early."

"By the way, it just started raining," Dustin said, cracking a smile.

"It's not funny. You know my hair frizzes when it rains," Hayley said.

Dustin nodded and then burst out laughing. "Yeah. You look like a Chia Pet!"

"You're so close to being grounded. Show some respect," Hayley warned but she knew it was pointless. Dustin was already doubled over, his face red, guffawing.

Gemma rushed out of the kitchen with two plates of shells and sauce sprinkled with some grated Parmesan cheese and handed one to her brother.

"Here's your dinner. Now scram and give Mom some space," Gemma said, grabbing the remote away from him with her free hand and shutting off the television. "And take Leroy."

The Shih Tzu had already sensed a car in the driveway and was yapping with all his might and running around in circles. Leroy talked a good game but he was a tiny wimp and could probably be taken out by a large Maine Coon cat.

Dustin reached down and scooped him up, then barreled past his mother with his dinner and disappeared upstairs to his room.

Gemma saw the panicked look on her mother's face and put down her plate on the coffee table and gave her a hug. "You look beautiful. Honest. You do."

Hayley wasn't quite ready to believe her.

Gemma smiled. "He didn't ask out your dress or your hair or your makeup. He asked *you* out. And you're great. So there's nothing to worry about."

"Stop it," Hayley said. "You'll make me cry."

"Good. Maybe it'll wash away some of that crap on your face," Gemma said as she picked up her dinner plate and bounded up the stairs.

"Tomorrow night we do a family dinner, just the three of us, at the dining room table. No more eating in your rooms and chatting with friends on the computer."

"Yes, Mother dear," Gemma said with her usual sarcastic tone as she slammed the door to her bedroom shut.

Hayley took a deep breath. She heard footsteps walking onto the front porch. She sucked her thumb and futilely tried to rub the stain out of her dress. No go. That sauce was there to stay. Her date would just have to deal with her disastrous appearance.

Of course, of all the men she could have gone out with, it would have to be Lex Bansfield.

Lex was tall, dark, sexy, and had a good job as a caretaker at one of the large sprawling seaside estates in the coastal tourist town of Bar Harbor, Maine, where they lived. He had only moved to the island four years ago, so he was still considered fresh meat by all the unattached women in town. And a few of the attached ones, too.

Hayley and Lex were planning to dine at Havana, an upscale Cuban restaurant at the end of Main Street, where the Obamas had dined when they vacationed in town one summer. Hayley and Lex would surely be spotted there by a few locals so she knew the whole town would be buzzing.

Hayley put on her brightest smile and opened the door. But Lex wasn't standing there for her to greet. It was two uniformed police officers. Both were young, no more than twenty-five, one tall and lanky, the other shorter and bald with a goatee. She instantly recognized both of them.

"Hi, Donnie. Hi, Earl," Hayley said, her smile

replaced with a look of confusion. "How can I help you?"

Hayley used to babysit both of them when they were little boys and she was a teenager. She couldn't believe how fast they had grown up. And she couldn't help but be surprised by the fact that both of them had become cops. Mostly because they were hell-raisers and a handful when she was put in charge of them—and she had expected them to both wind up in prison someday.

Donnie, the taller one, couldn't look Hayley in the eye. She noticed he was shaking a little bit. "We're here . . ."

He couldn't bring himself to say it.

"I'm in a bit of a rush so if you could just spit it out, please?" Hayley said.

Earl, the shorter one, cleared his throat and stepped forward. "We're here to place you under arrest, Mrs. Powell."

Hayley laughed. "I'm sorry, what?"

Earl unlatched some handcuffs from his belt. "You're under arrest."

Hayley still thought it was some kind of joke. "For what?"

"Murder," Donnie piped in, finally getting a little braver.

There was a stunned silence as Hayley processed what was happening. "This isn't funny, you guys."

"No, ma'am, it isn't," Donnie said as he gently turned her around. "Place your hands behind your back please, Mrs. Powell."

"You have the right to remain silent," Earl said as he snapped the handcuffs on Hayley. "You have the right to an attorney . . ."

Earl turned to Donnie. "Is that right? Is *attorney* next?"

"Yes, I think so," Donnie answered.

Hayley thought of her kids. She didn't want them to see their mother being carted off in handcuffs. She called out, "I'm leaving now! I won't be too late!"

She heard muffled grunts and replies from upstairs. They weren't really paying attention, and Hayley decided for once that was a good thing.

Donnie and Earl escorted Hayley toward a squad car, and she noticed a couple of neighbors peering out their windows, engrossed in all the action happening in her driveway. She thought it couldn't get any more humiliating.

And that's when Lex Bansfield pulled into the driveway in his jeep. He was wearing a nice blue dress shirt with a white T-shirt underneath, khaki pants, and shiny black shoes, a far cry from his usual Eddie Bauer work boots. He looked so handsome, and as he stepped out of the jeep with a shocked look on his face, Hayley noticed he was gripping a beautiful bouquet of red roses in his fist.

Hayley offered up her best smile. "Lex, would you mind if we postponed our date?"

Lex nodded, a little too stunned by the scene to reply.

"At least until I can make bail."

And with that, Officers Donnie and Earl stuffed Hayley into the back of their police cruiser and shut the door.

Chapter 2

One Week Earlier . . .

Hayley Powell was bored. She had been at the *Island Times*, one of two local newspapers in Bar Harbor, for almost four years. She loved the paycheck. Any single mother raising two kids and trying to keep a roof over their heads—even one that leaked into the dining room when it rained—would in this economy. A leaky roof on a house that still wasn't even completely paid for. A house in desperate need of a new coat of paint, with a front porch that had recently almost collapsed under the weight of her Shih Tzu Leroy. Yes, Leroy, who was barely ten pounds.

Okay, so the house wasn't in the best shape, but at least her car was running. A white Subaru Outback wagon with a brand-new transmission that cost her so much she now couldn't afford to buy new windshield wipers. Maybe there was a Native

American tribe nearby that would be willing to do some kind of dance to keep it from raining. You had to get creative when funds were low.

Making ends meet was becoming more and more of a challenge for Hayley, especially given her ex-husband's spotty track record with his child support checks. Danny Powell had been her high school sweetheart. Tall and good-looking. Wildly charismatic. She couldn't resist him. And as it turned out, not many other women could either. Tiger Woods could learn a thing or two from this guy.

After the divorce, Danny had moved to Iowa. He'd followed a girl half his age, who had dumped him within three weeks, but he'd decided to stay and make his fortune. In Iowa. Danny was never the brightest bulb in the chandelier.

Last she heard, he was a store manager at Target. With a steady job like that, you would think he could be on time with the check. But Danny was always a man of excuses, so Hayley stopped expecting him to come through on a regular basis, and tried to manage things on her own. Every cent she made went to new uniforms for Gemma's soccer team and art supplies and computer software for Dustin's budding career as a comic book artist.

But as the office manager at the daily paper, Hayley had the most duties to perform and made the least amount of money of anyone on staff. She spent her days putting out fires. Fielding phone calls from irate readers upset over the misspelling of their names when they appeared in the paper. Even in a blurb about their DWI charge in the

Police Beat section. Really? You actually want people to know the correct spelling of your name when you're arrested?

Then there were the reporters to deal with, who constantly argued over who got to cover what story. A high school football game was much more desirable than a city council meeting debating a new irrigation project. Who wouldn't rather be outdoors on a crisp, cool fall day?

And the Christmas party was a huge responsibility. With a paltry budget of a hundred dollars, Hayley was in charge of planning an elaborate office celebration featuring live carolers, a Secret Santa gift exchange, and an impressive set of goodies she would spend weeks baking and frosting. It had been a welcome change from that of her predecessor at the paper, who bought a box of wine and some stale sugar cookies, then absconded with the rest of the money and bought new ski boots at L.L. Bean.

There was no shortage of appreciation for all Hayley's hard work at the paper. She did her job with her usual trademark humor and good cheer. No complaints. Low maintenance. Her boss Sal Moretti, editor in chief, would always rub his eyes when tired and frustrated, and say, "At least Hayley is here to make sure this whole damn place doesn't fall apart."

Hayley repeated those words over and over in her head on the morning she marched into Sal's office to ask for a raise. It had taken her a whole week to work up the nerve. The only time Sal's temper flared seemed to be when someone asked him for more money.

Sal was a bit stocky, which made no sense considering that he hit the gym every morning, but he also had a sweet tooth and kept a stash of candy in his top drawer alongside a bottle of bourbon. He was also boisterous and loud, almost as loud as Hayley. Sal said it was because he was Italian. But others questioned his reasoning. Not all Italians have a wife who is partially deaf in one ear.

One night Sal and Hayley had stayed late at the office to finish putting the paper to bed to make up for a holiday, and someone called the police with a noise complaint. They said there was a party that was out of control at the *Island Times*. Probably fifty or sixty people. It was just Sal and Hayley and a couple of empty bottles of Blackstone Merlot.

Sal and Hayley talked in shorthand. After four years together, they had a routine and system on how to run the paper. In Hayley's mind, she was indispensable to the *Island Times*. And she prayed Sal would recognize that fact.

On her way into the office that day, she stopped at the coffeehouse next door for a hazelnut latte, which she knew was Sal's favorite. She handed it to him as she sat down in a creaky chair across from his desk.

Sal sipped his latte, his eyes closed, a smile on his face. "You're too good to me, Hayley."

"I know," Hayley said, taking a deep breath, drawing up her courage. "I need to talk to you."

Sal opened his eyes, a little wary over what might be coming. "I hate those six words. They seem so innocent at first but in the end they always manage to up the dosage of my blood pressure medication."

Sal put his coffee cup down and folded his arms. "Shoot. What is it?"

Hayley hesitated. She knew she had every right to ask for a raise. But she also knew the paper was struggling. Their rival across town had a larger readership, mostly because it had been the paper of record for Bar Harbor since the early 1900s. Sal was the upstart. He grew up in the town and wanted something new, something fresh, something different from the staid, boring news spoonfed to the locals. So after a stint writing for a large Boston paper, he had moved back home and started the *Island Times*. And now, ten years later, it was a worthy rival to the *Bar Harbor Herald*. But with the Internet and blogging and instant access to information, with newspapers across the country shutting down, or just going online, Sal knew he needed a new business model to keep up with the times, and to just survive.

"Hayley?" Sal leaned forward, a concerned look on his face.

Hayley was having severe second thoughts. She stood up. "Never mind. Now's not a good time."

She was halfway out the door when Sal said, "You can ask me anything. You know that."

Hayley stopped. He was right. Sal was her boss, but he was also her friend. She turned back around and decided to just go for it.

And then he added, "As long as you don't want a raise."

Hayley's face said it all. She just stood there frozen. Crushed.

Sal slumped down in his chair, shaking his head. "Oh, Hayley, I would love to give you anything you want, but you know I can't. Times are tough. We're barely above water here. Everybody deserves to be making more, but I just can't squeeze out a spare dime right now."

"I understand," Hayley said as she calculated in her head just how she was going to stretch her modest income a little more when it was already stretched so far it was ready to snap.

Even though he turned her down flat, Sal was a softie. And she knew it was killing him to see the look of despair on her face.

She tried to remain upbeat. "Not a problem."

Hayley spun around again and headed for the door.

"Wait," Sal said. "I may have an idea. Nothing big. Just a few extra dollars a week."

Hayley nodded, her excitement building.

"I'm sure you heard about Hattie Jenkins," Sal said, a solemn look on his face.

Hayley gasped, covering her mouth with her hand. "Oh, no. She died?"

Sal laughed. "Hell, no. She's already ninety-six. That old bag's going to outlive us all. She's retiring. Finally."

Hattie Jenkins had been a home and garden columnist for the *Bar Harbor Herald* since the 1940s, doling out helpful hints to housewives every week. She was an institution. So when the *Herald* fired her nine years ago for being old and outdated, there was a public outcry and Sal seized the opportunity and immediately put her on staff writing recipes.

"I can't believe Hattie is finally going to retire," Hayley said.

"Yeah, good news for everyone who likes their recipes without Spam as a main ingredient," Sal said. "I want you to take over the food and wine column."

"Me?" Hayley was floored. "I'm not a writer."

"Neither was Hattie," Sal said. "She could barely form a sentence. And that was before the short-term memory loss."

Hayley's mind raced. She was a whiz in the kitchen. All her friends told her so. They often said she would even make Martha Stewart proud. In fact, Hayley's house was usually saved for last during the monthly traveling potluck dinners because she could always be counted on to come up with the night's most mouthwatering favorite.

"This is nothing big," Sal said. "But it might help you out."

Hayley didn't have to think about it. She jumped at the offer. "I'll take it."

"Good," Sal said. "Now get out of my office."

Hayley was elated. She knew Hattie didn't make more than twenty-five bucks for each column. But maybe Sal would let her write two or three columns per week. She could sure use the extra cash.

As Hayley returned to her desk and sat down at her computer, she started to get nervous. People she knew were going to actually be reading what she wrote. What would she write about? What if she was a big flop? What if she was ridiculed and scorned as the worst writer in the history of journalism? Hattie may not have been Joyce Carol Oates, but she certainly had been a beloved figure in Bar Harbor for decades. And nobody likes a cheap imitation. Was a little extra spending money really worth risking her reputation in town?

Chapter 3

Hayley's mind raced as she made a quick stop at the Shop 'n Save on her way home from work to load up a cartful of ingredients. She had a lot of research to do. She wanted to get started right away by trying out a few recipes. She knew since this was a Maine newspaper her first column should probably have something to do with seafood. Maybe mussels. Or some kind of shrimp dip. Some interesting, fun, easy-to-make appetizer.

Still, it was one thing cooking for friends. But the whole town? What if people tried her recipes and then wrote letters of complaint? Maybe taking over for Hattie was a huge mistake. She needed some advice. So after paying for her groceries, she headed over to Drinks Like A Fish, a happy hour hot spot on Cottage Street, one of the three main streets in town. The bar also happened to be owned by her brother, Randy, who always had opinions about everything, and would make the ideal sounding board for this new development at the paper.

Hayley had already called her two best friends to join her for an after-work cocktail, so she was anxious to hear their take as well. She knew she had some time to hang out with her friends. Gemma was at an away game in Bucksport and Dustin was staying over at his friend Lenny's house to play video games.

Hayley parked the car in the Rite Aid parking lot three blocks from the bar (there was a spot in front but Hayley had never learned how to properly parallel park). She scurried past the last few remaining tourists of the season strolling the streets now that Labor Day had come and gone. Now the shops had only the occasional cruise ship that would arrive in the harbor throughout the fall and spill passengers out for an hour or two at a time.

Hayley blew into Drinks Like A Fish to find Randy behind the bar, wiping it down with a wet rag. There were a couple of college kids at the other end playing darts, and sitting atop two stools near the front were Liddy Crawford and Mona Barnes, her BFFs since kindergarten.

On the surface, the bar looked upscale with finished wood and leather bar stools and booths, soft lighting, and an overall tasteful décor. But nobody was ever fooled about this place for long. The clientele made the place what it really was, and many drunken fishermen smelling of trout and cigars were dragged out by the cops for disorderly conduct on pretty much every night of the week.

Hayley squeezed in between Liddy and Mona, and waved at Randy. "I need a Cosmo, pronto."

"Cosmo, Hayley? Really?" Liddy stared at Hayley incredulously. "*Sex and the City* was canceled years ago. Try a Lemon Drop Martini. Same as me."

Hayley opened her mouth to protest but knew it wouldn't do any good. Liddy had been bossy ever since she learned to talk. And she always managed to get her own way. It was no surprise she wound up a glamour puss real estate agent with a bunch of million dollar oceanfront listings. Some people were put off by her sometimes stinging directness and loud opinions, but they were mostly men who were threatened by her incredible financial success.

"Make that two, Randy," Liddy said, as she pulled out a hand mirror and checked her makeup. She always looked impeccable. Her twice a year New York shopping trips kept her in the latest fashions. Dr. Feingold, whose office was an hour away in Bangor, kept those wrinkles forming under her eyes at bay. And she had a standing Friday morning appointment with Carole, a local girl who managed to make the final cut as a contestant on Bravo's hair design reality show *Shear Genius.* She didn't win, but the notoriety made her somewhat of a local celebrity, so Liddy wouldn't have anyone else touch her lush auburn curls.

"Randy, I'll have some water. No fancy bottled crap. Tap is fine," Mona said.

"Mona, I'm stunned. What happened to Bud in a can?" Liddy said, one eyebrow raised.

"Can't," Mona said with a shrug.

They all knew what this meant.

"Oh, no," Liddy wailed. "Not again."

"Couldn't be helped," Mona said, rubbing her eyes with her fists. "I swore I was done but you know how Dennis is. We could be in the middle of a nor'easter and he'd still be in heat."

"You already have five rug rats!" Liddy said.

"That's right. What's one more? Congratulations, Mona," Hayley said, giving her a warm, tight hug.

"Thanks," Mona said. "I'm gonna kill Dennis."

"At least it'll stop you from getting pregnant again," Randy said, smiling as he delivered the drinks to the three women.

"Pretty soon you're going to be like that awful lady on TV with the eight kids and that hideous outdated haircut," Liddy said, taking a long, satisfying sip of her martini.

"I'll never be like her because I don't give a crap what my hair looks like," Mona said.

"We know, honey," Liddy said. "It's painfully obvious."

Liddy and Mona sometimes pretended not to like each other. But they had been friends for so long, their sparring was like a warm blanket. Comforting and familiar. And everyone knew if one was in trouble, the other would be the first on the scene.

Liddy was a success, but Mona was, too, in her own right. She was the owner of a lobstering business that had been passed down for generations in her family. Mona worked her butt off four months out of the year during the tourist season selling lobsters to restaurants and the private estates on the island, and then she would kick back and enjoy the fruits of her labor during the winter months. She tried going to Florida, but missed her hometown too much, even during the freezing cold blizzards that were commonplace in the early part of the year.

Despite her thriving business, Mona lacked even an ounce of pretension. She was always in a sweatshirt (usually with some dirty joke on the front) and faded jeans and work boots. She wasn't lying about her hair. She did it herself, cutting it into almost a pageboy look. And her fresh-scrubbed face was free of any makeup. She just didn't want to be bothered. And she refused to trade in her beat-up Dodge pickup for anything newer. Why would she? The truck got her where she needed to go.

She met her husband, Dennis, when he blew into town on his motorcycle after a stint in Iraq and got a job working on her father's lobster boat. But an accident involving his leg getting caught in a trap left him on permanent disability, so now Mona was the sole breadwinner for her family.

"Isn't anyone besides me curious to know why Hayley called this meeting of the minds?" Randy said as he poured himself a shot of tequila.

"Right. Enough about me," Mona said. "I hate talking about me."

"I've never understood that," Liddy said, without a trace of irony.

There was an uncomfortable silence. Finally, Hayley cleared her throat. "Okay, I went in to Sal today and asked for a raise."

"That's right," Randy said. "You told me you were getting up the nerve. So what happened?"

"He said no."

"You run that place," Liddy said. "He just doesn't appreciate you the way he should. Let me talk to him. Do you know how much I pay in advertising? I should be a shareholder! He'll listen to me."

"Thanks, Liddy, but no, there just isn't any money in the budget," Hayley said. "He did say, however, I could take over Hattie's food and wine column."

Another uncomfortable silence.

"She's retiring. I know. Bad idea. I mean, where do I get off thinking I can be a writer?"

"No," Randy protested. "I was just thinking how great it will be to finally have a column in the paper I actually look forward to reading."

God love Randy. He was Hayley's number one fan. The two of them had fought like cats and dogs when they were kids. Over everything. Then, during their teen years they simply ignored each other. Hayley partied with her friends. And Randy just wanted to stay home to watch his idol Tori Spelling on *Beverly Hills, 90210.*

Needless to say, after high school, Randy moved to New York to become an actor. He attended the prestigious Academy of Dramatic Arts, did a few Off-Off-Off-Broadway plays, and scored one United Airlines commercial playing a smiling, helpful flight attendant. Then he came out of the closet. Hayley was incredibly supportive except for the fact that Randy told their mother before he told her, which she took personally. Who tells his uptight mother before his cool worldly sister? But she forgave him.

Randy always expected to live in a big city where he would be free and accepted, but he desperately missed the small-town life, and it was Hayley who convinced him he could live openly in Bar Harbor. Besides, the town had just passed a gay rights ordinance to draw more tourists with diverse lifestyles. Randy worked as a stock boy at the Shop 'n Save for a while, saved his money, applied for a business loan from the Bar Harbor Bank and Trust because he gave the loan officer her first kiss back in seventh grade (it must have been good because the loan was approved), and opened his bar. Ten years later, Drinks Like A Fish was a local staple and very profitable for Randy and his boyfriend of ten years, Sergio.

So Hayley was with the three most important people in her life—besides her two kids—and was waiting to hear what they had to say about this new, exciting but scary opportunity.

"So, Liddy, say something," Hayley said anxiously.

"There really isn't anything to say," Liddy said.

"Then you think I shouldn't do it?" Hayley said.

"Of course you should," Randy shouted from the other end of the bar where he was serving the college kids another round of beer on tap.

"I'm just surprised they didn't ask me," Liddy said, shifting in her seat, clearly perturbed she was overlooked for the job.

"You don't cook," Hayley said.

"I know. But I have impeccable taste. Who wouldn't want to read what I have to say about entertaining?"

Mona raised her hand and Liddy quickly slapped it down.

"I think you should go for it, Hayley," Mona said. "And who knows? Maybe somebody besides me and your brother might actually read it."

High praise indeed.

Chapter 4

Hayley stared at the blank computer screen. She had been sitting there for well over an hour, her paper cup of coffee long since swallowed, tiny beads of sweat forming on her brow. She chalked it up to Bar Harbor experiencing one of the hottest fall seasons on record. Temperatures in the low nineties with stifling humidity.

But no, it wasn't the weather. It was nerves. She had no idea what to write about. After testing some appetizers at home, she knew which one she wanted to use to kick off the column. Maybe build up to a main course dish and then finish off with a cool refreshing dessert. Do seven courses over the next couple of weeks. Made sense. Readers would have a full-course meal to try out at their next dinner party. She was beginning to doubt she'd even get to the salad course before Sal fired her and replaced her with someone who knew what she was doing.

Hayley couldn't just jot down the recipe and be done with it. She had to talk about something first. Introduce herself. A lot of the locals already knew her, but there were visitors to the island who had no idea what her qualifications to write this column were.

Probably because she had none.

Hayley needed more coffee. And her break was coming up, so she knew she could kill some more time by running a few errands, like buying stamps at the post office and running home to let the dog out so he could do his business. Wait. She was just delaying the inevitable. No. She was going to sit here and not get up until she had at least written the opening sentence.

Tick. Tick. Tick.

The phone rang and she lunged for it.

"Island Times," Hayley chirped, grateful for the distraction.

It was Liddy, placing an ad for her latest listing. But really she was just calling to gossip about the dirt she picked up while getting a facial at the local beauty shop.

"Guess whose husband came home from a trip out of town early to find his wife in bed with a local contractor who was putting a new roof on their house?"

Hayley feigned interest, but her mind was elsewhere. This was torture. She should just march into Sal's office and remove herself immediately from this potentially humiliating situation.

Liddy would've prattled on for at least an hour if Hayley didn't stop her. "Liddy, I really need to hang up. Sal wants this column by three. We're going to press."

"Our little Hayley has her first deadline. That's so adorable," Liddy cooed.

"I need it by noon!" Sal bellowed from the back office, clearly eavesdropping on her conversation.

Hayley dropped the phone and could faintly hear Liddy still chattering away. "Noon? You said three."

"I'm going fishing with Bruce on Long Pond and want to leave early today, so you better come up with something. And fast," Sal yelled.

Hayley pictured him in the other room, smiling, enjoying the fact that he was adding pressure to her already frayed nerves. She knew exactly what he was doing. Sal was old school. Pounding out a story in two minutes and racing it over to the printing press. He always did his best work while under the gun. Deadline looming. He loved the chaos of big-city newspaper reporting. Unfortunately, he didn't realize when he moved back to Bar Harbor to start his own paper that things never moved quite so quickly on the quiet coast of Maine. And this kind of tactic was not going to work on Hayley. Or was it?

Suddenly, after what seemed like an eternity, Hayley just started typing. She had to write something. And whatever came to mind was certainly better than a blank page. So she wrote. And kept writing. And before she knew it, she was writing the recipe. And then she was done.

Hayley read it over for typos and then e-mailed it to Sal. She could have made a big production of printing it out and delivering it in person, but she was too scared about his reaction. What if he hated it? She would just have to stand there as he read it,

and then get screamed at for doing such a lousy
job. But what if he actually liked it? What if her
fears were dead wrong? She thought the column
was kind of cute. Maybe he would find it charming.
As it turned out, her first instinct was right.

"What the hell is this?" Sal hollered as he came
bounding out of his office. Sal was a big guy, so
the fact that he actually stood up from his desk
and walked all the way out to the front office to
yell at her meant he really, really hated it.

"I can't print this!"

"Why not?"

"It's all about your personal life. Where the hell
are the recipes?"

"I include them at the end."

"This isn't supposed to be about you. Or your
dog. You spend half the column talking about
your dog, Leroy! This is a cooking column. For
people who want to cook. Not read some precious
diary entry."

That's when Sal's fishing date, Bruce Linney,
blew through the door.

Oh, great. Bruce. Just what Hayley needed.

Bruce was the crime reporter for the paper.
Which meant he was only a part-time employee, because there wasn't that much crime in Bar Harbor
to cover. A lot of women in town found Bruce to be
a stud. Especially when he would put on a Speedo
to go biking around Eagle Lake shirtless. Women,
including Liddy, would actually hike the six miles
around the lake just to catch a glimpse of him
zooming by on his mountain bike. He was muscu-
lar, with close-cropped brown hair, always with

some stubble on his face, and a pair of puppy dog brown eyes that made a girl's heart melt.

Hayley didn't get the appeal. *I mean, sure he was good-looking,* she thought, *but then he would open his mouth.* It was like getting hit in the face with a bucket of cold water. And he loved the sound of his own voice.

Bruce believed he had the most important job at the paper, which Hayley found annoying. But mostly, she couldn't stand the fact that the two of them had dated briefly in high school when he and Hayley had been paired as lab partners in biology. Hayley was terrible in science and when the class was surprised with a pop quiz, she didn't know one answer, so she winged it and wrote down whatever came to mind. The teacher told them to exchange papers with their partners so they could each grade the other's paper. When she got hers back, she had an A. Bruce had changed all her answers to the right ones so she wouldn't fail.

Okay, not the most noble reason to fall in love, but fall she did. Hard. For about a week. Until she discovered he was dating three other girls, one in algebra, one in typing, one in drivers' ed. And all of them scoring A's on their pop quizzes.

Despite the death of their torrid affair (Hayley at least let him get to second base), there had been some lingering sexual tension between them ever since. Hayley insisted it was just indigestion. There was no way she could ever have feelings for Bruce Linney. Ever.

"Ready to go, Sal?" Bruce said, eyeing Hayley with a smile. "Looking good, babe."

Hayley was too busy trying not to burst into

tears over Sal's horrible reaction to her column to acknowledge the compliment.

"I can't go," Sal said, sighing. "Hayley royally screwed up her first column and now I have to walk her through the basics of journalism."

Bruce shook his head. "Why do you need a cooking column anyway? It just takes up space. You should've canceled it the second old lady what's-her-name announced her retirement."

"People like Hattie's column, Bruce," Hayley said, her cheeks burning with anger. "I get calls all the time from her fans."

"Blue-haired ladies with nothing better to do," Bruce sneered. "Has nothing to do with what's really going on in the world."

"Maybe people want to be entertained sometimes instead of getting hammered constantly by bad news," Hayley said.

Bruce ignored her. "You should be focused more on hard news, Sal. Forget the fluff."

"Hard news?" Hayley laughed. "Your last two *hard news* scoops were a stolen moped and a sting to arrest Mrs. Sheldon on Hancock Street for refusing to curb her Labradoodle."

"A two hundred dollar fine is nothing to sneeze at, Hayley," Bruce said proudly. "She won't be messing up my lawn again."

"You know the only reason Bruce is pushing for more crime reporting is so you'll make him a full-time employee and he can finally get health benefits," Hayley said.

"Don't listen to her, Sal," Bruce said. "One of these days something big is going to happen in this town, and you won't have me around to cover it. Now, are we going fishing or what?"

Sal furrowed his brow, debating with himself.

"Come on," Bruce said. "Just print what she wrote. It's one column. If you get a complaint, then it will be cause to celebrate. That means one person read it."

"Yeah, you're probably right," Sal said. "It's not like one bad column will stink up the whole paper."

"In case you two have forgotten," Hayley said, glaring at the two of them, "I'm sitting right here."

"Okay, Hayley, you win," Sal said, putting on his Red Sox baseball cap and grabbing a fishing pole from the hall closet. "We'll run it as written, but I want it buried in the back of the issue. And from now on you write recipes. And only recipes. Plain and simple. Got that?"

"Yes, fine," Hayley said, feeling like a complete and utter failure.

Despite her fantasies of becoming the Maureen Dowd of Down East Maine, it was becoming painfully clear that Hayley's career as a newspaper columnist was going to be astonishingly short-lived.

Island Food & Spirits

by
Hayley Powell

First of all, for those of you who haven't heard the news yet, I would like to announce that our own Food & Wine columnist, Ms. Hattie Jenkins, is retiring after many wonderful years of writing mouthwatering recipes for all us lucky island residents. Good luck, Hattie! It will be truly hard following in your footsteps, but I will try my best!

So last night after I got home from work, I was in my kitchen trying to unwind, which I'd like to add here is not always the case when my Shih Tzu Leroy is barking at every passing dog out the open window and I'm yelling at him, "This is why you don't have any friends!" I honestly think I've seen some of the dog owners roll their eyes as they walk past our house.

Anyway, now I've got to come up with another idea for dinner. And it's not easy when you have kids with completely different tastes in food—one won't eat anything but pasta and the other has a more sophisticated palate. And she's the one who will be coming home within the hour from soccer practice demanding a time check on when her dinner will be ready because she is absolutely starving! It's a lot of pressure for one single working mother to take.

So to relax and regroup, I made myself a great Lemon Drop Martini, which I tried for the first time with my friends the other day after work at the Drinks Like A Fish bar right here in town, and let me tell you, I ran right out and bought a martini shaker and glasses because this is my new favorite beverage. I'll share the recipe with you later on.

Anyway, as I was still trying to come up with a dinner idea for my two hungry teens and enjoying my second martini (and let me say once again these are really wonderful drinks!), I happened to hear on my police scanner that four visitors from "out of state" were in distress and very sick at the Jordan Pond House, our lovely tea and popover restaurant in the heart of Acadia National Park. They had made their way there after coming out of the woods where they had been picking and eating wild mushrooms. Who on earth from "away" would actually come here and try to eat wild mushrooms unless they knew something about them?

I must admit I should have felt sorry for them, but it gave me a good chuckle for the night as I sipped on my Lemon Drop. Oh, and in case you were wondering, all of them survived, but won't be straying too far from their RV toilet anytime soon.

It struck me that for my first recipe this week, I have a great crab stuffed mushroom appetizer recipe to share with you! The perfect starter for any New England dinner party. And many thanks to the four people from away for helping me come up with this idea for my first recipe column! So enjoy your Lemon Drop Martini with this tasty appetizer. And remember, don't go looking for your mushrooms out in the woods. It's easier and safer to just pick some up at our local supermarket.

Lemon Drop Martini

Three parts vodka to one part simple syrup (equal amounts of sugar and water dissolved together by simmering briefly) and one part lemon juice; fresh is best but not necessary. Simmer lemon rind in with the simple syrup, or use ginger or whatever to add flavor. So if you use 1 cup of vodka, you would add ⅓ cup of lemon juice and ⅓ cup simple syrup (I always go a bit lighter on the simple syrup because I like a tart flavor).

Maine Crab Stuffed Mushrooms

8 Tablespoons (1 stick) unsalted butter
1 small onion, minced
1 clove garlic, minced
2 pounds large mushrooms, stems
    removed and chopped (buy them from
    your local store)
¼ cup dry sherry
½ stack Ritz crackers, crushed
1 Tablespoon minced parsley
½ pound fresh Maine crabmeat
Freshly ground pepper and salt to taste
Freshly grated Parmesan cheese

Heat oven to 350.

Melt the butter in a large skillet over medium heat. Add the onion, garlic, and chopped mushroom stems. Sauté until the onions are transparent. Add the sherry and cook for 2 minutes more. Remove from the heat and add the cracker crumbs and parsley. Fold in the crabmeat. Add salt and pepper to taste. Mound the crabmeat mixture onto each mushroom cap and top with a bit of Parmesan cheese. Bake until the cheese turns golden and the mushrooms are cooked through, about 15 minutes. Serve warm.

Chapter 5

Sal Moretti was never one to admit he was wrong. He would probably rather have a wisdom tooth extracted. Twice. But when the paper hit the stands and appeared online with Hayley's first column, the avalanche of e-mails, letters, and phone calls from new fans of Hayley Powell was just too much to ignore. People liked Hayley talking about her dog Leroy. Hearing about the tourists who ate the poisoned mushrooms was a kick. And so typical of tourists. And more than a few ran out to the Shop 'n Save to load up on the ingredients so they could make that cool tasty refreshing Lemon Drop Martini. It was also reported that the produce section ran out of mushrooms because too many shoppers wanted to try out Hayley's Maine Crab Stuffed Mushrooms recipe.

"Fine. You were right. People like that crap," Sal said, taking a big bite of a poppy seed bagel smeared with cream cheese and washing it down with a cup of black coffee.

Hayley stood in his office doorway, trying to act

nonchalant, but inside feeling euphoric. "I'll take that as a compliment."

"Don't get too cocky, and I'm telling you right now, they can give you a Pulitzer Prize for all I care, I'm not paying you a cent over fifty dollars per column," Sal said, wiping some spilled cream cheese off his blue shirt with a napkin.

"Absolutely. Understood."

"Now get out of my office and get to work on your next column."

Hayley returned to her desk and sat down. The sales department (which was basically one person, Eddie Farley, who sat in the back and watched Fox News all day on his portable TV that he kept hidden in a desk drawer) e-mailed Hayley to let her know the paper was on track to enjoy a fifteen percent sales boost that week. And he was convinced it was because word was spreading about Hayley's entertaining musings.

Hayley glanced out the window to see Bruce Linney pull up in front of the building. She'd heard on the police scanner that there was a break-in at Razor Rick's Barber Shop the night before, so Bruce had been out most of the night following up leads and interviewing the cops. He looked beat, especially since he had been out fishing with Sal late and then worked all night.

She didn't expect him to be in a good mood, but he was more distracted and short-tempered than usual.

"Morning, Bruce," Hayley chirped, keeping things light and pleasant.

He grunted his reply, and marched into the back toward the desk he shared with the arts and leisure editor, a kid who was barely out of high school and only did the job part time when she was home from college. There was even less arts and leisure to cover in Bar Harbor than crime, especially with the busy summer season winding down.

Eddie, who never liked Bruce and let him know it at last year's Christmas party after too much bourbon-spiked eggnog, was itching to rib him about Hayley's successful first column. Hayley winced as she heard Eddie shuffle over to Bruce, who was at the coffee machine pouring himself a cup.

"Looks like we have a new star here at the *Island Times*," Eddie said.

"Don't start with me, okay? I've been up all night," Bruce growled.

"I saw Hattie Jenkins this morning. She was with that group of seniors who wear the red hats and hike around town before dawn."

"So?"

"Even she said she loved Hayley's column," Eddie said, nudging Bruce. "Big dog lover, I guess. Plus, I hear Hattie likes to tip a few while watching Diane Sawyer, so she probably loved that Lemon Drop Martini recipe, too."

"Are you going to bore me all day talking about Hayley's column or are you going to go out and sell some ad space before this whole paper goes under?"

"Sounds to me like somebody's jealous."

Hayley couldn't take anymore. She jumped to her feet, and called out to Sal, "I'm going to go withdraw some petty cash at the bank. Be back in five."

And she was out the door.

Hayley couldn't help but be happy about people actually reading, let alone liking, her column, but she certainly didn't want to upset the reporters in the office. She decided to downplay it, and just get through the day doing her real job, serving as the paper's office manager. She didn't really need to drive to the bank. It was only a few blocks away. But it was sweltering and humid, and her hair was already starting to frizz like a Chia Pet, according to her son.

Was Bruce really jealous? The idea made her chuckle. He had been a journalism major at the University of Maine in Orono. He had worked for a major Bangor paper before moving back to the island and taking over the crime beat for Sal. How could he possibly be threatened by her? And why was she wasting her time thinking about Bruce now anyway? She should be enjoying her fifteen minutes of fame. Not focusing on some old high school fling who didn't really like her anyway. No, she was going to forget about Bruce.

And it was a good thing, too, because as she raced into the bank someone else immediately became the focus of her attention. Someone who looked a lot more put out with her than Bruce.

Karen Applebaum.

Karen was the cooking columnist for the *Times*' rival paper, the *Bar Harbor Herald*. Karen was very prim and proper, always dressed to the nines, and had the hint of a British accent, even though she was born and raised in town, and didn't even have a passport. Karen fancied herself a local institution, running sewing circles and scrapbook clubs, and went all out when it came to bake sales and fundraisers. She was in her early fifties and knew everything that went on in town. But the one thing that got by her until today was that the *Times* was going to introduce a new food and wine columnist.

Hayley could see the storm clouds gathering.

Karen had enjoyed little competition from Hattie Jenkins, who she laughed at for peddling her tired and tasteless green bean casserole and ambrosia salad staples. In fact, Karen was instrumental in getting Hattie bounced from the *Herald* for being out of step with the times, and then she wasted no time in offering herself up as a replacement. There was never any love lost between the two.

When word got out that Hattie was retiring, Karen just assumed the *Times* would let the column die a quick, deserved death. And then she would be the premier voice when it came to cooking and entertaining and arts and crafts. So it came as a rather rude awakening when Hayley blew onto the scene so quickly and stole her thunder.

And it was especially tense this early morning in the bank when the hefty, sweet as pie bank teller Pam Innsbrook, with her bright smile and cherubic face, looked up and practically screamed at the sight of Hayley.

"Hello, Hayley! I loved your column. I can't wait to read it next week! I have a Chihuahua named Cricket who drives me crazy, too!"

"Thank you so much, Pam," Hayley said, feeling Karen Applebaum's eyes burning a hole in the back of her head.

Hayley just wanted to get out of there, but Pam was taking her sweet time counting out the money for Hayley.

"I'm going to try and make your Crab Stuffed Mushrooms tonight, but it's already been a long day, so I may add a full cup of dry sherry instead of a quarter cup," Pam said giddily. "I can't believe I've lived in Maine all my life and never made Maine Stuffed Crab Mushrooms. Isn't that the craziest?"

This was interminable. Karen was standing directly behind Hayley. It would be awkward to ignore her, so when Pam finally handed the cash over to her, Hayley scooped it up, stuffed it into an envelope, and twirled around, plastering on her biggest, friendliest, warmest smile.

"Good morning, Karen," Hayley said. "How have you been?"

The whole bank was watching.

Karen looked at Hayley, her stone face giving nothing away. Then, she stepped around Hayley and slapped a check down on the counter.

"I'd like to deposit this, please, Pam," Karen said flatly. "And I'm in a bit of a hurry, if you don't mind, so I don't have a lot of time for chitchat."

There wasn't a sound in the bank. Karen had completely snubbed Hayley.

Hayley kept the smile plastered on her face, but her cheeks were red, and it was obvious she was embarrassed. Hayley looked straight ahead and marched out of the bank, refusing to give Karen the benefit of causing a scene. Hayley had certainly made a few enemies in town over the years. Who wouldn't, living in the same place your whole life? But Karen Applebaum was someone you just didn't mess with. She had a vicious mean streak. It was not a good idea to get on her bad side.

Gemma's favorite Disney movie growing up was *Sleeping Beauty,* and Hayley always thought the evil witch—who pricked Princess Aurora's finger and sent her reeling into a years' long coma before turning herself into a fire-breathing dragon to take on the prince at the end of the movie—always bore a faint resemblance to Karen Applebaum. So this was a potentially disastrous situation. Her day was off to an ominous start. But she had no idea at the time it was about to get a whole lot worse.

Especially when she hit that poor man with her car.

Chapter 6

Hayley hurried out of the bank, jumped into her Subaru wagon, and peeled out of her parking space, heading straight back down Main Street to the office. Her mind was on Karen Applebaum, and how rude she had been.

She was also thinking about her next column. What would she write about? And speaking of food, what would she feed the kids for dinner? Her head was so full of random thoughts she just didn't see the man step into the crosswalk. And the next thing she knew, he was staring at her through the windshield on top of her hood. Then when she instinctively slammed on the brakes, he rolled off and hit the pavement, because he didn't have a good enough grip on her windshield wiper.

Throwing open the driver's side door and screaming, Hayley raced over to the man, who was now standing up, his pant leg torn, and his knee bloodied.

"Oh my God, are you all right?" Hayley screamed.

"I'm fine. Just a small cut," the man said, wiping gravel off his plaid shirt.

"I need to get you to the hospital," Hayley screamed.

"You need to calm down and stop screaming. I'm okay."

But Hayley was already steering the man toward the passenger side of her car. Despite his protests, she physically shoved him in the car, slammed the door shut, scurried back around to jump behind the wheel, and tore off toward the hospital.

"Slow down or you're going to hit somebody else," the man said, buckling himself in for the roller-coaster ride.

Hayley glanced down at the man's bloodied knee. "I can't believe I did that."

The man put a comforting hand on her shoulder. "I think I'm going to live."

She felt a charge from his gentle touch, but she kept her eyes on the road. "We'll let a doctor decide that."

Hayley knew who the man was. Lex Bansfield. The caretaker at the Hollingsworth estate. The Hollingsworth family became filthy rich from a line of frozen seafood dinners, and had purchased a sprawling property along the shore with lush gardens, a stone mansion, and several guest houses, including the one where Lex lived that was twice the size of Hayley's tiny two-story structure with the leaking roof.

Lex was tall, a good foot and a half taller than Hayley, and he had dirty blond hair that was thick and wavy. Most women who met him imagined running their fingers through it. Hayley included.

He had an easy comforting smile and at the moment was using it to try and get Hayley to relax a little bit. But she was so frazzled she barely remembered to switch on her blinker as she took a sharp right and roared up Hancock Street toward the hospital's emergency entrance.

"Please tell me you're not taking me around back to the emergency entrance," Lex groaned.

"You may have a concussion from the fall," Hayley said. "We're not taking any chances."

Hayley nearly sideswiped a parked ambulance as she squealed up to the large glass doors, and jumped back out of the car to escort Lex inside. He was halfway out the door by the time she got to him. She took him by the arm, and to her surprise, he didn't try to shake her off. She couldn't decide if he needed her help to walk or he just liked her touching him.

Once inside, Hayley pounded on the desk, demanding Lex be seen right away. A burly balding orderly barreled around the corner with a wheelchair and a clipboard full of paperwork.

"I'm not sitting down in that thing," Lex scoffed.

But he barely got the words out before Hayley shoved him down in the wheelchair and they were rolling him off down a long hallway to get checked out by a doctor.

Lex called back to Hayley. "Could you call my boss, Edgar Hollingsworth, and tell him I'm going to be back a little late?"

"You don't worry about a thing," Hayley said. "I'll take care of everything."

Hayley whipped out her cell phone and immediately called the Hollingsworth estate. She got a

maid on the phone, and was told Mr. Hollingsworth and his grandson were out boating but
would be back in an hour and she would give
them the message.

Then Hayley called Sal at the paper to explain
her delay in coming back to the office from the
bank.

Once the calls were made, Hayley's thoughts
went to more pressing matters. What if Lex Bansfield sued her for mowing him down with her car?
She was barely hanging on by a thread financially
at the moment, and the last thing she needed was
an expensive civil lawsuit. And what if she was
charged with reckless driving? Neither one of her
kids had their driver's license yet. How would she
get them to and from all their school activities?
No, she was not going to start worrying until there
was something to actually start worrying about.

And then she went back to worrying.

Hayley waited about forty-five minutes for an
update on Lex's condition before she noticed her
stomach growling, so she told a nurse where she
was going and wandered down the hall to the hospital cafeteria for something to eat.

There wasn't much of a selection. Some stale-
looking ham and cheese sandwiches slathered
with mayo. Tiny boxes of sugary cereals and a few
pint-size milk cartons sitting atop a serving bowl
full of ice. She was about to give up when she noticed a large round silver canister with a matching
cover on top. There was a strip of masking tape on
the cover with "New England Clam Chowder"
scrawled over it in magic marker.

Classy joint.

Hayley picked up a ladle, took the top off, and served herself a small bowl. She had barely eaten her first spoonful when she realized she had made a terrible mistake. The chowder was pasty and bland and the one small piece of clam she got was rubbery and disgusting. Hayley looked around to make sure no one was watching, and dumped the whole thing into the garbage can near the register. She knew a much better recipe for New England clam chowder.

Maybe that would be her next column.

Lex ambled around the corner looking for her. She could see a white bandage wrapped around his knee through the big tear in his pants. He smiled as he approached her.

"Doctor said it's a good thing you brought me in when you did because I might not have made it."

"Seriously?" Hayley's mouth dropped open.

"No, I'm teasing," he said. "It's nothing. Just a scratch."

There was an awkward moment. Hayley hated those moments and usually filled them with endless chatter.

"I am so sorry again for what happened."

"I know you are."

"There was no excuse for my bad driving, and I don't know what to say except . . ."

"Listen, there's something I need to ask . . ."

"Please, please don't sue me!"

"Say what?"

"I'm a single mother with two growing kids, an astronomical heating bill in the winter, and a car that barely gets me to work without overheating. I have insurance but my payments have been spotty mostly because I used up my savings to send my daughter, Gemma, to soccer camp in July, but I promise I will make it up to you. You name it. I'll do it. I'll come work part time for you at the Hollingsworth estate raking leaves, or watering plants, or walking their dogs. Anything."

"How about you go out with me?"

Hayley was stunned. This was not what she was expecting. And it threw her.

She didn't know how to respond. She wanted to say yes. But she had been through such a stressful morning, and she hadn't been out on a date in so long, and she was in such a confused state at the moment that she heard herself say, "No, I don't think that's such a good idea right now."

Really? Did she actually just turn him down? What was she thinking?

She opened her mouth to retract her rejection when a voice called out from behind them, "Ouch!"

Both Lex and Hayley spun around to see Edgar Hollingsworth and his grandson Travis walking down the corridor toward them.

Edgar was in his early seventies and had somewhat of a hunchback, white thinning hair, and a long face with a pronounced nose, and there was almost a grayish hue to his complexion. He wasn't the most handsome older man on the island, but he didn't have to be. He was worth three hundred million. He was also grouchy and a man of few words.

His grandson Travis, on the other hand, was young, probably mid-twenties, sexy, well built, and ten times more charismatic than his grandfather. He was a little spoiled, but how could anyone blame him? He didn't have to work a day in his

life. He just traveled the world having adventures
and spending his family's money.

"Oh man, that's sad, Lex," Travis said, laughing. "The woman hits you with her car and you
still can't close the deal. I would've thought you at
least had a shot by guilting her into a date."

Travis was howling now, and Lex just stood
there and took it. How could he not? The kid's
granddaddy signed his paychecks.

Hayley felt awful. But the moment was now in
the past and it seemed a little too late to try to
backtrack and rectify it.

"If you need anything . . ." Hayley's words
trailed off.

"Thanks, I'll be fine," Lex said softly.

Edgar Hollingsworth never even bothered to
ask how Lex was doing after such a near tragedy.
He was more concerned with Lex clearing some
brush from one of the walking paths on the property and was already barking new marching orders
for the afternoon shift.

As the three men headed out, leaving Hayley
just standing there and feeling awful, Travis said
to Lex, "Maybe she's just into younger men."

He turned his head around and gave her a
wink. "I'm in town for a few weeks. You know where
to find me."

Hayley forced a smile. She knew she had blown
it with Lex big-time.

Chapter 7

Hayley decided not to worry about Lex Bansfield. Unless she got served papers, or worse—was charged with assault with a deadly weapon.

Maybe her first instinct was right. Maybe it was not the right time to be going out on a date. She had way too much on her plate, plus she had to think about her column.

She decided to feature a decent New England clam chowder as a soup course. After nearly barfing up the rancid goop she'd tried at the hospital cafeteria, she knew her mother's tried and true recipe would be a bona fide winner.

That's what she would go with.

She sent her mother a message on Facebook. But after a few hours, she decided to call her in Florida since her mother rarely used the computer and got nervous thinking every website she went to had an insidious virus waiting to infect her HP desktop.

Everything to Hayley's mother was some kind of evil conspiracy.

Hayley punched in her mother's cell phone

number and waited for her to pick up. She thought she was going to get her mother's voice mail but on the fourth ring, a suspicious voice said in a deep tone, "Hello? Who is this?"

"Relax, Ma, it's just me," Hayley said.

"Who?"

"Your daughter?"

"Who?"

"Your only daughter. Hayley, Mom. It's Hayley."

"Oh, hello. I'm about to go play a round of golf with Stan so make it quick."

Hayley's mother, Sheila, wasn't one of those needy mothers who expected their kids to call a few times a week or even a few times a month to check in on her. She had a busy life, with a new beau she'd met at her retirement community near Melbourne, and very little time for small talk in between senior cruises and early bird specials.

"So did you go to the paper's website and read my new column?"

"Yes. They should put a better picture of you in there. Your teeth look crooked."

Always so supportive.

"Anyway, I'm doing a soup course next and I want your clam chowder recipe."

There was a long awkward pause.

"You don't mind giving it to me, do you?" Hayley said.

"No. I just don't feel comfortable giving it to you over the phone. You know Homeland Security is listening in to everything we are saying right now."

"Ma, I'm going to print it in the paper. If they really want to know your recipe, they can just read my column."

"You know we've been on their list ever since your brother started dating that boy from the Middle East."

"Sergio is Brazilian, Ma. He's not from the Middle East. And he's not a boy. He just turned forty."

"Those CIA spooks are everywhere. Stan went to call Time Warner to complain about not having the Military Channel on his lineup and he swore he heard a clicking sound like his phone was being tapped. The cable woman said he was just being transferred. They'll say anything to cover their tracks."

Hayley took a deep breath. "So are you going to give me the recipe or not?"

"Fine," Sheila sighed. "They know everything already anyway. What's my panty size, Agent Triple X, you want to tell me that? I know you're listening to us right now!"

"Ma!"

"Fine. You got a pen?"

Hayley rummaged through her bag and found a pen, but she couldn't find any paper so she scribbled down her mother's instructions on a used lotto ticket, yet another one she'd bought with her hard-earned cash that came up empty.

After indulging her mother for another few minutes discussing senior profiling at airport security, Hayley hung up and left the office to buy what she needed at the Shop 'n Save to try out the clam chowder recipe.

She pushed her cart down the spice aisle and was eyeing her list on the lotto ticket. She only needed one last ingredient and was hoping to beat the after-work rush in the checkout lines when she suddenly slammed into another grocery cart.

One that was being wheeled by Karen Applebaum.

Hayley dropped her lotto ticket and her open bag. All the contents went scattering across the tiled floor.

Karen just stood there, eyes flaring, her white knuckles gripping the handle of the cart, not saying a word.

Great, Hayley thought, first the bank and now here.

"I'm so sorry, Karen," Hayley said in a concilia-tory tone.

"You really should watch where you're going," Karen said haughtily.

Hayley shrugged and then knelt down to scoop up the contents of her bag.

Karen sighed. "Do you need some help?"

"No thanks," Hayley said. "I got it."

An elderly woman rounded the corner with her cart and stopped, unable to get past the two other carts and Hayley's belongings littering the floor.

Karen hissed, "You're blocking the aisle. I'll help. Just hurry up."

Hayley felt her face burning again. This woman was insufferable.

Karen knelt down and picked up one eyebrow liner and waved it in Hayley's face. "Here."

Hayley clenched her teeth. "Thank you."

Hayley went to take it from her, but Karen's hand was wrapped around it in a viselike grip and she wasn't letting it go. They struggled for posses-sion of the eyebrow liner for a few seconds before Karen leaned forward and whispered in Hayley's ear, "That was my recipe. You stole it."

Karen suddenly let go of the eyebrow liner and

Hayley fell back, slamming into the spice rack and knocking over a few bottles of paprika.

"I don't know what you're talking about," Hayley said.

"That was *my* recipe for Maine Crab Stuffed Mushrooms. I don't know how you got your hands on it, but this means war."

"I can assure you, Karen, that was my recipe. It's been in my family for years."

"You're a lying bitch. And if you even dare come near my pan fried dumplings or Swedish meatballs, I will take you down."

"You really are bananas, you know that?"

"You're on my radar, Hayley Powell. You just better watch yourself."

And with that, Karen Applebaum stood back up and pushed her cart past Hayley's and stormed down the aisle.

Several shoppers, their mouths agape, watched the scene with rapt attention.

Hayley hated scenes. Karen looked so evil. Just like that Disney villain. And Hayley was suddenly afraid of winding up sleepwalking during the night and coming across a spinning wheel where she would prick her finger and slip into a deep coma never to awaken unless her lips were touched by a true love's kiss.

Fat chance that would happen. There was only one guy in town she was attracted to and as for him, she had just nearly killed him with her car and then stupidly turned him down flat when he asked her out on a date.

Life sure could be depressing sometimes.

Chapter 8

By the time Hayley arrived home from the market with her ingredients for the clam chowder, Gemma and Dustin were already eating day-old pizza warmed up in the oven and watching an Adam Sandler comedy on TV.

"I'm making a clam chowder so stop snacking on pizza!" Hayley said as she hurriedly unloaded her grocery bags.

A few grunts were heard from the living room. At least they were acknowledging she was actually in the house. Unlike her children, her dog, Leroy, was running around her in his usual circles, nipping at her pant leg, acting as if she had just returned from a two-year journey around the world. She tossed him a doggie treat as a reward for his utter devotion to her.

Hayley rifled through her bag for the lotto ticket where she had written down all the ingredients and instructions her mother had given her, but couldn't find it. She emptied the bag on the counter, sorting every hairbrush and silver wrapped piece of chewing gum, but there was no sign of it. She then searched through all her pockets.

Nothing.

She knew she had it when she was at the store because she was holding it in her hand to make sure she didn't forget any of the ingredients she needed.

Maybe she dropped it when she slammed into Karen Applebaum's grocery cart. That's the only explanation that made sense. She didn't want to call her mother again, so she decided to re-create the cooking instructions from memory.

By the time she was finished, the kids were drawn into the kitchen by the delicious smell and began chowing down on it. They didn't even wait for Hayley to sprinkle those cute little fish crackers on top, they were so ravenous. Hayley knew her chowder was a hit if her kids liked it. They were the pickiest eaters in the world.

Hayley sat down at the dining room table and began pounding out her column on her laptop. Leroy nestled in her lap, snoring softly. The kids went upstairs to do their homework. Or at least that's what they told her. It was going on midnight when Hayley finally finished and e-mailed the column to the office.

Two down.

Hayley was finally starting to feel like a real bona fide writer.

She slept surprisingly well given how much was on her mind. Hitting Lex in the crosswalk. The altercation with Karen at the grocery store.

And she even leapt out of bed the following morning without waiting for the alarm clock to annoy her into crawling out of bed. That was definitely a first.

She took Leroy out for a brief walk around the block, and even had time to iron her blouse before she was in her car by 7:45 A.M. and on her way to the office.

That's when all hell broke loose. When she arrived at work, Sal was already there with a tall, lanky IT guy who was busily working on his computer. Eddie and Bruce were there as well, watching nervously. This was definitely another first. Hayley was always the first one to arrive at the office in the morning.

"What's going on?" she asked as she went to pour herself a cup of coffee.

"There was a power surge in the building last night. Blew out the whole network of computers," Bruce said.

"What?" Hayley said, nearly spilling hot coffee all over Bruce's shirt.

"Sal's got a guy working on it. Says we should be back up and running by noon, but we'll be behind schedule, which means the paper's going to be late coming out today," Eddie said.

The paper had come out late before. When Sal's wife had a baby. When a snowstorm swept through town with such force one February morning that everybody had to stay home. So it didn't seem like such a crisis.

Little did Hayley know just what kind of crisis would balloon after this seemingly harmless office setback.

The IT guy was true to his word. By noon, the computers were humming like new, and the next issue was back on track again. Bruce had taken the morning to go interview the chief of police about the Razor Rick break-in, and when he returned to the office, he had a copy of the *Bar Harbor Herald* tucked under his arm.

Apparently they didn't have a power surge at their office.

"I wonder what scrumptious delicacy Karen Applebaum wrote about this week," Bruce said, thumbing through the paper. "I just love her column."

"Don't start with me, Bruce," Hayley sighed. "I'm not in the mood."

Bruce cleared his throat and skimmed Karen's column. "Looks like a yummy recipe for a delicious New England clam chowder."

"You can't be serious," Hayley said, grabbing the paper from Bruce.

Hayley's mouth dropped open as she perused the column. Karen Applebaum's recipe was an exact word-for-word replica of Hayley's own. This could not be happening. The *Bar Harbor Herald* was already plastered all over town. When the *Times* came out, it would look like Hayley was copying her. How did this happen?

The supermarket! When Karen banged her cart into Hayley's and all the contents of her bag went scattering across the floor, Hayley must have dropped the lotto ticket. And when Karen bent down to pick up the eyebrow liner, she could easily have seen the recipe and pocketed the ticket. But Karen Applebaum couldn't possibly be that sinister and devious.

Of course she could!

Hayley was fuming. She had been outplayed. And she wouldn't be surprised if Karen somehow caused the power surge that delayed the paper. Who knew what that scheming witch was capable of? She had a lot of connections in town.

Hayley dashed into Sal's office to stop him from running her column, but it was too late. The paper had already been put to bed and was now being printed and, worse, Hayley's column had already been posted online.

Within minutes, her phone started ringing with people wanting to know why Hayley had stolen poor Karen Applebaum's New England clam chowder recipe. Much to Hayley's horror, it was quickly becoming obvious that the whole town was not only going to eat up two identical recipes for New England clam chowder, but also this delicious dishy feud between the two dueling kitchen divas of Bar Harbor.

Island Food & Spirits

by
Hayley Powell

Have you ever had one of those days? Well, I certainly had a long one today, after fighting my way through the grocery store and losing my shopping list, then trying to remember everything on it. I couldn't wait to get home and have a relaxing cocktail. Which reminds me. Last night when I was watching the Food Network, Sandra Lee made a fantastic concoction of vodka, club soda, and a splash of cranberry juice garnished with a lime, so I decided to try that and, wow, what a refreshing way to relax and begin your evening.

I envy that woman, with her cute little chic outfits that always match her kitchen décor, plates, glasses, and even her napkins so perfectly. When I get home, I grab the first pair of sweats I find lying on the bedroom floor and a t-shirt three sizes too big, which lately hasn't seemed so big (note to self: start using the gym membership I transferred from my son's name to mine and swore I was going to start using regularly).

So having a few minutes to myself before

starting dinner (which is rare at my house because usually my kids cannot wait for dinner and start munching on leftovers before I even have a chance to get one frying pan on the burner), I decided to take my dog Leroy for a quick walk to the shore path and back in an effort to try and loosen up that T-shirt.

After filling my "To Go Cup," we headed out. I was hoping not too many people would be there as Leroy can be quite a handful. But just my luck, as soon as we arrived, he began barking at seagulls and lunging at other dogs passing us by. My dream of relaxing and sitting by the water was completely shattered so when he pulled extra hard on his leash and broke free, I just gave up and sat down to watch him dig up every clam and mussel he could find.

Watching Leroy dig up the clams reminded me of a recipe I wanted to share with you this week.

I thought of it recently while looking for a small snack in the hospital cafeteria. I was there visiting a dear friend who had the unfortunate experience of being struck down by a car. Not to worry though. With the fast, highly skilled excellent care he received at our local hospital, I know he will be absolutely fine with just a scratch that shouldn't even leave a scar. So I'm absolutely positive that it's in my dear friend's best interest and health that he should just forget about this small bump in the road and move forward and not look back and dwell on it.

Well, on to the secret recipe that has been safe-guarded in my family for generations. One that I got from my mother and plan on handing down to my own children. But it's just so good, I've decided to share it with you.

I thought my family's secret New England clam chowder recipe would be the perfect recipe for our soup course. I hope you will enjoy it as much as we do. So make yourself a cocktail, relax, and eat up this delicious recipe.

New England Clam Chowder

2 ½ cups water
20 to 30 fresh clams (which I buy at my
    friend Mona's shop so I know they'll
    be fresh)
2 strips thick sliced bacon
1 medium yellow onion, chopped
1 stalk celery, chopped
4 Tablespoons flour
1 clove garlic, minced
4 medium red potatoes, peeled and diced
1 bay leaf
1 teaspoon salt
½ teaspoon black pepper
2 cups half & half

Pour 1 cup of the water in a large stockpot and bring to a boil over high heat. Add clams, cover pot; reduce heat to medium and steam for 5 to 7 minutes or until clams start to open. Remove clams from pot as they open. Throw out any unopened clams.

Remove clams from shells, chop clams, and set aside.

Cook bacon in large saucepan until crisp. Remove bacon to paper towels, leave dripping in pan. Crumble bacon when cool enough to handle.

Add onion, celery, flour, and garlic to bacon drippings. Cook over medium heat, stirring occasionally, about 2 minutes or until veggies are crisp tender. Remove from heat.

Add potatoes to onion mixture. Stir in remaining 1 ½ cups of water, bay leaf, salt, and pepper. Bring to a boil, then reduce heat to a medium low and simmer uncovered until potatoes are tender, about 10 minutes.

Stir in half & half and chopped clams, heat through over medium heat, stirring occasionally. Throw out your bay leaf. Stir in bacon. Serve with your favorite crackers (my kids prefer the Goldfish over the traditional Oyster Crackers).

Enjoy!

Chapter 9

Hayley kept her head down while running errands in town, hoping all the drama involving Karen Applebaum and the identical recipes would just die down by the time the next issue of the twice-weekly paper hit the stands. In hindsight, that was just wishful thinking.

Things quickly went from bad to worse.

Hayley had completely forgotten about the Library Bake Sale, an annual event she had long participated in to raise funds for new books. The city council had continually slashed the library's budget year after year and they were no longer capable of buying the latest John Grisham or Stephanie Meyer best-sellers and were increasingly facing complaints from locals and tourists alike, who wanted something a little more contemporary than Jane Austen or Oscar Wilde. So every September, the library hosted a bake sale, and as she did every year, Hayley made her delectable almond fudge brownies.

She had been up late the night before baking

because Gemma and Dustin didn't see the "Do Not Touch" note scotch taped to the batch she had made the previous night that was sitting wrapped in cellophane on the kitchen counter. Or at least she chose to believe they didn't see the note. There was probably a fifty-fifty chance they did see it and just ignored it. But she opted to give them the benefit of the doubt.

So Hayley didn't get to sleep before 1 A.M., and was groggy the next morning when she bolted out of bed just after dawn to shower, slip into some jeans and a red print sleeveless blouse, comb out her hair, and get the brownies to the library before the doors opened for the sale at 8 A.M.

There were several ladies already setting up on the main floor of the library when Hayley arrived. Agatha Farnsworth, the librarian since the early 1960s, was barking orders like a drill sergeant. Two strokes and a replaced hip had done little to dampen the eighty-year-old's controlling nature.

Hayley always shuddered at the sound of Agatha's booming, intimidating voice. It brought back a lot of memories from her childhood of that same bellowing voice ordering her to hush up or get kicked out of the library permanently. Time hadn't really made Hayley less afraid of Agatha and she always had a tendency to stutter when she was forced to have a conversation with her.

"Brownies? You brought brownies, Hayley? Didn't you get my e-mail?" Agatha said, a put-out expression on her face.

"Y-Y-Yes, I always bring b-b-brownies. It's sort of a t-t-tradition," Hayley said.

"Keep your voice down, Hayley. Don't forget this is a library."

"S-S-Sorry," Hayley said, looking at all the other women who were talking in normal voices.

Maybe it was just her that Agatha didn't want to hear talking in the library.

"If you had bothered reading my e-mail, you would have known I have too many people bringing brownies this year. Peanut butter brownies, blonde brownies, five different kinds of fudge brownies. We need some variety. I was hoping you would make cupcakes, or blueberry squares, or hell, at this point I would take marshmallow Rice Krispie treats," Agatha said, sighing.

"You sent me an e-mail?" Hayley said, trying to keep her voice to a whisper.

"I sent it to your office. You didn't get it? I find that rather strange. I've sent you e-mails before and there was never an issue," Agatha said, folding her arms, eyes filled with judgment.

Hayley remembered she had been so thrown by the whole dueling divas with identical New England clam chowder recipes crisis, she never bothered to check her account before leaving the office yesterday. And she missed it in the morning because the computers were down.

Well, it was too late now. She couldn't very well run home and whip up another dessert in forty-five minutes.

"Do you think you could run home and bake something else before we open the doors?" Agatha asked, not even cracking a smile.

She wasn't joking.

"Ummmm, I-I-I really don't think that's possible,"

Hayley said in a tiny whisper. "It's already a quarter past seven and by the time I get home . . ."

"Oh, forget it, Hayley. I'm not interested in excuses. I just assumed you were a miracle worker in the kitchen because of all the brouhaha surrounding your new column in the *Times*," Agatha said, practically drooling sarcasm.

Hayley suddenly felt an evil presence in the library, like some dark force casting a shadow over her.

"Here we are, Agatha. Four cherries jubilee pies, priced at ten dollars apiece," Karen Applebaum said as she placed a cardboard box down on a table right next to Hayley and began unloading her bright red desserts. "I just want to add a little whipped cream along the sides before we put them up for sale. As if they could possibly look more delicious."

"I knew I could count on you, Karen," Agatha said, turning to Hayley. "At least somebody got my e-mail."

Hayley was steaming mad and wanted to tell both Agatha and Karen off, but held her tongue. Now was not the time to cause a scene.

Hayley was grateful to see Liddy sweep into the library, dressed to the nines, wearing a giant floppy pink hat to protect her light complexion from the intense sun, and carrying a matching bag. She marched right over and gave Hayley a hug. The tension drained out of her. Finally, she had an ally.

"Thank God you're here," Hayley said.

"I wouldn't miss it. Well, actually I would, but I want to butter up Aggie and rent this place next spring for my birthday party. I want to throw a costume party and have everyone show up as their favorite literary characters. I'm going to come as Scarlett O'Hara. Big shock, right? I've already ordered the dress."

"What'd you bring for the sale?" Hayley asked.

"Oh, I almost forgot." Liddy reached into her pink bag, fished around, and pulled out a bag of Pepperidge Farm oatmeal cookies. "Here you go, Aggie."

She tossed the bag to Agatha, who managed to catch it. Agatha stared at the label, an irritated look on her face.

"I can't sell these to people. They're store bought. Everything at the sale is supposed to be homemade," Agatha said.

"It says homestyle, right on the bag. Close enough," Liddy said dismissively before turning back to Hayley. "Such a bitch."

"You sure you want to tick her off? What about your birthday party?"

"Please. I've got dirt on her. Remember last year's sale? She served rum balls so soaked with booze, five twelve-year-olds tested over the legal limit."

Suddenly there was a squirting sound and Hayley heard a tiny giggle from behind and someone said, "Oops."

She turned around to see Karen holding a canister of whipped cream. A couple of her friends from her coven of witches were covering their mouths and trying not to laugh.

"What?" Hayley asked, her eyes narrowing, suddenly a little suspicious.

"Just a small accident," Karen said. "Nothing, really."

Hayley decided to ignore them and continued unpacking her brownies from her Tupperware when Liddy stepped behind her to take a look.

"She just nailed you in the ass with whipped cream," Liddy said.

There was a wall mirror next to the mystery section, and Hayley spun around to see for herself.

Sure enough. Her entire backside was covered with frothy whipped cream.

"Seriously, Karen, is this what it's come to?" Hayley said, wiping the cream off the butt of her jeans. "What are we, back in the third grade?"

"It's not like I did it on purpose," Karen said, eyeing her friends, who were all now trying their hardest to stifle their laughter. And not succeeding.

"No, of course not. First you threaten me in the supermarket, and now you go out of your way to make me look foolish."

"I never threatened you, so stop making things up. And as for looking foolish, darling, you're doing a bang-up job all by yourself," Karen said with a self-satisfied smile.

Oh, no, she didn't.

Liddy saw what Hayley was about to do and hurried over and put a comforting but firm hand on Hayley's shoulder. "Honey, I don't think that's such a good idea."

But Hayley was through being nice. She picked up one of her almond fudge brownies, walked over to Karen, and mashed it on the front of her white cashmere sweater. There was utter silence in the library.

For once.

"Oops. Sorry. Accident," Hayley said.

Karen looked at the chocolate stains on her sweater, then picked up one of her cherries jubilee pies and reared back. But Hayley saw what was coming and just as Karen flung it, Hayley ducked, and the pie sailed across the library and splattered all over Agatha Farnsworth's face.

Liddy howled with glee, only making Agatha madder than a wet hornet. Agatha picked up a white chocolate bundt cake and hurled it at Liddy. Liddy grabbed the sides of her big floppy pink hat and ran screaming for the front door as the flying cake chased her. It missed its target by two inches and went crashing to the floor. But Liddy slid on the frosting and her legs flew up into the air and she landed flat on her ass.

The coven of witches rushed to Karen's defense and started pelting Hayley with some vanilla bean scones. She fired back with a plate of no bake cookies, which were hard and would probably hurt if her throwing arm was as good as it was when she played softball in high school.

It was a free-for-all, and the few locals who showed up early to get their pick of the best desserts in the sale stood motionless outside the glass windows of the library, staring in awe at the food fight that was in full swing inside.

Finally, there was a lull because the only dessert left to throw was a lone fruit cake and nobody really liked fruit cake.

Everyone was covered with bits of brownie and cream and frosting and cake, and there was a feeling in the room that they had just done something that would go down in the annals of Bar Harbor history.

And it was something nobody should be proud of.

Karen Applebaum was still in a state of shock as she stared at the damage to her three-hundred-dollar white cashmere sweater. She dropped the last small piece of pecan pie she had scooped up to use as a weapon, and glared at Hayley, who was picking bits of angel food cake out of her hair.

"This is all your fault, Hayley Powell. You've ruined the bake sale for everyone," Karen spit out.

Every last instinct told Hayley to keep her mouth shut and just walk away. But Karen insisted on egging her on, and she had finally reached her breaking point.

So she stepped over Liddy's crushed bag of Pepperidge Farm oatmeal cookies, and, fists clenched, approached Karen, who slowly stepped away from her, now regretful for stirring Hayley up into such a fit of anger.

"I'm done playing games with you, Karen. So back off," Hayley said, her voice seething. "Or else."

"Or else what?" Karen scoffed.

"Or else I might just have to kill you," Hayley said.

She didn't really mean it. She just wanted to show Karen how pissed off she was. And nobody there actually took her seriously. But the words were now out there and they were words that would soon come back to haunt her.

In a really big way.

Chapter 10

It may come as a surprise, but the annual library bake sale turned out to be a smashing success. The spectators standing outside the library were so entertained by the food fight, they wrote checks for new books on the condition the women repeat the same show next year.

Hayley also wound up forking over a nice chunk of change out of her own pocket, in an attempt to make things right, and as an apology for her own participation in trashing all the treats before the official sale opened to the public.

By the end of the day, after all the checks and donations were counted, Agatha proudly announced that this year's earnings were on par with last year's, although they did fall short when she subtracted the cost of the cleaning supplies the women used to mop up the mess. And there was one first edition Mark Twain that got smeared with peanut butter fudge, so restoring the binding might cut into the final take as well.

Hayley was exhausted when she pulled into the driveway later that night. After making some macaroni and cheese and salad for the kids, she plopped down in her rocker on her outside deck, and sipped a cocktail while staring up at the shiny stars that dotted the black sky.

What a day.

At least she had tomorrow off, and could re-group, and then hit the ground running on Monday doing damage control over her very front and center role in the disastrous scandal that would surely be the talk of the town.

After finishing her cocktail and wrapping her-self in a comfy shawl her grandmother gave her, Hayley fell into a deep sleep.

When she woke up twenty or thirty minutes later, she went inside and sat down at her com-puter to check her e-mail. There was one deliv-ered at 10:15 P.M.

It was from Karen Applebaum.

That caught Hayley's attention. She opened the e-mail and read it.

Hello, Hayley, I know I'm the last person you expected to hear from, especially after what happened today, but I've thought about everything, and I owe you an apology for my appalling behavior today and at the supermarket this past week. I really think it is in both our best interests to bury the hatchet. There is absolutely no reason there can't be two food and wine columns in town, and I was hoping you could come over to my house to talk. I know it's late, and it's a Saturday, and I was going to call you, but I'm embarrassed and it's easier for me to write you. I'm sure you might be out with friends or on a date . . .

Boy, she really didn't know Hayley at all.

> But if you do get this e-mail, please, please, just
> come on over. I'm only a few blocks away. I feel
> awful and I want to hash things out and nip this
> escalating feud in the bud. Thank you, Hayley.
> Yours, Karen.

Hayley was leaning toward dealing with all of this tomorrow, or even on Monday. Maybe Karen was setting her up. Maybe she would show up at Karen's house and Karen would greet her with a twelve gauge shotgun. She watched enough true crime shows on cable to know that was a very distinct possibility.

Finally, Hayley decided she didn't want to wait until Monday. Why not clear the air now? Both of them could just move on with their lives, acknowledge each other with a smile if they happened to dine at the same restaurant, compliment each other's columns publicly while trashing them in private, and just live a peaceful coexistence with no more drama.

Yes, that was the best course of action, and Hayley was going to do her part and drive over to Karen's. She'd resolve the situation and be back home before the kids even realized she was gone.

It was getting chilly, the temperature dipping below fifty, so Hayley threw a coat over the torn sweats she was wearing (she certainly wasn't going to gussy up for Karen Applebaum), fired up the wagon, and drove the four blocks to Michigan Avenue where Karen lived.

Hayley pulled the car up front and was surprised that all the lights were off in the house. She got out of the wagon and walked up the steps to the front door and rang the bell.

No one answered.

Had Karen gone out? Hayley rang the bell again. Nothing. She could just wait in the car until Karen got home. But what if she was there half the night waiting? What if Karen never came back?

Hayley tried the door. It was unlocked. She poked her head in.

"Karen, are you home? It's me, Hayley Powell," she said.

Still nothing.

Hayley stepped inside.

"Karen?"

Hayley had the urge to bolt back outside, jump in the car, drive straight home, and just pretend she never got Karen's message.

But curiosity was getting the best of her.

She looked around in the dark but couldn't see much. There was a glow coming from the den and the faint sound of a woman's voice. Probably the TV.

Just to double check, Hayley made her way through the living room to the den and there on the screen was a repeat episode of the *Barefoot Contessa* on the Food Network. Figures. Hayley watched the show regularly and knew Karen stole half her recipes from that show. There was a quilt balled up on the sectional couch. Someone had been lying there recently watching TV. Suddenly something big and furry jumped at her and she screamed. It was a cat. A really fat cat. But its hefty size didn't slow him down when he scampered up the stairs to hide. Hayley calmed down. She continued looking around.

Still no sign of Karen.

Hayley was about to leave when the thought occurred to her that Karen might be upstairs sick or incapacitated. She decided to make a quick check of the bedroom before she left. She rounded the corner into the kitchen and was heading back to the hallway to head up the stairs when she slid on something and fell facedown, smashing her forehead on the hardwood floor.

Ouch.

Hayley felt for blood on her forehead. There was none, but she knew a nasty bruise was sure to follow.

What had she slipped on? She felt around on the floor. Hayley's hands suddenly felt wet and sticky. She felt some more and picked up a small rubbery object in her hand.

She crawled to her knees. She didn't know where the switch to the overhead lighting was, so she opened the oven door. The light inside came to life, and illuminated a body sprawled out on the floor.

Hayley gasped.

It was a woman's body.

Hayley shook the left shoulder. "Karen, is that you? Are you okay?"

Then she remembered the wet and sticky substance on her hand.

Dear God. Please let it not be blood.

But it wasn't. It was milky and white. She smelled her palm. It was clam chowder. The rubbery object she had picked up was a clam.

Hayley placed her palm down on the stovetop and pulled herself up to her feet. The light from the oven was bright enough so that she could see the light switch next to the range. She reached over and snapped it on. A blinding light flooded the room, and Hayley, squinting, stepped back away from the body.

She recognized Karen Applebaum instantly.

Even though the poor woman was facedown in a turquoise-colored porcelain bowl of New England clam chowder.

She was still wearing the dessert stained white cashmere sweater.

And she was very much dead.

Chapter 11

Hayley gasped and threw a hand to her mouth. She couldn't believe it. She knelt down and shook Karen, but instinctively she knew it was too late.

Hayley looked around, spotted a telephone on the wall next to the kitchen counter and stumbled over to it, grabbed the receiver, and dialed 9-1-1.

Bar Harbor being such a small town, several police officers were dispatched instantly and were banging at the door within seven minutes. Hayley ushered them in, and led them into the kitchen and over to Karen's body.

Officers Donnie and Earl were among them, two young wet-behind-the-ears patrolmen. Earl gently took Hayley by the elbow and steered her into the living room away from the body. He sat her down on the couch and asked her to stay put until the chief got there. He wanted to question her himself.

Hayley knew Police Chief Sergio Alvares would want to personally talk to her for two reasons. For one thing, she was the one who had found the body. And second, they were related. Sort of.

Sergio Alvares was a strapping, impossibly good-looking man from a tiny town in southern Brazil called São Francisco that was nestled along the coast three and a half hours from the nearest metropolitan area of Curitiba. He was the only son of a poor farming family, who worshipped him and wanted great things for him. But Sergio quickly fell into the party scene and spent his early adult years bouncing between the wild, un-inhibited nightlife of the two biggest urban areas of Rio de Janeiro and São Paulo.

One spectacular night during Mardi Gras in Rio, he found himself on the private jet of an American mogul flying to Miami Beach for a party on Star Island, thanks to the lustful maneuvers of the businessman's beautiful college-age daughter. The excitable girl thought she had found her future husband, and her father, seeing how excited his baby girl was over her new plaything, offered to groom Sergio as an executive in the family business as long as he kept her happy.

But Sergio had an independent streak, and had no intentions of marrying the rich girl. And being the hot-blooded outspoken Brazilian he was, he had no qualms about telling both father and daughter to back off. He was only twenty-one at the time and the last thing he wanted was to get tied down so young. That moment would prove fateful. The girl and her mega rich daddy took off back to Dallas in their jet, leaving Sergio stranded in Miami. He had no friends. No place to stay. And most importantly, no money to get back to Brazil.

So Sergio started working odd jobs off the books to get himself an apartment and scrape together some cash. He made some pretty influential friends from the South Beach club scene, and soon was being wooed by a famous fashion designer, whose company had just gone public, making him an instant billionaire. Sergio always knew he was gay, but never labeled himself as such because in Brazil, especially at the hot spots where he hung out, it really wasn't much of an issue. He had dated girls, boys, and some who you couldn't tell what they were, especially during Mardi Gras. He was young and carefree, and just went with the flow, whatever felt right at the time.

The designer, who immediately fell in love with Sergio, would whisk him off on fabulous weekend getaways around the world, but soon became possessive and controlling, and Sergio was one man who didn't take to the idea of being kept.

Especially by another man.

On one weekend trip to Maine where the designer and Sergio went to visit the estate of a wealthy blue blood in Northeast Harbor who adored the designer and his fashions, Sergio slipped away to explore on his own. He fell in love with the glorious mountains and peaceful carriage trails of Acadia National Park, the stark rocky shores, and, across the island from the more stuffy, old money Northeast Harbor, the down-to-earth, eccentric, colorful tourist town of Bar Harbor. Drinking at a bar with a few locals, Sergio felt right at home. The live-and-let-live attitude of the people reminded him of his own home in São Francisco.

So when the designer sent a driver to find him

and deliver him back to the estate so they could fly home to Miami, Sergio refused to go. He knew he didn't want a future as the boy toy of a famous fashion designer. He wanted to be his own man. So once again, Sergio started from scratch.

He bussed tables at a number of restaurants that buzzed with activity in the summer, cleared brush for the National Park Service in the fall, and shoveled snow out of driveways for cash in the cold, dreary winters. He did anything to scrape together enough money to pay for his one-room apartment above a hair salon on a tucked away side street off one of the busier main drags. He lived on Ramen noodles and sent whatever spare money he could to his parents back in Brazil.

It didn't take long for Sergio to become well-known in town. How many strikingly good-looking Brazilian men were there in Bar Harbor, especially in the freezing winter months, who actually liked to go ice fishing with friends?

Lex Bansfield got plenty of attention for his good looks, but Sergio was in another category altogether and the single women flocked to him. But it quickly became clear he played for the other team. This was never a big deal in Bar Harbor, being one of the first towns in the nation to pass a gay rights ordinance; it was mostly to draw the gay tourists, who had a lot of disposable income they could throw at the local businesses during the busy summer season. But New Englanders also prided themselves on keeping out of other people's business, so, like in his beloved Brazil, Sergio happily found that very few people cared about his sexual orientation.

It was right about this time he landed a job as a dispatcher at the local police station. The chief's wife, who everyone suspected had a thing for Sergio, strong-armed her husband into hiring him. The only trouble was, English was not Sergio's first language. A few of his friends called him "Ricky Ricardo" because everyone had trouble understanding him, especially after he had a few cocktails. So the dispatcher gig turned out to be a disaster because if there was a domestic disturbance call, nine times out of ten the officers would show up at the wrong address because they didn't understand what Sergio was saying.

Still, the chief loved Sergio's personality and work ethic, and made him a patrolman. That was ten years ago. When the chief retired three years ago, there was only one person everyone in town felt deserved the job.

Right about the time Sergio became a patrolman, Hayley's brother, Randy, returned to town to start anew after abandoning his ill-fated acting career in New York. There were only so many gay people in town so it didn't take long for the two of them to hear about each other. But the last thing either of them wanted at the time was a relationship, so they tended to avoid each other. That's when fate intervened. Randy threw a party for all his old high school friends, and it got a little out of control, and a noise complaint was called into the station. Sergio answered the call, and when Randy opened the door, it was practically a done deal. Sergio still charged Randy with making a public disturbance just so it didn't appear he was playing favorites, and the court summons was now framed above their fireplace in the nicely appointed waterfront home they shared together, as a reminder of how they first met.

When Sergio marched through the door of Karen Applebaum's house, a wave of relief swept over Hayley. She stood up and threw her arms around his neck.

"Thank God you're here!" Hayley said, near tears.

Sergio comforted Hayley for a few moments, but then pulled away, trying to remain professional. After all, this was a potentially sticky situation.

"Please, sit down, Hayley. I have some questions for you," Sergio said.

"Do we have to do this now? I'm totally stressed out, Sergio. Why don't I just come over to your house tomorrow and we can go over everything then? I'll bring bagels and coffee."

"We have to do it now, Hayley," Sergio said, stepping away and gesturing for her to sit down on the couch.

Hayley's sense of relief was now slipping away, replaced with a queasy feeling in her stomach.

"Okay," Hayley said, following instructions and sitting down. "Shoot."

"What were you doing here tonight?"

"Karen sent me an e-mail. We had a little disagreement earlier . . ."

"The food fight at the library bake sale."

"You heard about that?"

"Everyone heard about it."

"Oh," Hayley said, not too surprised.

"Go on."

"Anyway, after I got home, I got an e-mail from Karen apologizing and asking me to come over to her house so we could talk about it."

"So soon?"

"I know. I thought it was strange, too. I wasn't going to go, but she sounded so desperate to resolve our differences in the e-mail, so I decided just to come over and work it out and be done with it."

"And that's when you found the body?"

"Yes."

"What about the clam chowder?"

"What about it?"

Sergio paused, thinking about what he was going to say next very carefully.

"Don't you find it a bit iconic that you found Karen face down in a bowl of clam chowder?"

"Iconic?"

"Yes."

"You mean ironic?"

"What?"

"Iconic is someone who has made a cultural impact like Madonna or Lady Gaga," Hayley said, smiling. "I think you mean ironic. Like the Alanis Morissette song."

Sergio thought for a second.

"Okay. Yes. Ironic," he said, frustrated, then growled something to himself in Portuguese.

Hayley really didn't want to know what he said.

"What was the question again?" she asked.

"The clam chowder," Sergio said, trying not to raise his voice.

"Oh, right. No. Not really. Why do you say it's ironic?"

"Because Karen had just accused you of stealing her crab stuffed mushroom recipe."

"How did you know that?"

"Everyone knows it."

"Oh."

"You two were moral enemies."

"I wouldn't go that far," Hayley laughed, deciding not to correct Sergio by telling him he probably meant to say mortal enemies.

"You threatened her at the library in front of everyone," Sergio said. He was dead serious.

"You heard about that? Wait. I know. Everyone did."

"And now you're in her house, with her body, her face drowning in a big bowl of clam chowder, which you wrote about in your columns."

"Wait just a second, Sergio. You're questioning me like this is some sort of murder investigation."

"It's not a murder investigation, Hayley," Sergio said.

"Good," Hayley said.

"Yet."

"What do you mean, yet? There's no evidence of foul play. Where's the blood? She wasn't stabbed or shot or anything like that!"

"All I'm saying is, I think it's a bit odd you being here and the circumstances surrounding her sudden death," Sergio said.

"I suppose," Hayley said. "But what seems odder is you treating me like some kind of suspect. Like this is a *Law and Order* episode or something. How can you imply something like that? Especially after we kicked ass playing trivia together at Randy's bar last weekend."

"I'm sorry, Hayley," Sergio said calmly, putting an arm around her. "I don't mean to make you feel uncomfortable. But I'm just doing my job. I need to ask the tough questions. But I'd be lying if I told you your presence here is not going to jump-start the rumor factory."

"Rumor mill."

"What?"

"It's not rumor factory. It's rumor mill."

She just couldn't help herself that time.

Sergio sputtered something to himself in Portuguese again.

"I think you're overreacting, Sergio," Hayley said confidently. "Everyone in town knows I wouldn't hurt a fly."

Hayley had been wrong before.

But she had no clue how wrong she was now.

Chapter 12

The news of Karen Applebaum's untimely death swept through town with the force of a category five hurricane. Hayley even overheard a couple of tourists from Canada gossiping about it when she stopped off at the local book and stationery store to buy a few art supplies for her son, who was drawing a portrait of Batman for a school project on world figures he most admired.

When Hayley checked out with her items, the clerk gave Hayley a smile, but then Hayley noticed the woman quickly averting her eyes, signaling a coworker, alerting her to the fact that Hayley was in the building. Suddenly Hayley felt as if she was becoming a local celebrity for all the wrong reasons. People knew she had found Karen's body, and they certainly knew all about the strained history between the two of them.

Hayley kept a smile plastered on her face, paid the woman, and walked out of the store with her head held high. She knew once the preliminary autopsy on Karen was completed, she would be in the clear. They would confirm it was some previously undetected health-related issue that got her in the end, something completely innocent and unforeseen.

"Poison?" Hayley said the next day as she stood in the doorway of Sal's office, a stunned expression on her face.

"Coroner up in Bangor found traces of cyanide in her system," Sal said.

"But I don't understand. How did she ingest it?"

Sal looked over at Bruce, who put his head down.

They knew Hayley wouldn't like the answer.

Sal cleared his throat. "It was in the clam chowder."

"What?" Hayley screamed. Not good. Not good at all. "You're saying someone actually did murder Karen Applebaum?"

"Looks that way," Bruce said quietly.

"Who would do such a thing?"

There was dead silence in the room.

Sal and Bruce kept their mouths shut. Hayley stared at them, the uncomfortable truth finally dawning on her.

"You don't think I actually had anything to do with this, do you?"

"Of course not," Sal said.

"Don't be ridiculous," Bruce chimed in.

They had answered her too quickly, and Hayley knew in her gut they just didn't want her getting more upset. But maybe, deep down, they had a small feeling, some tiny notion that Hayley might have reached her limit with Karen, and just done her in. The thought of anyone, especially her colleagues at the paper, suspecting her sickened Hayley.

"Karen and I may not have been the best of friends, but there is no way I would do anything that might harm her, so let's just make that clear right now," Hayley said firmly.

"Of course," Sal said.

"Right. The idea is preposterous," Bruce said.

Bruce never used words like preposterous unless he was feeling uncomfortable. He was nervous. So was Sal. Were they now afraid of her?

"Would you like me to get you two some coffee?" Hayley said.

"No," Sal said, standing up. "I'll get it myself."

"Yeah, me, too," Bruce said, nodding.

Getting their own coffee? Hayley suddenly felt like she was in the Twilight Zone.

Hayley folded her arms, furious.

"Don't worry, boys. I left my vial of cyanide in my other purse."

They froze in their tracks, exchanged glances, and laughed at the joke. But then they both scurried past her out to the coffee machine to pour themselves their own cups.

Hayley managed to get through the day with only two calls from anonymous locals asking her point-blank if she had poisoned poor Karen. But two was almost more than she could handle.

She decided to ditch her errands after work. Why put herself through shopping for dinner and endure the stares of the other shoppers and checkout clerks? Why buy that duct tape she needed to reattach her rearview mirror after she smashed it into the brick wall of the bank pulling up too close to the drive-through ATM machine? The owner of the hardware store would just think she was really buying the duct tape to tie up and gag her next victim.

No, Hayley drove straight home to hide in her house until all of this nonsense blew over.

She ordered a pizza to be delivered for dinner since she had avoided the grocery store, and Gemma and Dustin, who had already heard the rumors—but of course dismissed them—were excited about chowing down on pizza instead of having to be lab rats for another one of their mother's recipes which she was trying out for her column.

Both Mona and Liddy called to offer their support. Mona especially was riled up by all the rampant speculation, and nearly punched out one of her longtime customers who said right in front of her that Hayley should get the death penalty. Liddy was more politically savvy than Mona, and simply scoffed at the accusations while getting her hair colored that day.

Later that night, Randy called Hayley, who was becoming deeply depressed about the prospects of being a hermit until the case was solved.

"Why didn't you stop by for a drink tonight?" Randy asked.

"I was afraid you might have other customers besides me, and I just couldn't take the judgmental looks," Hayley said.

"It was pretty quiet tonight. I closed early."

"Oh, you're home now? You and Sergio having a quiet romantic dinner for two?"

"No, he had to work late."

"Oh, that's too bad. Is he working a big case?"

There was an uncomfortable pause.

"Um, yeah," Randy said.

"Somebody's dog run away?"

"No. Nothing like that."

"Well, what is it?"

"What do you think, Hayley?"

It was like a kick in the stomach.

"Karen Applebaum," Hayley said, sighing.

"It's his only case at the moment. It's all anyone is talking about. He's under a lot of pressure to find who killed her."

"I wish he would just make a statement saying I'm no longer a person of interest so people will stop staring at me and whispering about me behind my back," Hayley said.

Another uncomfortable pause.

"Do you think he'd do something like that for me, Randy?"

"Um, I don't think so."

"Why not?"

"Because you *are* a suspect, Hayley!"

"He thinks I did it?"

"No, of course he doesn't think you did it. But look at the facts! If he takes you off the list of suspects, then it looks like he's favoring you because you're his sister-in-law."

"I guess I understand that. Who else is on his list of suspects?"

Cue uncomfortable pause. Hayley sighed.

"Randy?"

"There isn't anybody else."

"Oh my God!"

"But that's why he's working late! He's going over all the evidence and he's out knocking on doors trying to find someone else who might have had a motive to off Karen."

Hayley knew in her heart that Sergio would do everything in his power to find the real killer and clear Hayley. But she worried that so many people already thought she was guilty, it would do irreparable harm to her reputation. Not that she cared much what other people thought about her, but it was really tough living in a small town where a good portion of the population avoided eye contact.

Hayley barely slept that night, tossing and turning, coming in and out of dreams of being in a courtroom, a judge sentencing her to life in prison without the possibility of parole, getting processed into a dark and dingy women's prison, brawling with an imposing inmate named Big Aggie, who chooses Hayley to be her bitch behind bars.

Hayley bolted upright in bed, sweat pouring down, a wild-eyed look on her face. She checked the clock on the bedside table, 4:30 A.M. Hayley knew getting more sleep was a fruitless ambition, so she petted Leroy who snored softly next to her, crawled out of bed, put on her slippers, and walked downstairs and turned on her computer.

She had been so distracted by all the events involving Karen's murder she hadn't written her next column yet. She decided to write it as if nothing was happening. She was not going to make any allusions to the incredible strain she was under from the locals suspecting her of some heinous crime. After all, despite all her troubles, it was poor Karen for whom she felt sorry. Karen probably had a lot of good years left to live if someone hadn't decided to spike her soup with that cyanide.

Hayley focused on the salad in her seven course series, and just pretended nothing was wrong. Why give people more reason to gossip? She banged it out in less than an hour, and then made a pot of coffee and turned on the morning's news. She heard the weather report. Another chilly fall day. The college basketball scores. And then at the top of the hour, the headlines.

That's when her mouth dropped open and she spilled coffee on her ripped gray sweatpants because a local news anchor was saying her name and then they aired an interview with Sergio at the police station. He downplayed Hayley's presence at the murder scene and tried deflecting questions about her obvious motive. But she knew it wasn't going to do her any good. People were going to jump to conclusions.

When she got to the office a few hours later, she happened to see Bruce's own local crime beat piece that he had already included late last night in the layout file on her computer.

Another shock. Bruce couldn't resist mentioning her as well in his coverage of the case, how one of their own at the *Island Times* had been caught up in the intense investigation due to her very public rivalry with the victim.

Hayley knew if she confronted Bruce, he would say he was just doing his job. As a journalist, it would be irresponsible of him to leave her name out of it. And as mad as she was that her own colleague, in her mind, was throwing her under the bus, she knew he was right to include her in his column. The *Bar Harbor Herald* wouldn't have any qualms about trumpeting Hayley's name as a suspect. Or publishing an unflattering photo.

It was all spiraling out of control. And things were just going from bad to worse.

Island Food & Spirits

by
Hayley Powell

Once again this year we had another successful bake sale for the library's fundraiser to help raise money for some much needed books and to also bring our volunteer bakers and community together. Let me tell you this. I truthfully have never tasted such delicious pies, cakes, and brownies. Believe me, I had it coming out of my ears! I would just like to give a big thumbs-up to all of the ladies that baked these delectable treats.

As you know from all of the people who attended the sale, a good time was had by all!

This also reminds me of one of the pies I tasted today. It was a really scrumptious strawberry pie. So after arriving home with a slight headache from my busy day, I remembered that while I was out shopping at our local farmer's market a few days ago, I happened to see the most delicious looking strawberries. Well, true to form, I overbought and walked away with an entire case of those yummy looking berries.

By the time I arrived home, I had two thoughts.

My first was daiquiris (big surprise) and my second was desserts!

After a few trials and errors, I am proud to say I made the best strawberry daiquiri ever! After polishing off my first batch, my headache was completely gone! I also regret to say that I forgot to write down exactly how I did it so a do-over was definitely in order.

Then I went on to making homemade biscuits just like my grandmother used to make for her strawberry shortcakes. Unfortunately, my biscuits turned out a little dry. But with the syrupy sauce, fresh strawberries, and whipped cream piled on top, it didn't much matter. And since the kids weren't home, I found myself eating enough of these sweet and delicious concoctions for a small church social. You might say I satisfied my craving for strawberries.

Then I settled down in my chair promptly at 8:00 P.M. to watch my favorite crime drama of the moment on TV. *NCIS* with that sexy Mark Harmon. He's one man who gets even more handsome with age. Sigh. Why does it seem that men just get better looking as they get older while we women have to start dealing with wrinkles and our skin sagging in places which should be illegal? The other day when I saw a friend drive by my house and I waved at her, I almost knocked myself unconscious with the loose skin on my arms. It just does not seem fair!

Anyway, my daughter casually strolled in the room just as the show started and announced that it was her turn to provide the snacks for the next day's away soccer game. But not to worry, she told me, it was only the boys and girls varsity teams going as the junior varsity was staying home, so it shouldn't be too much of a problem for me to whip something up at the last minute. Now as most of you know, this is still roughly 50 people. I'm not proud to say this, but after some major huffing and puffing, I heaved myself out of the chair and marched into the kitchen and started grabbing a bowl and pans with a little banging for dramatic effect (which was totally ignored, by the way) and began making strawberry granola bars for the soccer teams. It's required that all snacks be somewhat healthy, which, unfortunately, reminded me of the ever-growing tightness in the waistband of my pants this week. Who puts on all this extra weight just eating healthy fruit? It dawned on me that for this week's third course, which is the salad course, you can have your strawberries without all of the cream fillings, pastry, and sugary extras just by having a nice refreshing light salad. So here's a recipe for a strawberry and spinach salad, and I highly recommend making a strawberry daiquiri as well so you'll have something to chase it down with.

Strawberry Daiquiri

 2 ounces rum
 Your favorite drink glass filled with ice
 6 fresh strawberries (or a quart if you're
   like me and make a few mistakes)
 2 teaspoons sugar

Blend all ingredients together in a blender until

smooth (taste and add more rum if needed).
Pour in your glass, sit back, and enjoy!

Strawberry and Spinach Salad

2 Tablespoons sesame seeds
½ cup white sugar
½ cup good olive oil
¼ cup distilled white vinegar
¼ teaspoon paprika
¼ teaspoon Worcestershire sauce
1 Tablespoon minced onion
10 ounces fresh spinach—rinsed, dried,
   and torn into bite-size pieces (support
   your local farmers)
1 quart strawberries (cleaned and sliced)
¼ cup almonds toasted and slivered (warm
   up a small pan and toss your almonds
   and toast them until golden brown)

In a medium bowl, whisk together the sesame seeds,
sugar, olive oil, vinegar, paprika, Worcestershire
sauce, and onion. Cover, and chill for one hour.

In a large bowl, combine the spinach, strawberries,
and almonds. Pour dressing over salad, and toss.
Refrigerate 10 to 15 minutes before serving.

Chapter 13

Hayley was determined not to let the town's suspicions about her guilt in the murder of Karen Applebaum consume her. In fact, when the day for the funeral service for dear departed Karen arrived, Hayley decided to accompany Liddy and Mona to the church.

"Are you friggin' nuts?" Mona asked in her usual ladylike way.

"If I don't go, everyone will speculate it's because I have something to hide," Hayley said, sifting through her closet for something appropriate to wear.

"But everyone knows you two hated each other," Mona said, sitting on the edge of her bed chugging down a can of Miller beer.

It was ten o'clock in the morning.

"Mona, you can't be drinking that. You're pregnant."

"You're right," Mona said, spitting it out in Hayley's bathroom sink. "I'm pregnant so often I sometimes forget."

"Look, I know it might appear hypocritical of me to go, but before this whole rivalry started, Karen and I were actually friends. Sort of," Hayley said, pulling out a long print skirt and modeling it for Mona. "I want to pay my respects."

"Suit yourself," Mona said.

"What do you think? This skirt with a black sweater? Tasteful, understated, black top for mourning, but the skirt lets me be a little stylish."

"Why are you asking me? I'm wearing what I've got on right now," Mona said, standing up and twirling around to show off her dungarees and oversized gray sweatshirt with her lobster shop logo on the front.

"America's Next Top Model," Hayley said, laughing as she took the skirt off the hanger and slipped it on.

"We picking up Liddy on the way?" Mona asked.

"Uh, no, I don't think Liddy is going to ride in the back of your pickup truck while wearing Donna Karan. She'll meet us there."

"Miss High Maintenance. Whatever," Mona said, crushing her beer can in her hand after emptying it out in the bathroom sink.

Hayley threw on her sweater, fixed her hair, and applied a bit of makeup and within ten minutes she and Mona were riding in Mona's truck to the church. When they arrived at the Bar Harbor Congregational Church, they had trouble finding parking. The whole lot was full and there wasn't any street parking available.

"I can't believe how many people are here," Hayley said.

"It's just a matter of giving the people what they want," Mona said, cackling.

"Stop it, Mona. Karen might not have been the nicest person . . ."

"She was a world-class pain in the ass," Mona shouted. "Any way you cut it."

"I hope Reverend Staples doesn't ask you to get up and say a few words," Hayley said, shaking her head.

Frustrated, Mona double-parked in front of the church and hopped out.

"What are you doing?" Hayley asked.

"Parking."

"You can't leave your truck here. You're blocking the hearse. How are they going to transport Karen's body to the cemetery if your truck's in the way?"

"Like I'm going to stay for the whole thing. I'll be long gone by the time they drag out Karen's coffin."

"But you'll get a ticket," Hayley said.

"The boys at the police department know not to ticket me if they see my truck double-parked. They'll just think I'm making a lobster delivery."

"To Karen's funeral?"

"Mourners got to eat," Mona said, losing patience.

"Fine," Hayley sighed, getting out of the truck. "Let's go."

Hayley and Mona walked up the stone steps to the church's front entrance and went inside. The organist was playing a somber hymn and it was standing room only. A crowd of people, mostly in black, were gathered around the coffin.

Hayley immediately spotted Liddy. She was in designer black, very chic. But Liddy also had an innate need to stand out everywhere she went, so she also wore a flashy diamond pendant that was almost blinding, along with a matching pair of earrings.

Hayley, however, wasn't focused on her outfit. She was more concerned with Liddy's face. It was contorted into a silent scream and her eyes were wild with fury as she stampeded over to Hayley and Mona.

"What's up her butt?" Mona asked as Liddy descended upon them.

Liddy grabbed Hayley by the arm and squeezed it tight. "We have a situation. Outside."

Liddy steered Hayley right back out the door. Curious, Mona followed.

Liddy led Hayley down the steps and across the lawn, out of earshot of the few stragglers still filing into the church.

"What is it?" Hayley asked.

"It's an open casket," Liddy said, near tears.

"What, is Karen's face scaring the children?" Mona said, before busting out laughing.

"Mona, please," Liddy said sternly and then swiveled her head back to Hayley. "I've been freaking out waiting for you to get here."

"What, Liddy? What? Just tell me," Hayley said, her stomach twisted all in knots.

"Remember my grandmother's brooch, the silver one in the shape of a dragonfly?"

"Yes, I love that brooch," Hayley said.

"I know. Which is why I lent it to you a few months ago to wear to the surprise birthday party

Mona and I threw for you, but ended up telling you about a week in advance so you could dress appropriately."

"Right. I looked so good that night," Hayley said.

"Thanks to my brooch," Liddy interjected. "Do you remember what you did with it?"

"I gave it back to you."

"No, you didn't."

"I'm sure I did."

"Trust me, Hayley. You didn't."

"Well, did you look for it?"

"I don't have to. I already know where it is."

"Well, then, what's the problem?"

"The problem is, Karen Applebaum is wearing it. In her casket."

"What?"

"It's fastened right to her ugly maroon wool knit dress."

Mona guffawed so loudly she had to cover her mouth.

Liddy spun around and glared at Mona. "You're not helping."

"That's impossible. How did Karen get ahold of your grandmother's brooch?"

"I was hoping you could tell me," Liddy said, trying to remain calm. "When I got here, I did what everybody else was doing and got in line to pass by and take one last look at Karen. Mostly because I wanted to make sure she was really dead. When I got to the front of the line, I practically screamed my head off. Everyone was looking at me in horror so I mustered up some tears and just said I was overwhelmed with grief over losing such a dear, sweet friend. Like anybody would believe me! I hated the cow!"

"Wait a minute," Hayley said. "Karen was at my birthday party a few months ago, and I remember she complimented me on the brooch and . . ."

"And what?" Liddy asked.

". . . and asked if she could borrow it to wear to the Way Back Ball and—oh, no . . ." Hayley said, her voice trailing off. "I gave it to her but forgot to get it back. It all happened long before this whole feud between us erupted."

Mona was having trouble breathing at this point, she was laughing so hard.

Hayley grabbed Liddy by the shoulders. "Oh, Liddy, I am so, so sorry. This is all my fault."

"It's fine," Liddy said, patting Hayley's hand with her own. "I understand. These things happen."

"I'll make it up to you, I promise," Hayley said. "I'll replace it."

"You don't have to do that," Liddy said.

"No, it's the least I can do."

"You don't have to replace it because you're going to get it back for me."

"What?"

"That brooch is priceless. It's been in my family for generations. You can't just replace it."

"What am I supposed to do? Go back inside that church, march up to Karen's coffin, and just rip it off her chest?"

"See, you already have a plan," Liddy said.

"Are you insane?"

"I will not allow my grandmother's brooch to be buried with that hag Karen Applebaum!"

Mona was now in such a state of hysterics, she

lost her balance and stumbled into the hedges lining the church property.

"Liddy, I can't. I just can't," Hayley pleaded.

"Yes, you can. Now you better go do it now because they're going to close the casket once the service starts and then we'll be royally screwed!"

"Want me to pull the fire alarm to distract everybody?" Mona asked, finally able to catch her breath.

"Liddy . . . ," Hayley pleaded.

But Liddy just stared at her, and Hayley knew there was no getting out of it.

"All right, fine, Liddy. You win. I'll get the damn brooch back," Hayley said, sweeping back across the lawn and up the stone steps.

"Oh, this I've got to see," Mona said, chasing after her.

Liddy checked herself out in a compact mirror before following behind both of them.

Inside the church, Hayley slowly walked down the aisle toward the casket. At first she thought swiping the brooch might be easy, especially since there were only two people left in front of the casket. Most of the other mourners had already taken their seats.

But Hayley had forgotten about one key fact.

Her recent history with the deceased.

Everybody knew there was no love lost between the two. And all eyes were fixed on her. How was she going to steal the brooch with everyone watching?

Hayley lagged behind the last two people who stood at the casket. They cried softly, lingering a bit too long. Hayley started to sweat, worried

Reverend Staples would start the service and she would lose her one chance to get the brooch back.

Finally, the two mourners walked away and sat down in a pew.

Hayley was the last one there.

Her back was to the congregation. She lowered her arm inside, as if to stroke Karen's face. She began to shake her shoulders slightly to make it look like she was overcome with emotion and tears.

Her fingers slowly, methodically encircled the brooch. She gave it a quick yank but it was stuck on the fabric. She yanked again.

She heard murmurs behind her. What was she doing? Why was she taking so long?

She gave one last yank.

The brooch broke free, but it tore the fabric. She was about to surreptitiously pocket it when she noticed the good Reverend Staples, having already taken his place in front of the podium next to the casket to deliver his sermon, with a clear view of what she was doing.

His mouth was open in shock.

Hayley burst into tears. For real. This wasn't happening.

Reverend Staples stepped over to her and put a comforting arm around her.

"Reverend, I can explain," Hayley said, sniffling.

"I'm listening . . ."

This was not going to end well.

Hayley decided the best course of action was to lie. "I was just adjusting it. It was crooked. But it got caught on my sleeve and . . ."

Reverend Staples smiled at Hayley as if to say,

"Dear, it's probably not in your best interest to lie in the house of God."

And it didn't help that they were just a few feet away from a statue of Jesus on the cross.

Hayley decided to try a different approach. The truth.

"You see, the brooch doesn't really belong to Karen," Hayley said.

She was trying desperately to talk in a low voice, but everyone in the front pew was leaning forward, on the edge of their seats, straining to hear whatever words they could.

Hayley knew they would pick up enough to seal her fate forever as *that woman who stole the jewelry off a dead woman.*

"Hayley, my best advice to you is to just come clean."

"That's what I'm trying to do, but I know we shouldn't hold up the service any longer so why don't I just sit down . . ."

Reverend Staples leaned in closer and whispered into her ear. "I'm not talking about stealing Karen's jewelry. I'm talking about her untimely death."

Hayley stared at Reverend Staples, not knowing how to respond. A minister was telling her he thought she was guilty of murder.

"If you confess, He will take that into account come Judgment Day," Reverend Staples said, pointing upward with his right index finger.

Then with one hand, he closed Hayley's hand with the brooch in it and said, "I want you to keep that. As a reminder of your responsibility to Karen."

He then turned her around, and sent her down the aisle to the pews toward the back where Liddy

and Mona waited for her. Hayley was so distraught
and embarrassed she didn't watch where she was
going and slammed right into someone. The impact
nearly knocked her off her feet, but a strong pair
of hands steadied her.

"Whoa, Hayley, easy does it. You okay?" It was
Travis Hollingsworth, the handsome young grandson of Lex's boss.

"I'm fine, thank you, Travis. I'm just a little
overwhelmed right now," Hayley said, knowing all
the eyes in the church were still fixed on her.

"She was a fine woman," Travis said solemnly.

"Yes, yes she was," Hayley said, giving Travis a
thin smile as she slid into the pew next to Liddy
and Mona and Travis took a seat on the opposite
side of the aisle.

She didn't notice Liddy grab the brooch from
her and stuff it into her Christian Louboutin handbag. Nor did she hear a word of the reverend's
sermon. She only had one thought in her head
and she kept repeating it over and over. Hayley
knew now, with every bone in her body, that it was
up to her and only her to prove to the entire town
that she was innocent. That it was somebody else
who killed Karen Applebaum.

Maybe even someone in this church at this very
moment.

Hayley was now determined to find out who
that someone was before her brother's boyfriend
booked her for first degree murder.

Chapter 14

There was a parade of friends and colleagues who got up to speak about Karen, and reminisce about her. What a wonderful woman she was. How she was a stalwart, outspoken member of the community. How she was such a warm and loving person. It's funny how someone's entire personality can be whitewashed after they die. Suddenly they magically transform from a royal pain to a revered royal.

Hayley was still smarting from her run-in with Reverend Staples, who stood off to the side during the service as people remembered Karen in glowing terms. The reverend didn't take his eyes off Hayley, and she wondered if he was afraid she was going to also try to steal the copy of the hymnal that rested on a small shelf on the back of the pew in front of her.

This was an utter disaster. The reverend wasn't such a big mouth, but his wife certainly was, and there was no doubt in Hayley's mind that she would spread the tale of Hayley Powell prying

Karen's most beloved possession out of her cold dead hands at the poor woman's own funeral.

No one would care to know the real truth. That Karen probably didn't even know she still had the brooch. That one of her friends must have found it among her things and thought it would look nice on her. That Hayley didn't really pry it out of her cold stiff fingers. Hayley was certain once the story made the rounds she would look nothing short of a grave robber.

Hayley was snapped out of her thoughts by some grief-stricken sobs coming from two rows behind her. She casually turned around to see Karen's despicable ex-husband, Martin Apple-baum, pressing a white cloth hankie to his face with his pudgy hand.

Martin and Karen had divorced over five years ago. He was shorter than his ex-wife and about a hundred and fifty pounds heavier. According to his doctor, he was a heart attack waiting to happen. Hayley found him completely repulsive. Beady eyes. Just a few wisps of hair left on the top of his head, which he combed to the side to give the illusion that he wasn't going completely bald. Martin's head was so big and shiny it could probably be picked up on satellite photos. And he favored bright pastel-colored golf shirts, even in the dead of winter.

Today he was wearing a tangerine jersey under-neath his black sports coat. Hayley chalked it up to Martin just wanting everyone to know he was the president of the Kebo Valley Golf Club going on fifteen years now. A position that didn't pay much, nor garner any real benefits outside of a free cocktail on the nineteenth hole. But Martin flaunted his title as if he were the CEO of Chevron.

Ever since the divorce, Martin had dated a lot and Hayley knew it was mostly because of his bank account. His father had made some wise investments in the stock market when Martin was a boy, and when he died, Martin inherited a few million that he immediately began throwing around town to make himself look like a big shot. In reality, he hadn't worked a day since he was in high school.

Martin not only dated a lot post-divorce, he dated a lot during his marriage to Karen, which might explain the acrimonious alimony fight. He spent so much time with so many women the locals recently began referring to him as the "Jewish Tiger Woods."

Martin was clutching the sleeve of an attractive older woman in her forties sitting next to him, who Hayley recognized as a waitress from Jordan's coffee shop on Cottage Street. Probably Martin's latest paramour. At least for this month.

Mona leaned in to Hayley. "Don't see why Martin's so upset. You should hear some of the names he's called Karen when he's drinking at your brother's bar."

"She got half his fortune in the divorce," Hayley said. "He knows he's not getting a penny of it back in the will."

"He's such a fake, crying his eyes out with snot running out of his nose like that. Why is he pretending to be so upset?" Mona said, craning her neck around to watch the spectacle. "Unless he's trying to cover something up."

Liddy was busy fastening her grandmother's

dragonfly brooch to her lapel. "Everyone knows they loathed each other. All the local restaurants knew to seat them in separate rooms if they showed up to eat on the same night."

"Liddy, please," Hayley said, ripping the brooch off her lapel and stuffing it back inside Liddy's handbag. "Could you at least wait to wear this until after the funeral? I'm humiliated enough."

Liddy threw up her hands, surrendering, and then said in a whisper, "I'm not going to have my funeral here. Too small. I need a much bigger space. I mean, I'm sure I'll draw one or two heads of state."

"How about friggin' Westminster Abbey?" Mona asked, a bit too loudly and with a snort.

"Shhhh," Hayley warned, gesturing to Reverend Staples, who was eyeing all three of them with a stern glare.

Liddy lowered her voice. "You know, I'm less surprised by who is here than who isn't here."

"Her son, I know," Hayley said solemnly.

"The Unabomber?" Mona asked, shaking her head. "What a freak."

Karen's only son was Bradley Applebaum, who was the polar opposite of both his parents. Martin and Karen enjoyed socializing and engaging in the community, but there was always something off about Bradley, even when he was a boy. He had a violent temper and was removed from his school for a semester after setting a girl's hair on fire on purpose in chemistry. His IQ scores were through the roof, but he was never able to adapt socially.

After high school, his father bought him a run-down cabin out in the woods on the other side of the island, hoping he wouldn't have to see him much. Bradley, who was now in his mid-twenties, lived like a recluse, with no electricity or running water, and he occasionally would write letters to the *Times* passionately exhorting his radical antigovernment views. Really, the only person who didn't think he was nuts was Hayley's mother, who always had a soft spot for Bradley before she moved to Florida, which wasn't much of a surprise given how close their political ideas were.

Bradley had been in trouble with the law a few times. Mostly for hunting deer out of season with a nonregistered shotgun. He was just trying to store extra meat for the winter since he refused to shop at the grocery store out of fear the government was poisoning the food supply.

Hayley knew Bradley's conspicuous absence would certainly get tongues wagging. There was no love lost between Bradley and his mother. She was supremely embarrassed about how he had turned out, and he knew exactly how she felt. Whenever anyone asked Karen about her son, she would deflect the question, mumble something about him being fine, and then quickly change the subject.

Hayley was curious to find out just what he thought about his mother's murder.

If she could find him.

Hayley shifted in her seat wondering if the service was ever going to end, when Reverend Staples led the congregation in singing one last hymn before finally inviting everyone for tea and coffee in the church parlor prior to driving out to the cemetery for Karen's burial.

"About time. I think my butt fell asleep," Mona

groaned, standing up and rubbing the back of her jeans.

"You're using your outside voice, Mona," Liddy sighed. "Everyone can hear you."

"Anybody want to grab something to eat? I'm starving," Mona said.

"No, I better get back to the office. I've been gone the whole morning," Hayley said, suddenly distracted by something. "Wait for me. I just want to apologize again to Reverend Staples."

"Forget it, Hayley. Let's just go," Mona said.

"I can't let him think I tried to steal jewelry off a corpse," Hayley said.

"But you did try to steal jewelry off a corpse," Mona said.

"No, she didn't. The brooch didn't belong to Karen," Liddy piped in.

"I'll just be a second," Hayley said, pushing her way through the crowd that was trying to file out in an orderly fashion.

Reverend Staples stepped down from the podium, and started to walk out through a side door to another room where the tea and coffee were to be served.

"Excuse me, Reverend Staples?" Hayley waved her hand, trying to flag him down.

But he either didn't hear her or was trying to get away from her. Hayley couldn't be sure. He didn't stop.

Hayley raced to catch up with him, and didn't see a large flower arrangement blocking her way. She crashed right into it, toppling the whole thing over, sending spring carnations flying everywhere.

This was just getting better and better.

Oh well. At least she didn't knock over the coffin.

Hayley began frantically picking up the strewn flowers and stuffing them back into the arrangement that was done up in the shape of a heart. That's when she noticed the card.

It was unsigned. But the sentiment was clear. *I will miss you forever. Today. Tomorrow. And always. With all my heart.* Whoever wrote the card dotted all of his or her "i's" with little hearts.

Too cute.

Hayley put the card back inside the plastic holder. She decided not to chase down Reverend Staples and embarrass herself any more.

No, she would join Liddy and Mona for lunch after all. The office could wait. She was too curious to see if she and her two BFFs could figure out if Karen Applebaum had a secret lover nobody in town knew about, and who it might be.

Chapter 15

When Hayley finally got back to the office, a little tipsy from the two Manhattans she had with Mona and Liddy at lunch, there was a message from Lex Bansfield.

Hayley debated whether or not she should call him back. Maybe he was going to tell her he had finally decided to sue her for plowing into him with her car. It might be better if she dodged him for as long as she could, or at least until she found herself a good lawyer.

On the other hand, he didn't seem all that put out when she last saw him at the hospital. In fact, he still seemed rather smitten with her. Smitten? Why did she think with words like that? It was as if she were trying to live in a Jane Austen novel.

Hayley picked up the phone and started to return the call.

And then she hung up.

No, after what she had been through today at Karen Applebaum's funeral, there was just no way she could possibly deal with whatever Lex Bansfield had to say.

Hayley began checking her work e-mail, but her mind soon drifted. What if Lex was calling for a professional reason? What if he just wanted to sell his jeep and was simply calling to place an ad in the classified section? It would be wrong for her not to respond.

Hayley picked up the phone again and started to return the call.

And then she hung up again.

Why was she so nervous? What was preventing her from just getting him on the line and finding out what it was he wanted? She began to feel foolish. This was ridiculous. Of course she should call him back. She had already turned him down for a date, so obviously he wasn't calling to ask her out again. A man has his pride.

No, Hayley's gut was telling her there had to be another reason why he was calling her at the paper, and so finally, with no more hesitation, she picked up the phone and called him back.

Lex picked up on the first ring.

"Hi, Lex," Hayley said, as casual as she could. "Hayley Powell at the *Times*. I see here you called me earlier."

"Yes," Lex said. "Why did you refuse to go out on a date with me?"

So much for her gut.

"I . . . I . . . Well, when you asked me . . . I was so flustered . . . because, well, in case you forgot, I ran you down with my car."

"Oh, I remember. There's no chance I'll ever forget that fun little memory," Lex said.

"Again, I'm so sorry . . ."

"You already apologized more than enough

times. I just find it mind-boggling that even after you sent me flying onto the hood of your car, and injured me enough that I needed multiple stitches, you still, even after all that, turned me down for a date."

"I . . . I really didn't think you would be this upset about it," Hayley said.

"I'm not upset. Do I sound upset?"

"A little bit, yes."

"Well, I wasn't at first. But the more I thought about it the more it ticked me off. And then it hit me. You owe me."

"I . . . what?"

"You owe me. You owe me at least one date after what you did."

"I really don't think we should discuss this while I am at the office," Hayley said.

"Oh, yes we should. The boss gives me one fifteen-minute break a day when he's in town and according to my watch, I've got five minutes left, so I need to wrap this up pretty quick. You going out with me or not?"

"Can I think about it?"

"No."

"No?"

"Hell, no! You hit me with your car! You should be scrambling to make it up to me! And if you're too thick in the head to see that, then maybe I should sue you for damages in order to drive some sense into you!"

Hayley was speechless. She had really gotten to this guy without even trying. She had no idea how to play this.

Bruce wandered into the bull pen. "Hey, Hayley,

you got any candy bars around? I got a hell of a craving for something sweet."

Hayley shook her head and then went back to her phone conversation. "Are you blackmailing me into going out with you?"

"Yes. Is it working?" Lex said.

"Who's that? Who's blackmailing you?" Bruce asked.

Hayley covered the mouthpiece. "None of your business. I don't have any candy. I'm sorry."

"Oh," Bruce said, disappointed. "I'm out of cash. You have any money I can borrow so I can run across the street and buy some?"

Hayley sighed. "In my purse. Now leave me alone."

Bruce picked up her bag and began rummaging through it.

"Who are you talking to?" Lex said on the other end of the phone.

"I'm sorry, but I am at the office and it's kind of busy and now is not a really good time to have this conversation," Hayley said.

"Fine. Say yes and we can both hang up," Lex said.

"Yes. Okay. Fine. When?"

"Tonight," Lex said. "I already made reservations at Havana."

"Tonight? Why so soon?"

"Because if I give you any wiggle room, you'll just come up with an excuse to get out of it. Man, I've never had to work this hard for one lousy date!"

Hayley looked up to see Bruce drop her bag on the desk. He was holding something in his hand but she couldn't see what it was.

"Did you find any?" Hayley said.

"Any what?" Lex asked on the other end of the line.

"I'm not talking to you. I'm talking to Bruce," Hayley said.

Bruce's face was ashen.

"Hayley? Are you still there?" Lex asked.

Hayley was now suddenly more concerned for Bruce. His face was pale and he looked as if he was about to pass out.

Hayley went back to her phone conversation. "Yes. Tonight. Pick me up at seven o'clock. A simple dinner. I can't stay out too late. It's a school night."

"Understood," Lex said. "Thank you. I'm exhausted from this conversation, you know that?"

Hayley couldn't help but smile. "See you tonight."

She hung up and looked at Bruce again. "What is it, Bruce? What's wrong?"

Bruce showed her a small glass vial with a colorless liquid in it. "What's this?"

"I don't know. Where did you get it?"

"Your purse."

"It's not mine."

"I found it in the bottom of your bag."

"Well, it's not mine, Bruce. I don't know how it could've gotten in there."

Bruce examined the vial more closely and popped it open. "Has an almond odor. I've seen enough true detective shows to know this could be cyanide."

Hayley couldn't help but laugh. "You're out of

your mind. I had an Almond Joy earlier. You're probably smelling that."

"Do you mind if I keep this?"

"Knock yourself out," Hayley said. Her mind wasn't really on Bruce's big discovery. She was more concerned with what she was going to wear on her date with Lex that evening. And did she have enough time to get her hair done? If only there was someplace that offered walk-in liposuction. She would have to try and slip out early to get everything done.

Bruce took the vial of liquid in the back and she heard him pick up the phone in his office and call someone. He talked very low and she couldn't make out what he was saying or with whom he was talking.

Hayley e-mailed Sal and asked if it would be all right for her to leave early, and once she got his okay, Hayley raced to finish up her work so she could get out of there.

As Hayley drove over to the hair salon, she did stop to think about the mysterious vial Bruce had supposedly found in her bag. Where did it come from? What was it? But then she pulled into the driveway of the salon and that unpleasant thought was immediately replaced by her wondering if Jessica would have time to do her face while her hair was under the dryer.

In retrospect, Hayley probably should have paid more attention to Bruce and the vial. Because she had no idea at the time that Bruce had called Police Chief Sergio Alvares at the station, and that Sergio picked up the vial, got in his car, and drove to Bangor to have the liquid tested. It turned out the substance in the vial was definitely cyanide.

The same poison that had killed Karen Applebaum.

And Hayley was also completely oblivious to the fact that Sergio then called two of his officers, Donnie and Earl, to drive over to Hayley's house and place her under arrest for murder just as Lex Bansfield pulled into the driveway to pick her up for their first date.

Well, looking on the bright side, it was one of those first dates neither party would soon forget.

Chapter 16

Hayley sat alone in the jail cell at the police station wondering how she had gotten to this point.

A murder suspect?

She had raised hell in high school, bought beer with a fake ID, bounced a check once at a local boutique when she needed some new lip gloss. But never in her thirty-five years had Hayley Powell ever come close to killing anyone.

But now it seemed like the whole town, even the police, were convinced she had gotten her hands on some arsenic and added a few drops to Karen Applebaum's homemade New England clam chowder. The recipe she apparently stole from Hayley.

Hayley stood up and brushed the dust off the back of her dress. The cell rarely got used except by an occasional drunk or teenage vandal so cleaning it was usually an afterthought.

Hayley walked over and grabbed ahold of the bars separating her from Donnie and Earl, who were eating sandwiches they had bought at a sub shop down the block.

"Excuse me, guys, don't I get to make a phone call?" Hayley asked.

Donnie and Earl looked at each other, waiting for the other to speak first. When Earl took another bite of his sandwich, Donnie figured he should probably say something. "Uh, I don't know. Do you?"

"Yes, it's the law, I think," Hayley said, unsure whether this was actually true or not. "I mean, I see it done on TV all the time."

No one except Lex knew she was in jail. Her kids were home and upstairs, oblivious, doing their homework. Scratch that. They were probably chatting on Facebook or playing with the Xbox. But, in any event, they had no idea their mother had been arrested. They might get a little worried tomorrow morning when no one was there to scream at them to get out of bed and ready for school.

"Can one of you give me my cell phone so I can let my kids know where I am," Hayley said, trying not to cry.

Donnie and Earl looked at each other again.

"Think we should call the chief?" Donnie asked.

"Yeah, see if it's okay," Earl said, nodding.

Hayley stepped away from the bars and sat back down, putting her head in her hands. She could only imagine the gossip mill tomorrow when word spread about her arrest.

A few minutes later, Earl came over with a big set of keys and began unlocking the door to the cell.

Hayley jumped to her feet. "So it's okay to make a phone call?"

"No. We got his voice mail. Cell service sucks between Bangor and Ellsworth. He's probably not getting a signal. You have a visitor."

For a moment Hayley thought it might be Lex. Her knight in shining armor. Here to assure her he would do everything in his power to fight these bogus charges and defend her honor if it was the last thing he ever did.

It wasn't Lex.

Bruce Linney appeared behind Earl as he slid open the door. Earl waved him inside and Bruce offered Hayley a weak smile.

Her heart sank.

Then she turned her back on him. "Come to gloat?"

"Of course not," Bruce said. "I came to see how you're holding up."

"That's rich," Hayley spat out. "You're the reason I'm in here."

"I didn't have a choice, Hayley," Bruce said, slowly approaching her, and gently putting a hand on her shoulder. "If I didn't hand over the poison, I would've risked being charged as an accessory."

"You really think I did this?"

"No. I don't. But how do you explain the cyanide in your bag?"

"I can't explain it."

"It killed me having to turn that evidence over to the chief. You must know that."

"How could I possibly know that? You're constantly ribbing me and giving me a hard time. I thought you hated me."

"Far from it," Bruce said, eyes downcast. "I think you're . . . Let me put it this way. If there is one silver lining in this situation, for me at least, it's that your arrest totally screwed up your date with that caretaker guy."

Hayley smiled. She appreciated his honesty. She had no idea Bruce was remotely interested in her.

"So you were jealous?"

Suddenly Bruce snapped out of whatever romantic notions were swirling about in his head. He never wore his heart on his sleeve, and decided for the sake of his own reputation that now was certainly not the time to start.

"No! I just meant I like you as a friend and I just don't trust that guy."

Hayley shook her head.

Typical Bruce. A macho jerk to the very end.

Then Hayley noticed Bruce holding his iPhone in the palm of his right hand. There was a small flashing red light on the screen.

"What's that?" Hayley asked.

"What?"

"That red light on your phone. What is that?"

Bruce's face turned beet red. Hayley snatched the phone out of his hand and looked at the screen. It was an application for an audio recording device.

"Are you taping our conversation?" Hayley asked.

Bruce noticed the phone. "Oh. Yeah. I forgot to mention that when I came in."

"What for?"

"I'm a reporter, Hayley. It's what I do."

"So this is an interview for the paper? I can't believe you! I wouldn't be surprised if you planted that evidence just so you'd have yourself a big scoop!"

"You know that's not true," Bruce said.

"We're done talking, Bruce," Hayley said and sat down on her cot with the thin, musty mattress. A puff of dust floated up from the impact.

"What are you going to do, Hayley? Talk to the *Herald*? Sal will fire your ass if you don't give us the exclusive."

"Exclusive what?"

"Your story. How you're feeling about being the chief suspect in Karen Applebaum's murder."

Hayley knew it was true. But hearing it out loud brought it all home. She was the focus of the investigation now. And there was no escaping that reality.

"Get out."

"Don't do this, Hayley," Bruce pleaded.

"Out! I'm not saying another word to you until I talk to my lawyer. I can only imagine what you'll say about me in the article."

"Do you need anything?"

"No! Not from you, anyway. Just go."

Defeated, Bruce called for Earl, who shuffled back over, and after fumbling with his keys again for a few seconds, let Bruce out of the cell.

Hayley fought back tears as she curled up in a fetal position on the cot and debated her next move. Someone put that poison in her bag to frame her for the murder. She had to get out of jail somehow.

Because, she knew she was going to have to conduct her own investigation to prove her innocence.

Chapter 17

Sergio arrived at the station shortly after Bruce left, and Hayley was finally able to make her phone call. She quickly got in touch with Mona and told her to get over to her house and fill her kids in and then call Ted Rivers, a local lawyer, in fact one of the only lawyers in town, and see what he could do about getting her out of jail. He had an office right upstairs from Liddy's real estate business.

Soon after, Liddy called the station. Word was spreading fast. She insisted she be able to talk to the prisoner, so after getting the okay from Sergio, Donnie handed Hayley the phone.

"This is the worst thing that's ever happened to me and it's not even happening to *me*," Liddy cried through the phone.

"It's all right. Mona's calling Ted Rivers. Judge Carter is an old family friend. I'm sure he'll let me post bail until all of this is straightened out."

"How could Sergio, of all people, have you arrested?"

"He didn't have much of a choice. The evidence is kind of overwhelming."

"Well, still, he's your brother's boyfriend. Don't you worry, Hayley, I'm going to organize a protest demanding they spring you immediately."

"You know, Liddy, I'm not sure that's really such a good . . ."

Liddy had already hung up.

Hayley handed back the phone to Donnie.

Sergio appeared outside the cell. He had a pained expression on his face.

Hayley knew this couldn't be easy on him.

"I'm sending Donnie out for some food. I thought you might be hungry," Sergio said.

"I can't possibly think about food at a time like this."

"Okay. I understand," Sergio said and turned to walk away.

"Where's he going?" Hayley quickly asked before he got too far.

Sergio shrugged. "I'm not sure. I told him to drive around town to see what's still open."

"I was on my way to Havana when Donnie and Earl arrested me."

"We can't afford Havana, Hayley. I'm sorry."

"That's okay. How about some fried clams?"

"Sure," Sergio said, just grateful she was still speaking to him.

"With french fries. Maybe a salad. Dressing on the side. No, forget it. Why bother rationing my salad dressing with all the fried food I'll be eating?

Just have them pour it on. But make it a light dressing. And I'd like extra croutons."

Sergio was trying to remember the entire order. "Extra croutons. Got it."

"And something sweet. Chocolate. Chocolate makes me feel better when I'm stressed out. And do you have any Jack Daniel's around?"

"I can't give you alcohol, Hayley. I'm sorry."

"I figured. Thought I'd give it a shot."

Sergio smiled. "I'm going to make your time here as comfortable as possible, Hayley. I promise you that."

"Thank you, Sergio. I know you're just doing your job."

Sergio reached through the bars and took Hayley's hand and gave it a squeeze. Then he headed back to his office.

Forty-five minutes later, Hayley heard what sounded like chanting coming from outside the station. Sergio was shouting and there was a lot of commotion out in the reception area, but she couldn't tell what was going on.

Finally, Earl ran back near the cell, a look of panic on his face. He flung open a storage closet door and began rummaging around.

"What's going on out there?" Hayley asked.

"A bunch of unruly women are protesting! Chief's trying to get them under control! I'm seeing if we have any riot gear."

Liddy and the cavalry had come to her rescue.

"Oh, Earl, relax, you have nothing to fear from Liddy Crawford," Hayley said.

"She just hit me in the head with her sign!"

Hayley stifled a laugh. Liddy had a flare for the

dramatic. Plus, she always felt she had been born too late, and would have really shined as a late sixties radical advocating free love and protesting the evils of corporate America.

That was before she made a killing in real estate and discovered the personal benefits of tax cuts for the rich.

"Damn, we don't have any bulletproof vests or helmets or anything. How can a police station not have any riot gear?" Earl asked.

"Probably because there's never been a riot in Bar Harbor," Hayley said.

That satisfied Earl.

He slammed the closet door shut and ran back outside.

Hayley paced back and forth. She intermittently heard Sergio trying to reason with the crowd and then a chorus of shrill, deafening voices drowning him out. She felt bad for him. But at the same time, she had a warm feeling about the dedication of her friends to get her out of the slammer.

A few minutes later, Mona arrived in a huff, and was allowed to see Hayley.

"There must be fifty women out there waving signs. How'd Liddy get them organized so fast?" Mona wondered.

"I'm sure all it took was one posting on Facebook," Hayley said. *"Project Runway* is on tonight and they all chat about it online, so I'm sure she had an entire army of bored women on call."

"Gemma and Dustin are fine. They're over at my house right now watching a movie with my kids," Mona said. "I tried to bring you a lobster dinner, but Barney Fife out there was afraid you'd use the cracker to loosen the bars and escape. Dimwits!"

"It's okay. They're bringing me fried clams."

"We're going to get you out of here," Mona said. "Liddy said Ted Rivers has already called Judge Carter and they're arranging a hearing for eight o'clock tomorrow morning. It'll be their first order of business."

Donnie arrived with a brown paper bag with grease stains on it. He had his keys in his hand and was about to open the cell door, but Mona blocked his way. She stepped closer toward him, mustering up the most intimidating stare she could. Mona was even taller than Donnie and far more imposing and her breasts were practically smothering him.

Hayley noticed Donnie's hand shaking slightly.

Once Mona made her point, which Hayley assumed was *Don't mess with my best friend*, she moved aside and allowed Donnie to enter the cell and hand Hayley the bag.

"It might be a little cold. It took me awhile to get through the crowd out there," Donnie said. "One of them tried to give me a wedgie. I mean, come on, it's been years since high school!"

"That's okay, Donnie. Thank you," Hayley said, and removed the container of fried clams from the bag.

"Where's the tartar sauce?" Mona asked.

"What?" Donnie's voice cracked.

"How do you expect her to eat fried clams without tartar sauce?" Mona bellowed.

"I-I can go back and get some. It'll only take me a few minutes. If the protestors let me through."

"No, I don't need tartar sauce, Donnie. This is just fine. I appreciate all you've done," Hayley said.

Donnie nodded and smiled. Mona threw him one last threatening look. His smile quickly faded and he retreated to the front office.

Mona then turned to Hayley. "Anything else you need while I'm here?"

"No," Hayley said, popping a fried clam in her mouth. "If everything goes well with Judge Carter, I should make it home before the kids go to school."

"Cool beans. Now try to get some sleep. You'll be out of here first thing tomorrow morning."

"I wouldn't survive without you, Mona. Both you and Liddy."

"But me more, right?"

Hayley laughed. "Just don't tell her."

"Are you kidding? I live to make her crazy jealous."

Mona blew Hayley a kiss and left.

The protest died down around 10 P.M. due to the fact that most of the women wanted to get home to see who was going to be eliminated on *Project Runway*.

Hayley tried to get comfortable on the cot, and had just begun drifting off to sleep when she was jolted awake by more shouting. This time it wasn't a gaggle of her would-be activist girlfriends.

It was one voice. One very recognizable voice. It was her brother, Randy. And he was hopping mad.

"I have to hear from one of my customers that you've arrested my sister for murder?"

Sergio was speaking low, and trying to keep a lid on the escalating situation with his boyfriend.

It wasn't working.

"Why didn't you call me? I was at the bar all night!" Randy yelled.

"Because I had to drive back from Bangor after I got the poison tested and you know there is not good cell service on the way, and when I got back I had to deal with all of these Protestants . . ."

"Protestants? What Protestants?"

"Hayley's friends showed up with signs and were blocking the entrance to the station . . ."

"You mean protesters!"

"Isn't that what I said?"

"I'm living with Ricky Ricardo!"

Hayley felt terrible for Sergio. The poor guy was under a lot of pressure and she was obviously the only one who understood why he had to make such a difficult decision to arrest her.

"If it's any consolation, the clams were delicious!" Hayley called out.

Randy pounded down the hall to the holding cell. When he saw Hayley behind bars he gasped. "I tried to mentally prepare myself all the way over here to see you like this, but you can never truly be ready."

Like Liddy, Randy also had a flair for the dramatic.

"I'm fine, really," Hayley said, trying to give her brother a hug, which proved impossible given the metal bars separating them.

So she settled for petting his shoulders to comfort him.

Randy spun around to Sergio, who had followed him, a hangdog expression on his face. "My own sister . . ."

"Randy, I'll be out before breakfast," Hayley said, trying to be reassuring. She was handling her own arrest better than everybody else in her life.

Randy was still focused on Sergio. "It's inexcusable that you are taking out our relationship issues on a beloved family member."

Sergio's mouth dropped open. "What relationship issues?"

"You know exactly what I'm talking about," Randy said.

Hayley studied Sergio's face for a moment. "Actually, I don't think he does, Randy."

"Well, this isn't about the cracks in our relationship," Randy said. "This is about you. And how we're going to make all this go away."

"What cracks?" Sergio said, starting to get upset.

Randy ignored Sergio and focused on his sister. "Do you have bail money?" Randy asked.

"Depends. If it's under twenty dollars, we're good," Hayley said, forcing a smile.

"Well, don't worry. I can put up my bar as collateral."

"Oh, I don't want you to do that," Hayley said.

"I trust you not to skip town," Randy said, smiling.

"Don't assume anything," Hayley said with a wink.

"You call me if you need anything. Fresh sheets, a DVD player, some air freshener . . ."

"I'm only going to be here one night."

"Okay. I love you, Hayley."

"Love you, too."

Randy turned and flashed Sergio an angry look before marching out.

Sergio turned to Hayley.

"I don't see cracks! What cracks is he talking about?"

Sergio chased Randy outside, finally leaving Hayley alone.

Hayley was confident that in just a few hours she would be standing before Judge Carter, who would immediately grant bail, and then she would be out with enough time to get the kids to school and make it to the office without having to take another personal day.

And she would finally be free to find out just who wanted her to take the fall for Karen Applebaum's murder.

There was also the matter of her column. She couldn't ignore what was happening anymore. She had to address the scandal head on . . . along with a tasty recipe of course.

Island Food & Spirits

by
Hayley Powell

By now I'm sure some of you have heard all about my unfortunate (and might I add) very short stay in our local jail. I can honestly say some people didn't even know I was gone (like my kids).

I will address the jail situation head-on in just a bit but first, because of my brief encounter with our local law enforcement and subsequent lockup, let me tell you that my eyes have been opened to a very serious crisis that we have brewing right here in our very own town, and in our very own police station. And that is, our local jail food, or should I say, the lack of it, when it comes to the all important four food groups.

Frankly, I was appalled that our local law enforcement was not prepared to serve some kind of healthy and decent meal to anyone that might have a minor incident, and have to be detained for the evening, or God forbid, a few days.

Now, I'm not saying we need to treat the incarcerated with a seven course meal. Which reminds me. I have the most wonderful orange sorbet recipe for our fourth course this week that is to die for! Well, I guess I wouldn't go that far given recent local events, but I swear you will love it!

And I would also like to publicly thank Martin Applebaum for giving me this great idea for the sorbet when I saw the spiffy bright orange shirt he was wearing just the other day. It inspired me. I must say Martin's bold color choices just suit that man, and really make him stand out and be noticed in a crowd!

Well, back to the situation at hand.

I think our local police force, which otherwise does an outstanding job (shout out to you, Sergio!), is a little behind on this issue. So I'd like to suggest that volunteers sign up to prepare a quick, light, and healthy meal for those who have been unforeseeably detained. I don't think we will have to do this very often, but with this one small gesture, our visitors should go away with a better appreciation of our town and our law enforcement, not to mention a full stomach.

I have some really simple meal recipes I'd be willing to share with you and I'm sure many of you have some great ideas of your own! So give me a call and let's get the ball rolling on this project.

Now unfortunately, I do have to address another matter that has been getting quite a bit of unwanted attention around town. There has been a lot of talk that the dear late Karen Applebaum and I were having a sort of nasty feud. Suffice it to say, Karen and I were not friends. But I would like to go on record as saying that no matter how much I may detest someone (detest is a strong word, but some people just don't make it very easy to be civil), there is no way I would or could actually do harm to that person.

And I am also secure in the knowledge that I will be proven one hundred percent innocent of the crime that many of you may be thinking I committed.

But let me repeat. I have never broken the law. Wait. Let me rephrase. I have never brought harm upon anyone. And I never will.

So enough of this unpleasantness. It's time to unwind with a well-deserved, relaxing, and refreshing cocktail or two, and then move on to our fourth course, this week!

The Orange Blossom

2 ounces of good gin (or a bit more, depending on what kind of day you had)
1 ounce orange juice
1 teaspoon superfine sugar

Combine your gin, orange juice, and sugar in a shaker glass that you have half-filled with ice cubes. Shake and strain into a chilled martini glass. Garnish with a slice of orange and enjoy! A hint: These are so good you won't want to drink just one, so make up a nice big batch of them and you can sip on them at your leisure.

For our fourth course in our seven course meal, it's time to cleanse our palates before we move forward, and you are really going to enjoy this mouthwatering orange sorbet.

Mango Orange Sorbet

4 cups cubed chilled mango
½ cup cold water
¼ cup orange juice
½ cup white sugar

Blend your mango, water, and orange juice in your blender until smooth, then add your sugar until all blended together.

Pour mixture into an ice cream maker and freeze according to your ice cream maker's directions and enjoy!

Chapter 18

After posting bail, Hayley got a lift home from Randy, who insisted they have breakfast and decide on a course of action for mounting her defense. Hayley couldn't believe she was living in some *Law & Order* nightmare, and that she actually had to think about a defense. But Randy was insistent.

Hayley knew Gemma and Dustin were fully aware of their mother's predicament when she picked them up at Mona's and drove them home earlier and they wanted to hear all the gory details. But Hayley wasn't about to share her harrowing night behind bars.

Okay, it wasn't that harrowing. She was in the cell alone. The fried clams she had for dinner were actually not bad. And the cot wasn't nearly as uncomfortable to sleep on as she had feared. In fact, her lower back always ached after falling asleep watching the Lifetime Movie Network on her lumpy couch. But this morning, after a good night's rest on that jailhouse cot, her lumbar was feeling just fine.

"If you go to prison, are we going to have to go live with Dad in Iowa? Because I don't want to start over at a new school," Dustin sighed.

"No one's going to prison," Hayley said.

"Isn't that what Martha Stewart said?" Gemma asked.

"She only had to go for five months," Hayley said.

"So prison is a real possibility?" Gemma asked, gasping.

"Don't be so dramatic, Gemma," Hayley said, laughing. "Martha Stewart was convicted for investment fraud. What I'm dealing with here is . . ."

"Murder!" Gemma cried. "You could seriously get the death penalty! Wait. Does Maine even have the death penalty?"

Hayley realized she probably should have thought more carefully about what she was going to say before she opened her big mouth.

"Everything's going to be fine because your mother didn't kill anyone," Randy said, putting a pot of coffee on the burner and turning up the heat.

"Your uncle's right," Hayley said calmly. "I'm completely innocent. Now, I see the bus coming up the street, so get your butts in gear, or you'll miss it."

"You're not driving us?" Dustin said, frowning.

"Court made me really late. No time. Now go. And stop worrying, because there's absolutely nothing to worry about."

Hayley gave both her kids quick pecks on the

cheek and they grabbed their backpacks and headed out the door.

The second the door shut behind them, Hayley spun around to Randy.

"Holy crap, do you really think I could get the death penalty?" Hayley wailed.

"Of course not," Randy said. "Maine doesn't have the death penalty. Besides, you didn't touch a hair on Karen Applebaum's head. And neither did any self-respecting stylist in a hundred mile radius."

"Randy, don't speak ill of the dead!"

"It's a nervous joke. You know I make nervous jokes when I'm upset. And thinking of you showing up on one of those weekend *Lockup Raw* shows is scaring the hell out of me."

"You just said I had no reason to worry!"

"I was just putting on a brave face in front of the kids! The poison was in your bag, Hayley!"

"I appreciate your calming influence," Hayley said. "Is nine in the morning too early for a cocktail?"

"It's happy hour somewhere in the world."

"No, I'm not going to get all worked up over this," Hayley said as she grabbed a half-eaten donut from an otherwise empty white box. "I don't need alcohol to deal with stress."

Hayley took a big bite of the donut.

"Especially when sugar is so readily available," Randy said.

Hayley threw him an irritated look and then went to the cupboard to get two coffee mugs. "Look, I can't explain how that vial of cyanide showed up in my bag. I didn't put it there. Someone else did."

"Whoever killed Karen."

"Right. So all we have to do is find out who, besides me, hated her guts," Hayley said, taking another bite of the donut.

"That's most of the town."

"Let's face it. Karen was kind of a bitch when you get right down to it," Hayley said. "I'm sure she had no shortage of enemies."

"Yeah, but you were the only one who got caught with the same poison that killed her," Randy added helpfully.

"I'm trying to remain upbeat and positive and constantly repeating observations like that are really starting to bring me down, okay?"

"Got it," Randy said, a sheepish look on his face.

"We need to look for clues, anything that might suggest someone in Karen's circle who had a concrete motive to get rid of her."

"Too bad the police have cordoned off her house," Randy said. "I'm sure if we got a chance to poke around in there we could turn something up."

Hayley didn't answer Randy. She was too busy thinking.

Randy looked at her and suddenly felt queasy. "But obviously it would be foolish of you to try and get in there, because it is an official crime scene, right?"

Hayley's mind was still racing.

"Right?" Randy said, a bit louder.

"We should probably wait until after dark to go over there. I mean, Sergio doesn't have the manpower to watch the house all day and all night."

"Hayley, you're not serious."

"What? All it will take is a pair of scissors to cut through the yellow tape and ten minutes tops to go through the place. It's really not a big deal. She lived alone. And it's not as if Karen will come home and find us."

Randy just looked at her, aghast. "Us? What *us*? I'm not getting involved in this."

"Somebody needs to keep watch in case there's a patrol car in the area or a neighbor walking a dog who could tip off the police that we're there."

"Stop staying *we*! I can't go with you. Quick reminder. My boyfriend is the chief of police. If I got caught breaking and entering, do you know what that would mean?"

"Yes, I wouldn't have to spend the night in jail alone next time. You'd be there as moral support."

"No, I'd be there as a codefendant!"

"You're overreacting, Randy. Sergio would never arrest you," Hayley said.

"That's what we all said about you, and look how that turned out. You're out on bail, Hayley. If you do anything illegal, it will be revoked and you will be tossed right back inside, and there will be no getting out the next time."

"Randy, listen to me. Karen's house is set off from the main road. You drive by there all the time. The closest streetlight has been busted for months. There is no way anyone will see us enter if we approach from the woods behind the house."

"No!"

"Can we stop playing this game? We both know you're going to cave and go with me."

"Well, see, that just proves you don't know me so well anymore, because I've changed over the years and I've developed a very strong backbone and I will no longer automatically do everything you say just because you're my big sister."

Hayley just stared at him, waiting for him to break.

It took another minute of his hand-wringing before she knew she had him.

"Promise me we won't get caught," Randy said quietly.

"We're not going to get caught. I promise," Hayley said.

"You also promised me when we were kids that N Sync would never break up!"

"Trust your big sister," Hayley said, pouring a cup of coffee and handing it to him.

Randy took a big gulp of the hot coffee and eyed Hayley warily.

She knew she just had to wait him out.

Once, when Randy was four years old, she convinced him her mud pies were really made of Godiva chocolate. This breaking and entering scheme was a breeze in comparison.

"You in?" Hayley said, handing him the last bit of her donut.

Randy nodded and tossed the piece of donut in his mouth.

Hayley smiled.

Their secret raid was officially set in motion.

Chapter 19

As it turned out, Randy had very little to fear when it came to breaking into Karen Applebaum's house after dark. Everything Hayley had predicted turned out to be true. The nearest streetlight was broken. The woods behind the house provided the perfect cover for the brother and sister team of would-be investigators to approach. And they effortlessly slipped under the yellow police tape that cordoned off the property. They were at the back door within seconds.

Neither of them really expected the door to be unlocked and it wasn't. Hayley jiggled the handle a couple of times before giving up.

"Should we break a window?" Randy wondered.

"No," Hayley said. "Nobody can know we were ever here."

"Then how are we going to get inside?"

Hayley pulled a flashlight out of a side pocket in her dark blue sweat jacket and clicked it on. She waved it around and caught something in the darkness.

"What's that?"

"What? I don't see anything," Randy said, squinting.

"Over there."

Hayley steadied the flashlight and moved closer to the object to get a good look.

It was a little bearded man, no more than a foot tall, in a green jacket and red pants with a matching cap, standing on the lawn, waving at them.

Hayley jumped back from fright, nearly losing her balance.

Randy steadied her. "Relax. It's just a gnome. Karen has a whole collection of them."

"I had no idea Karen was so . . . tacky," Hayley said.

"I think he's kind of cute. Look at him waving. Like he's welcoming us," Randy said, waving back.

Hayley thought about this for a moment. "Right. He's Karen's version of a welcome mat. And what do some people keep hidden under a welcome mat?"

Randy looked at her blankly for a second before the lightbulb in his head snapped on. "A key!"

Randy bounded over to the gnome and turned him over. Sure enough, there was a silver key sticking up just enough from the dirt for him to see. He brushed it off with his hand and ran over to the back door. He slipped it in the lock and turned. The bolt retracted and he pushed open the door.

"When did you become such a good detective?" Randy asked.

"I had a good teacher," Hayley said, smiling.

"You went to school to become a detective?"

"No. My imaginary boyfriend Mark Harmon. You know I never miss an episode of *NCIS*."

"Okay, the next mystery we need to solve is 'The Case of Your Missing Life,'" Randy said.

Hayley smacked him on the shoulder and then pushed past him and went inside.

Randy was close on her heels.

They were in the kitchen. Hayley flipped on a light. There was a chalk outline of a body drawn on the floor.

"Is that where you found her?" Randy asked.

Hayley nodded.

"I had no idea she was so thick around the middle. She was tasting too much of her rich sauces, I guess," Randy said.

"Randy!" Hayley said, smacking him again.

"I know, I know, don't speak ill of the dead. These are my nervous jokes," Randy said. "And right now I'm a bundle of nerves."

Hayley put the flashlight back in her pocket and looked around. "Okay, you look around down here and I'll go upstairs."

"Okay," Randy said, as he began opening drawers in the kitchen searching for clues.

Hayley walked down the hall and ascended the creaky steps to the second floor. She started with Karen's bedroom. It was neatly appointed, but had a musty odor. And there were a few more smiling gnomes on top of her dresser. Hayley noticed the bland yellow paint peeling from the wall. Karen was such a perfectionist, she was surprised Karen hadn't repainted. There were other signs that perhaps Karen was distracted lately, and not so fastidious about everything. There was a pile of bills on her dresser, a few of them late notices. That was so unlike Karen. The *Herald* paid her a decent salary. Enough to cover her cable bill, at least.

Randy called from downstairs. "Did Karen have a cat?"

"Yes," Hayley answered. "Why?"

"There's a small maid's quarters off the living room with a litter box, bowls for food and water and a little round bed with a paw print design. So what happened to it?"

"I heard Karen's cousin took him in after she died," Hayley said.

"Spoiled cat had his own room! Didn't even have to leave for his meals!"

"No self-respecting chef would ever allow pet food in her kitchen," Hayley said.

Hayley continued going through drawers, then turned to the closet, sorting through the clothes. She wrinkled her nose at an ostentatious fur coat draped over a plastic hanger. Leave it to Karen to wear roadkill.

Hayley pushed it aside, but the coat slid off the hanger and dropped to the floor. She picked it up and noticed something nestled in a pocket inside the lining. It was some kind of card. She pulled it out. It was a Mother's Day card. It had to be from her son, Bradley. He was her only child.

Hayley opened it. Inside were the words, *Get out of town now or you're going to die.* It was scrawled in red ink. And it wasn't signed. But it was a Mother's Day card, so who else could it have been from but Bradley?

Why was Bradley threatening his own mother? What had she done to him?

Hayley stuffed the card in her pocket and cased the rest of the bedroom. There was a copy of the *Island Times* crumpled up on the floor next to the bed. Hayley picked it up and thumbed through it and noticed that the page with her own column had been ripped out. She searched some more and found the missing page wadded up and thrown into the adjoining bathroom's trash can. No big mystery there. Karen was definitely not a fan of Hayley's new cooking column.

Hayley was just about done searching the bedroom when she noticed a cordless phone on the opposite night table. She decided to see if there were any messages that came in right about the time Karen was killed. She knew the police wouldn't have erased them. That would be compromising the crime scene.

Hayley pressed the button for voice mail and there were three messages. The first was from her dentist confirming an appointment next Wednesday for her six-month cleaning. The second was a hang up. And the third was from a woman whose voice Hayley thought sounded familiar.

"Karen, it's me. I know you're there. Pick up right now! You cannot avoid me forever. I know what you've done and it's despicable. Do you think I'm going to just stand by and let this happen? You've destroyed me! And believe me, I'm going to make sure you never do anything like this to anybody else ever again. Do you hear me, Karen? You've crossed the wrong woman!"

End of messages.

Why did this woman's voice sound so familiar? And what had Karen done to make her so upset?

Hayley checked the caller ID. Dentist's office. Private number. Albert Cornbluth.

Whoa.

Hayley knew exactly why the voice was so familiar now. Albert Cornbluth ran the local pharmacy and his wife was Winnie Cornbluth, who just happened to be Karen Applebaum's dearest friend. Or at least, she was. They power-walked together, shopped together, and even took vacations together. But apparently they were on the outs and Winnie was now threatening her.

There was one more interesting fact about Winnie Cornbluth that was to prove useful to Hayley. Winnie worked at the local middle school.

And she also happened to be Dustin's homeroom teacher.

"Hayley! Get down here now!" Randy called from the first floor.

Hayley pounded down the steps and joined Randy in the living room where he sat on the couch with a stack of papers spread out on the coffee table.

"I found this inside a filing cabinet in Karen's library," Randy said. "It's a life insurance policy she took out years ago when she first started working at the *Herald.*"

Hayley sat down next to Randy and studied the papers.

"Look here. Martin is the beneficiary," Randy said.

"Of course he is," Hayley said. "They were married at the time. I'm sure she's changed it since then."

"No," Randy said. I went through her mail and

found an annual statement the insurance company sent her just a few weeks ago. Martin is still listed as the beneficiary."

"But Karen loathed Martin," Hayley said. "She would never have left his name on the policy after they divorced. Unless she just forgot about it."

"And maybe Martin found out he was still the beneficiary of a million dollar payout if anything ever happened to Karen. Like a rival kitchen diva poisoning her clam chowder."

"Don't call me a kitchen diva," Hayley said. She began pacing back and forth in the living room. "But wait a minute. Martin is loaded. What's a million dollars to him?"

"Maybe not so loaded. I had breakfast at Jordan's coffee shop the other day and I heard his new girlfriend saying the only reason she couldn't quit waitressing was because Martin's investments had taken a big hit lately. He could be overextended and just making it look like he's financially secure."

"Which would be a strong motive to knock off Karen," Hayley said, suddenly excited.

Hayley ripped the life insurance policy out of Randy's hands, folded it up, and put it in her pocket along with Bradley's Mother's Day card.

A treasure trove of clues.

And they were just getting started.

A passing light flashed across both their faces, and Hayley and Randy dropped to the floor to avoid being spotted.

The light disappeared and it was dark again. Hayley lifted her head and peeked out the window. She saw the red taillights of a car driving down the road past the house.

"It was just a car going by," Hayley said. "Come on. Let's get out of here."

They slipped out the back door again, secured the bolt, and placed the silver key underneath the waving gnome.

As they made their escape into the darkness of the woods, Randy turned to Hayley and smiled. "You were right. No one will ever know we were there. Maybe Older Sister does know best."

"You've just got to learn to trust me," Hayley said.

Famous last words.

Chapter 20

When Hayley walked into her house after Randy dropped her off around nine-thirty, Gemma and Dustin were still up and they were both very excited.

"You were just on the news again!" Gemma squealed.

"What for?" Hayley asked, as if she had to.

"What else? For murdering Karen Applebaum!" Dustin said, sitting at the kitchen table in front of his laptop.

"I did not murder Karen Applebaum!" Hayley insisted.

"They showed your mug shot and everything. Oh, Mom, I recorded it, but you really don't want to see it," Gemma said, putting a comforting hand on her mother's shoulder. "I mean, your hair is so frizzy you look like the Joker."

"And apparently I commit as many crimes," Hayley said.

"I just Googled you and you're all over the Net," Dustin said.

"Well, don't worry, when this is all over, you can write a book about this whole scandal and it will be a best-seller and we'll be rich and I won't have to worry about taking out any college loans," Gemma said.

Hayley closed her eyes, hoping she would wake up and find out all of this was just a horrible dream.

"You know what's funny?" Gemma asked, pouring herself a glass of milk.

"No. I really don't see anything funny about this," Hayley said as she removed the papers from her sweat jacket pocket and sealed them in a manila envelope for safe keeping.

"I was so mortified at the thought of going to school today. I didn't know how people were going to treat me. Was I going to be shunned for being the daughter of a homicidal maniac?"

"Alleged homicidal maniac," Hayley offered helpfully.

"Right. Alleged homicidal maniac. Would people at school think 'like mother, like daughter'? Would an angry mob drive me out of school like some leper?"

"I'm so happy you were able to find a way to make this all about you, dear," Hayley said, shaking her head.

"I know, right?" Gemma said, the sarcasm not quite registering. "But people thought it was totally cool! All my friends are dying to come over so they can tell everybody they were in our house. And Danny Forbes sat next to me at lunch! Danny Forbes! He's so hot and he has this sexy artistic side that is so deep and inspiring. I've been working

up the nerve to talk to him since freshman year!
He told me he's working on a new documentary he
wants to post on YouTube."

"What about?" Hayley asked.

"Us! He wants to record our family and show
how we're coping with all these false accusations
like in *The Crucible*, which we're reading in English
lit right now. He wants to come over tomorrow
after school and start filming us," Gemma said.

"Absolutely not," Hayley said.

"But, Mom, if I spend enough time with Danny
and he sees just how smart and witty I am, he'll
ask me to the prom."

"I thought this was a documentary, not a fantasy
film," Dustin said, howling.

"Zip it," Gemma said, her eyes boring into her
younger brother.

"This is enough of a circus already, Gemma,
and I need to keep a low profile. At least until they
find who really killed Karen. I'm sorry, but no.
Danny Forbes can't come over."

"You're ruining my life!" Gemma wailed, downing her glass of milk and neglecting to close the
refrigerator door.

"You know, you're both forgetting a woman has
died!" Hayley said, a stern look on her face as she
slammed the refrigerator door shut. "Doesn't that
affect you in the slightest?"

"No," Dustin said. "I mean, I never liked her. She
always yelled at me for cutting across her lawn."

"That's right," Gemma said. "And when I'd pass
her on the street she always told me to button the
top button of my shirt because I looked like a slut."

"She did?"

"She was a mean bitch, sorry, I mean witch, Mom, so stop pretending you feel bad now that she's gone," Gemma said.

"Okay, so maybe Karen had personality issues and she wasn't the nicest person in town, but we don't know her whole story. Maybe she suffered a lot in silence. I just think that at the end of the day she was a human being with real feelings and real passions, and it's a shame we belittle that just because we didn't get along with her."

Gemma twisted her mouth and thought about what her mother was saying.

Hayley began to smile. She knew she had raised her daughter right.

"Sorry, Mom," Gemma said. "You're right. I get it."

Hayley smiled at her daughter proudly.

Dustin piped up. "Hey, I found an online forum discussing who should play Mom in the Lifetime TV movie!"

Okay, one out of two wasn't so bad.

"No way! Seriously?" Gemma said, racing over to hover behind her brother.

"Mom, come see," Dustin said, waving her over.

"I'm not the least bit interested in who people think should play me in some stupid movie. This is a real life tragedy," Hayley said, walking out of the kitchen toward the living room.

"Forty-two percent voted Valerie Bertinelli," Dustin said.

"What? Really? She's like fifty years old now," Hayley said, spinning around and making a bee-line back to the kitchen.

"But, Mom, she's lost all this weight and even

appeared on the cover of *People* magazine in a green bikini a few years ago. She looks really good," Gemma reassured her.

Hayley squeezed in behind Dustin to glance at the computer screen. "*Terror in a Small Town?* That's what they're calling it? They couldn't think of something more original?"

"Who's Meredith Baxter Birney?" Dustin asked.

"An actress who is way too old to play me!" Hayley screamed. "This is ridiculous. Can't we write in our own names, like Scarlett Johansson?"

Dustin rolled his eyes.

"Natalie Portman?"

"Now you're just deluded, Mom," Dustin said, laughing.

Hayley tapped Dustin on the back of his head with the palm of her hand to show her annoyance.

"Okay, okay. But I can't live with who they're picking," Hayley said. "Wait. Someone once told me I look like Blake Lively's mother on *Gossip Girl!* She's attractive. Let's find out her name and get her on that list."

"I love that show!" Gemma said.

Hayley watched her son google *Gossip Girl* for a moment before she noticed an official-looking piece of paper sticking out of Dustin's knapsack, which he had flung on the kitchen table.

She went to pull it out to see what it was just as Dustin saw her.

"Mom, no!"

He tried to snatch it out of her hands, but she was too fast for him and stepped out of his reach.

Hayley skimmed the page, her eyes narrowing.

"An incomplete on your first history assignment of the semester?" Hayley asked in her sternest motherly voice.

"I can explain . . ."

"Keep reading. Science, too," Gemma added.

Hayley turned to her daughter. "You knew about this?"

"Well, yeah, but I wasn't going to rat him out," Gemma said. "I'm no snitch."

Gemma then picked up the phone to call one of her friends.

Hayley slammed the paper down on the kitchen table and glared at Dustin. "This letter is dated over a week ago. Is that how long you've been hiding it from me?"

"I haven't been hiding it. I just kept forgetting to give it to you," Dustin said in a chastised tone. "Sort of."

Hayley headed for the stairs.

"Where are you going?" Dustin asked.

"I'm taking the Xbox out of your room and locking it in the hall closet," Hayley said.

"What? No!" Dustin cried, jumping up from the kitchen table and chasing after her.

"I'm also putting a lock on your computer except for monitored sessions when you do your homework," Hayley said, pounding up the steps. "And first thing in the morning I'm going to call the school and make an appointment to go in and talk about this."

"Mom, Parent–Teacher Conference is next week," Dustin said. "You might as well just wait until then. There's no point in making two trips."

"Fine. But you're grounded until then," Hayley

said as she marched into Dustin's room to unplug the Xbox.

Dustin, standing at the foot of the stairs, sighed. "At least that's one less time I have to get balled out by Mrs. Cornbluth."

Hayley scurried back out of Dustin's bedroom and shouted down from the top of the stairs. "Mrs. Cornbluth?"

"Yeah, didn't you read the whole letter? She signed it at the bottom."

Hayley came scrambling down the stairs. "Gemma, get off the phone! I need to call Mrs. Cornbluth and get an appointment to see her tomorrow. Her home number is right here on the letter."

"Mom! It's almost ten o'clock at night! You said it could wait until next week," Dustin cried.

Gemma huffed loud enough to show Hayley how inconvenient her order was, and said into the phone, "I'll call you back on my cell. My mother's having another one of her crazy spells."

Gemma clicked off her call and handed the cordless receiver to her mother.

Hayley checked the letter and began punching numbers into the phone.

"You're making too big a deal out of this!" Dustin said.

"A week is an eternity when it comes to your education. I don't want you falling behind, dropping out, robbing a convenience store, and spending the best years of your life behind bars," Hayley said.

"At least we'll be together," Dustin said, smirking.

Hayley threw him a look and waited for Winnie Cornbluth to answer. Of course she was concerned about Dustin not completing his school work. Any concerned mother would be and she was anxious to resolve the situation with Dustin's teacher. But if Hayley could also get Winnie Cornbluth to open up about that nasty message she left on Karen Applebaum's voice mail, well, then that would be a win-win.

Chapter 21

Dustin squirmed in his seat as Winnie Cornbluth read through the student evaluations from all of his teachers. Hayley squeezed his arm tightly to get him to sit still. The reports weren't a total disaster. He excelled in art and creative writing, and was for the most part well-behaved. He also scored exceptionally high on his IQ tests. But when it came to the basics like math and science and history, he was lagging behind.

"It seems whenever there is a pop quiz, Dustin goes to the nurse's office with a migraine, promising to make up the test later. Which he never does. Seems he only gets migraines in three of his classes," Mrs. Cornbluth said, lowering her glasses to the tip of her nose in the most admonishing manner possible. "Remarkably, his health improves just in time for lunch and recess."

"I see," Hayley said. "Dustin, what do you have to say for yourself?"

"Maybe you should pack an Advil with my tuna sandwich," Dustin offered meekly.

"Don't get smart," Hayley warned. She then turned back to Mrs. Cornbluth and smiled. "Dustin would be more than happy to make up all the tests he missed at your earliest convenience, preferably a Saturday so it doesn't interfere with his other classes."

"What? A Saturday?" Dustin cried.

Hayley squeezed his arm again. This time real tight. "How about we spread it out over a few Saturdays so you don't get overwhelmed?"

Dustin heard the threat loud and clear. He knew he wasn't going to win this one. "No. One is good."

"He'll have plenty of time to study because I am making it my personal mission to see to it that he has absolutely no distractions so we can deal with his teetering grades," Hayley said.

"I'm sure he'll be back up to speed in no time," Mrs. Cornbluth said.

"Well, I certainly appreciate your understanding and support, Mrs. Cornbluth. Dustin was right. You are a wonderful teacher. He's told me so on numerous occasions that you're his absolute favorite."

Dustin sat up in his chair, surprised. "I have?"

Another quick squeeze to his arm and Dustin quickly shut his mouth.

This news was so shocking to Mrs. Cornbluth, she actually removed her glasses completely. "Why, thank you, Dustin."

Dustin was totally confused but followed his mother's lead. "Sure. No problem."

"With so many people criticizing our public school system, it's so nice to be able to hold a teacher up as a shining example of someone who truly makes a difference," Hayley said.

"I'm flattered," Mrs. Cornbluth said, beaming.

"With teachers like you around, I don't have to worry about him flunking out and winding up in jail . . . like his mother!" Hayley joked.

Mrs. Cornbluth's smile faded.

"Oh, don't worry, Dustin knows all about my arrest," Hayley said. "Being completely honest with your kids is a crucial part of parenting, as you well know."

Mrs. Cornbluth didn't know how to respond. So she just sat there with a frozen smile on her face.

"I'm sure it will all get straightened out. Right, Dustin?"

Dustin nodded.

"Well, I guess we're just about done here. Thank you again for coming in," Mrs. Cornbluth said as she began to shuffle some papers.

"Okay, then," Hayley said, standing up and steering Dustin toward the door. She leaned in and whispered in his ear. "Wait for me outside."

Dustin shrugged and left the classroom. Hayley pretended to follow him but stopped just short of the door and turned around.

"We missed you at the bake sale," Hayley said.

Mrs. Cornbluth stopped rustling papers. "Oh, yes. I couldn't make it that day. But I heard it was a rousing success."

"I can't remember a year when you weren't there sharing a table with Karen Applebaum and making a killing with your delicious apple fritters and those delectable lady fingers."

"Well, as I said, I was otherwise engaged."

"I see. They corral you to do Saturday detention duty here at the school?"

"No. It was a personal matter. I'd rather not talk about it."

"I understand completely," Hayley said, turning around and pretending to leave again, but then stopping. "You and Karen always seemed so close. I'm curious. Did the two of you have a falling out recently?"

"Who told you that?"

"I heard something at the bake sale. You were so conspicuously absent and you know how people talk."

"Did Karen say anything?"

"Just that you were angry with her and she didn't know why."

"Of course she knew why!"

"So it's true. You two did have a falling out."

"How much do you know?"

"Well, I heard about the threatening phone message you left on her voice mail."

Mrs. Cornbluth fell back in her chair, stunned, her mouth hanging open. Then she tried to compose herself. "I already explained everything about that message to Chief Alvares. He heard it when he was at the crime scene. He knows exactly why I left it. Now, I have a class to teach, so if you don't mind . . ."

Hayley knew if she left the room now she would never get the answers she so desperately needed.

She decided to just go for it.

Like in all the good detective novels she curled up with in bed, Hayley pointed a finger at Winnie

Cornbluth and said, "Where were you on the night of Karen Applebaum's murder?"

"You have no right to ask me that. And quite frankly, everyone in town knows where you were. Standing over Karen's body."

Okay, this wasn't playing out the way Hayley had planned it in her head.

"I just don't understand what Karen did to you to make you so mad," Hayley said. "If you just tell me, I'll leave."

"She did nothing."

"But I heard the message."

"How did *you* hear the message?"

"I mean, I heard you were really upset when you left the message."

The last thing Hayley wanted to explain was what she was doing in Karen Applebaum's house listening to her voice mail messages.

Mrs. Cornbluth took in a deep breath through her nose. "Has Chief Alvares been telling you confidential details about his investigation? Because if he has, that's terribly unprofessional."

"Sergio hasn't said a word to me. I have my own sources. I work at the paper, remember?"

"You're a food and wine columnist!"

"If you've already told the police, why can't you tell me?"

"Because I don't want any of this showing up in the *Island Times*."

"It will be off the record. I promise."

Winnie Cornbluth was a shaky mess now. She thought for another few moments and then sighed. "Karen did absolutely nothing to me. It was a horrible misunderstanding."

"So what happened?"

"Karen and I took a predawn power walk every morning before work. We'd talk about everything that was going on in both our lives. We were very close and really cared about each other. I was very happily married, so I always kept telling Karen she should find herself a nice husband. Not like her first husband, Martin. That pig. Somebody like my Albert. She'd laugh it off and say she was perfectly content with the way things were, and so I stopped pestering her. A few months ago, I noticed a distinct change in her. She was dressing better, wearing more makeup. She had this glow, like someone who was . . ."

"Getting sex on a regular basis?"

"Try to remember we are in a public school."

"Sorry."

"Yes. I asked if she was seeing someone and she said no. But then one day, I ran into her at the bookstore and she was buying a card for someone. It was one of those romantic ones, with red roses all over it and the schmaltzy words in cursive, the kind you send to someone you're hopelessly in love with. That's when I knew for certain she was having an affair. She didn't deny it, but she also didn't want to discuss him, either. I couldn't understand why it was such a big secret. But you could tell she was distracted and thinking about him all the time. When I pressed her again, she began cutting me out. Our walks stopped. She didn't return my calls. That's when I figured it out."

"Who was it?" Hayley wanted to know.

"My husband."

Hayley gasped.

"Around the same time, my husband, Albert, was working late three, maybe four times a week. There was always some kind of emergency. Trust me. Pharmacies never have emergencies. How dumb did he think I was? Then I noticed lipstick stains on his collar. The same color Karen used. And he was also gaining weight. Ten pounds in a month. Hello! Karen was a gourmet cook! How could I not think it was her?"

"So you called her and left that threatening message."

"I wasn't in my right mind. I thought I had caught them red-handed."

"But you were wrong?"

"Dead wrong. When I accused Albert of sleeping with Karen, he just laughed in my face. He said I was way off. He told me he would never waste his time with an old hag like Karen Applebaum. Not when he was scoring with a local college girl who worked as a barista at that new-age coffeehouse on Cottage Street. Who had the same taste in lip gloss as Karen and liked ordering a loaded pizza every night for dinner, hence the weight gain."

"Oh, Winnie, I am so sorry," Hayley said.

"After twenty years of marriage, he just threw it in my face. Like he was proud of it. They met when she came in for a contraceptive prescription, can you believe it? It would be funny if it wasn't so tragic and sad."

Hayley took a step forward, wanting to hug Winnie Cornbluth. But she didn't, because Winnie Cornbluth didn't seem to be the kind of woman who would appreciate a hug.

"I told Chief Alvares if I was going to kill anybody, it would be Albert. Not Karen," Mrs. Cornbluth said. "I wasn't at the bake sale because I drove to Bangor that day to meet with a divorce lawyer. I want to squeeze every last penny out of that no-good bastard. And then I had dinner with friends and I didn't get back to the island until well after eleven. Chief Alvares made a few calls and when everything checked out, he knew I couldn't have had anything to do with poor Karen's murder. She was my best friend and I never got to say how sorry I was for thinking she had betrayed me."

Tears streamed down Winnie Cornbluth's face. She reached for a tissue and began dabbing at her cheeks.

"So do you know who the card was for?" Hayley wondered. "The one you saw Karen buying at the bookstore?"

Mrs. Cornbluth sniffed. "I have no idea who her secret boyfriend was. I mean, if it wasn't my husband, why on earth couldn't she tell me?"

Hayley thought about her night in Karen Applebaum's house. The unpaid bills. The bedroom in need of a fresh coat of paint. Easily explained if Karen was so consumed by a hot love affair she didn't have time to worry about life's messy little details. It all made sense. Karen was obsessed with this mysterious admirer. He had to be the one who sent that spectacular unsigned flower arrangement to her funeral. This was the lead that sealed Hayley's determination to find out this mysterious man's name and whether or not he was Karen Applebaum's true killer.

Chapter 22

Hayley wasn't sure Sal would want her back working at the paper, at least until all the controversy swirling around Karen Applebaum's murder died down. So she was delighted to get a call from him when she returned home from her meeting with Winnie Cornbluth ordering her back to the office immediately. The place was falling apart without her.

Hayley jumped back in her car and drove straight over to the office. She didn't know what to expect when she got there, but was pleasantly surprised to find the staff acting as they always did, complaining about the bitter coffee and stale bagels, maneuvering around each other to score the best vacation days, and mumbling about how hard it was to get by on the pennies Sal paid them.

Business as usual.

And Hayley loved it. Nobody once mentioned her arrest. Even the locals who called in to place ads for their local businesses were cheery and pleasant when they heard Hayley's voice on the phone. Maybe it was because no one seriously believed she was behind Karen Applebaum's murder.

At least that was what Hayley hoped was the case.

There were two crank calls during the day from blocked numbers. One sounded like a kid, who kept snickering and said he gave his dog a bowl of Hayley's clam chowder and it killed him.

Hardly original.

The other call was more insidious. Clearly it was from an adult with a harsh, raspy voice who told Hayley she would burn in hell for her sins. Hayley didn't mention either call to anyone at the *Times*. Why create any more drama? She just went about her day and tried not to think about the murder.

Around two in the afternoon, Sal buzzed her and called her into his office.

Hayley grabbed a pad of paper and pencil and went into the back bull pen.

She caught Sal at his desk playing Solitaire on his computer. He quickly shut it off when he noticed Hayley looking at the screen.

"I want to talk to you about your next column," Sal said, a serious tone in his voice. "Have you thought about what you're going to write?"

"No, I usually just sit down and write down whatever comes to me."

"That's obvious."

Hayley couldn't decide if he was complimenting her or insulting her.

For the sake of her sanity, she decided to take it as a compliment. "But I do have a few ideas about my next recipe since I'm doing a seven course series and . . ."

"That's nice, Hayley," Sal interrupted, not the

least bit interested. "I think you should write some kind of tribute to Karen Applebaum."

"Excuse me?" Hayley was floored.

"She was well-known in town. It would be irresponsible of us not to at least say something about her."

"Her name is plastered all over our front page."

"Yes, she's the number one local news story. But we don't have anything about her personally. I know there aren't a lot of people in town who liked her, but she did have her fans and we have to acknowledge that."

"But I'm the last person who should be saying anything. Everybody thinks I was the one who knocked her off!"

"Which is exactly why you should do it. Tackle the rumors head-on! Show everybody we're not taking these wild accusations seriously. Okay? That's all. I know you'll do a bang-up job."

Hayley studied Sal for a moment. He had trouble making eye contact with her. "You do think I'm innocent, don't you, Sal?"

"Of course I do!" Sal bellowed. "There's really no basis for suspicion. I mean, so what you had a public feud with Karen? So what you were at the scene of the crime? So what the same poison that killed her was found in your purse?" Sal stopped talking as soon as he realized he was arguing against his own point.

"I appreciate your support, Sal, I really do," Hayley said. "But do you honestly believe me paying tribute to Karen is the best idea? It seems desperate."

"Maybe," Sal said. "But it's going to sell a hell of a lot of papers."

"But is it a good idea?"

"Yes. Because now we can all pay our heating bills in the winter."

Hayley knew the discussion was over. Without having written down one word on her notepad, she left Sal's office acutely aware of her new marching orders. She had already addressed Karen's death in her previous column. Now Sal wanted a tribute? She had no clue how she was going to approach this herculean task of writing about Karen without making herself look self-serving and even more guilty.

Hayley returned to the front office and sat down at her computer. She stared at the blank screen.

She typed a few opening words.

And then deleted them.

The door opened and a gust of wind sent a few papers in her inbox flying.

Hayley swiveled around in her chair to grab them before they hit the floor, and froze at the sight of Lex Bansfield standing in the doorway.

"What are you doing here?" Hayley asked, as nonchalantly as she could.

"I'm here to reschedule our date."

"You do realize I am the number one suspect in a murder investigation?"

"I like to live dangerously."

"So you still want to go out with me?"

"Absolutely," Lex said, smiling. "Besides, you've got great legs."

"The Manson girls had great legs, too, from what I hear."

"Yeah, but they weren't so big on personal hygiene and you smell real nice."

Hayley smiled. Major points for that one.

Bruce wandered in from the back. He was scowling. "Hayley, I don't mean to interrupt . . ."

"Sure you do," Lex said, giving him a wink.

Now this was interesting.

Did Lex have some inside information about Bruce being jealous?

"She's on the clock and what I have to talk to her about is a business matter, not a personal one, so your charming little back and forth banter will just have to wait," Bruce said, glaring.

Hayley was a bit titillated by their obvious rivalry. High school was the last time two boys had fought over her. And it really wasn't much of a fight. They both asked her to the prom at the same time during a pep rally. It didn't lead to fisticuffs. They ended up flipping a coin.

But still, it made Hayley feel special.

"What is it, Bruce?" Hayley asked.

"Have you seen the office dictionary?" he said, a little too quickly.

"Got a close game of Scrabble going on back there?" Lex said, winking again.

"Do you have something in your eye?" Bruce asked, his nostrils flaring.

Lex threw his hands up to let Bruce know he was finished teasing.

"No, Bruce, I haven't seen it," Hayley said. "Just look the word up on the Internet. It's 2012."

"Listen, I know you're working, so I'm not going to bother you. Just say yes. We'll make a plan later," Lex said, opening the door to leave.

"Yes," Hayley said, almost singing.

Lex gave her a quick wave and was back out the door.

Hayley's smile faded as she was left with just Bruce. "Did you butt in on our conversation on purpose?"

"Of course not," Bruce said, watching Lex cross the street to his parked jeep. "But I told you, I don't trust the guy."

Hayley picked up her bag and handed it to Bruce. "Here."

"What are you giving me this for?"

"I thought maybe you could stuff a Colt .45 in there, and stumble across it whenever I end up going out with Lex."

Bruce shoved the bag back at Hayley, and stormed off. "Not funny."

Hayley turned back to her computer. She was excited that Lex hadn't been scared off. Actually she was the one who was scared now. Not over her impending date with the hottest bachelor in town. No, she was scared about the column saluting the late great Karen Applebaum. She was at a loss over what to say. She knew she had to write something, but until she learned the truth about Karen's murder, there was no way she could write anything honest or truthful.

She closed the file on the tribute column and started another one from scratch. She would tell Sal she needed more time. And in the meantime, she would continue writing as if nothing had happened.

Which, of course, would just make her look even more guilty.

It was a losing situation all around.

Island Food & Spirits

by
Hayley Powell

Let me tell you, this week has been just a tiny bit stressful, so last night when I got home from work, I decided to call my brother and check on how he was doing and to see what mischief he's been up to lately. But honestly, I also wanted to beg him to give me his delicious Pomegranate Cosmopolitan recipe that he offers at his bar Drinks Like A Fish.

Hanging up after a nice chat, I proceeded to whip up a batch of the Cosmos and carry them out to the front porch where I could sit, relax, and think about what would be a nice fifth course for our seven course meal. I'm sure Randy won't mind if I share the recipe with you, but don't forget to go into the bar and try his . . . only four bucks if you show up for happy hour! And Thursdays are 2 for 1 night!

On the front porch, I watched and listened to the different birds flapping around my bird feeders and also heard my neighbor's chickens clucking softly in their backyard pen. I never thought I'd see the day when Bar Harbor would allow people in town to raise their own chickens. But I don't make the laws.

Suddenly I heard a loud horrible growling, a deafening crash, and chickens clucking like crazy! I looked over to my neighbor's yard to see what was the cause of all the commotion.

Imagine my horror at spotting a giant stray hungry dog that had somehow managed to get into the chicken coop by tearing down one side of the fence! He was chasing all of the panicked chickens around trying to nab a few for his dinner. Well, I grabbed the closest thing in my reach, which was the broom I used to sweep off the porch earlier. And I climbed over the ripped-down fence myself and started to chase the big dog around swatting at him with the broom while yelling at the top of my lungs to my kids to call the police and get someone over to stop the dog before he killed all the chickens! Well, my daughter apparently didn't hear me because she opened the door and screamed, "What?"

The next thing I knew, Leroy shot out the door past my daughter and made a beeline for the chicken coop! So now here was one more excited wild-eyed barking dog chasing and nipping at the giant stray who was running around the coop snapping at the terrified chickens!

Well, wouldn't you know at this moment my neighbor pulled up and saw her chicken coop fence torn down, and two dogs, a bunch of scared chickens, and me with a broom all running around inside causing a loud ruckus. I could tell by her face she was a bit confused. At that precise moment, we all heard a wailing siren followed by the sight of a police cruiser screeching to a halt right in front of my poor neighbor, who by now looked like she was about to pass out from the shock.

Two of our finest, Donnie and Earl, jumped out of the car, guns drawn. They knocked the poor woman aside, and began racing for the chicken coop yelling at me to get out of the way and run for my life! Later I would find out my daughter, who has a slight tendency to overdramatize situations, called the police station and reported that there was a rabid monster dog attacking and killing her beloved dog Leroy, a bunch of panicked chickens, and, oh yeah, her mother.

And yes, it was in that order.

I waved my broom and yelled at the young officers to put down their guns, and to please not shoot, especially since word around town was Donnie is nearsighted and refused to get laser surgery, and what if he missed and someone was hit? Like, me for example, who was in the direct line of fire.

Donnie and Earl lowered their weapons and it became strangely quiet. I turned around to see the two dogs panting, lying on the ground side by side, utterly spent. The chickens were finally settling down as well. I was the only one making noise at this point, still waving my broom and screaming at the boys not to shoot. They looked at me like I was an insane woman, so I calmly picked up a very tired and very happy tail-wagging Leroy in one arm and casually climbed back over the fence that had been ripped down, asking Donnie and Earl to please see to it that the stray dog be examined by the local vet to make sure he didn't have rabies. Hopefully an owner would be found. Calmly passing my neighbor, I told her to have a lovely evening and no thanks were necessary because that's what neighbors are for. I don't think she said anything as I went home, head held high.

And this morning I saw her look away when I waved good morning.

But if anything good did come out of the Great Late Night Chicken Rescue, I will say thanks to those chickens for helping me come up with a great dish for our fifth course—Creamy Chicken Marsala.

But first you have to try Randy's delicious Cosmo. Believe me, it was the perfect way to relax after my chicken coop ordeal.

Pomegranate Cosmopolitans

2 cups of your favorite vodka
1 cup Cointreau
1 cup pomegranate juice
½ cup fresh squeezed lime juice

Mix together in a pitcher your vodka, Cointreau, pomegranate juice, and lime. Pour the mixture in to a shaker with ice and serve in your favorite martini glasses and enjoy!

Now for our fifth course—and this will have your dinner guests talking.

Creamy Chicken Marsala

4 boneless skinless chicken breasts
¼ cup chopped green onion
1 cup sliced fresh mushrooms
⅓ cup Marsala wine
⅓ cup heavy cream
⅛ cup milk
salt and pepper to taste

Sauté chicken in a large skillet for 15 to 20 minutes or until cooked through and juices run clear when pricked by a fork.

Add green onion and mushrooms and sauté until soft. Add the Marsala wine and bring to a boil.

Boil for 2 to 4 minutes, seasoning with salt and pepper to taste. Stir in the cream and milk and simmer until heated through.

Rachael Ray, eat your heart out.

Chapter 23

The moment Hayley e-mailed her column to Sal for his stamp of approval, along with a long explanation as to why she wanted to delay her Karen Applebaum tribute, she knew she had a little downtime. So she immediately called Liddy to update her on her own investigation into Karen's murder.

Liddy ate up all the details regarding the clues Hayley and Randy found in Karen's house, how the phone message led them to Winnie Cornbluth, and how Winnie confirmed Hayley's suspicions that Karen had a secret lover.

"So do you have any idea who it might be?" Liddy asked breathlessly.

"No," Hayley said. "That's why I'm calling you."

"There can't be that many men in town who would even consider romancing Karen Applebaum. I would make a list of local widowers with health problems who want a nursemaid and guys with really low IQs."

"Liddy, don't be that way. We both know Karen was a very attractive woman."

"Then ask yourself why this secret lover is so secret? Obviously because he didn't want anyone to know who he was slipping it to every night."

"I don't think that's the reason," Hayley said. "Maybe he's married."

"Hold on," Liddy said before screaming, "Move it, Alice! I've got an open house and you're making me late!"

"Who are you yelling at?"

"Alice Richardson. I'm in my car and she's taking her sweet old time in the crosswalk."

"She's eighty-eight years old!"

"And perfectly healthy. You know she's never liked me ever since I sold her that money pit on Glen Mary Road. She just does this to annoy me."

"So do you think Mona might know who Karen was having an affair with?"

Hayley heard Liddy honking her horn at Alice Richardson.

"Liddy, stop it!"

"The old biddy just flipped me the bird!"

One more short honk. "You have a nice day, too, Alice!"

"Liddy, are you still with me?"

"Yes. I wouldn't bother calling Mona. She doesn't even remember the name of her own husband half the time."

"Somebody must have some idea who Karen was secretly shacking up with."

"Well, what else did you find at Karen's house?"

"Well, I definitely want to go talk to her son Bradley . . ."

"Don't you dare go alone!"

"And I found out an interesting fact about her ex-husband . . ."

Hayley suddenly felt a presence behind her and looked up to see Bruce hovering in the doorway.

"Just a sec, Liddy," Hayley said, pressing the HOLD button and glaring at Bruce. "Can I help you?"

"Are you going behind my back conducting some kind of investigation into Karen Applebaum's murder?"

"That's none of your business."

"Because local crime is my beat and I don't appreciate you encroaching on my territory."

"Encroaching? I see you found the dictionary. What I do outside office hours has nothing to do with you or your job here at the paper. I can spend my free time however I choose," Hayley said cooly.

"But this isn't your free time. Look around. You're at the office. It's during office hours."

"Don't be so smart, Bruce. It's really annoying."

"You need to stick to your grandmother's angel food cake recipe."

"And you need to stop eavesdropping on my phone conversations and start actually covering the crime beat," Hayley said.

Bruce's nostrils flared. They did that a lot.

"Now if you'll excuse me," Hayley said, swiveling around in her chair and turning her back to him. "I'm in the middle of a phone conversation."

Hayley pressed the HOLD button again. "Sorry, Liddy, where were we?"

"I can't really talk now. I just got pulled over by Dumb and Dumber for making a rolling stop.

Can you believe this? Now I'm going to be late for my open house."

"Call me later. And say hi to Donnie and Earl."

Hayley hung up and turned back to her computer screen.

Bruce was still standing in the doorway.

"Bruce, please, leave me alone."

"I'm sorry, I wasn't eavesdropping, I just happened to come out of the copy room and I heard you say something about finding dirt on Martin Applebaum."

Hayley eyed him for a moment. "You look nervous."

"I'm not nervous. Why would I be nervous?"

"You're nervous that I might be making progress on the case and you've got zilch. And if I actually come up with some real answers it will make you look bad."

"That's got to be the most ridiculous thing I've ever heard," Bruce said, dramatically rolling his eyes for effect. "I am not in competition with a food and wine columnist."

"Food and spirits. I really don't know a lot about wine," Hayley said.

"Fine. Whatever. All I am suggesting is that we pool our resources, share what we've both found out so far, and maybe work together."

Hayley studied him and then called his bluff. "Okay. You go first."

"Why can't you go first?"

"I was right. You've got zilch."

"That's not true."

"Then why won't you go first?"

Bruce's head was about to explode. His face

was beet red, his fists were tightly clenched, and he was gritting his teeth.

"You want me to tell you everything I know so you can write it up and take all the credit," Hayley said, folding her arms.

"Is that the kind of guy you take me for?"

"No, you're the kind of guy who hands over evidence to get me arrested so you can get the scoop. I'm a long way from trusting you, Bruce."

Bruce lowered his voice, trying to contain his temper. "It is your obligation as an employee of this paper to hand over any information you might have if it pertains to a story we're tracking."

"No, actually it is my obligation to write about food, according to you. Now, if you don't mind, I need to go dig up my grandmother's delicious angel food cake recipe for a future column."

Bruce didn't move.

"Good-bye, Bruce," Hayley said, stone-faced.

Bruce marched off in a huff.

Hayley picked up the phone and called Randy at the bar.

"Hi, Randy, it's me."

"Hey, sis," he said.

"You wouldn't happen to know who the county coroner is, would you?"

"Yeah, why?"

"I thought I'd give him a call and see if he would be willing to give me a heads-up on Karen Applebaum's final autopsy report. I know the county just hired a new one and I was hoping we might know him."

"Oh, you definitely know *her*."

"A woman? Oh, good. Who?"

"Sabrina Merryweather."

Hayley's heart sunk.

Sabrina Merryweather was Hayley's arch-nemesis in high school, a former cheerleader and queen bee who made Hayley's life a living hell for four long years.

Now, after all these years, Hayley was going to have to play nice with her?

This case just got a lot more challenging.

Chapter 24

Hayley actually felt a ringing in her ear after Sabrina Merryweather stopped squealing on the other end of the line. She hadn't expected such an excited reaction from Sabrina when she decided to call her at home after work. She didn't exactly know why. Perhaps it had to do with Sabrina making it her personal mission during their sophomore year in high school to tear down Hayley's confidence and fill her with crippling self-doubt.

Whether it was a low test score, a bad haircut, or an unfortunate wardrobe choice, Sabrina was always around to point out Hayley's many imperfections. When Hayley tried out for the cheerleading squad, Sabrina, as head cheerleader, was on the judging committee alongside her easily pliable coach, and convinced the coach that poor Hayley just couldn't master the splits and was a tad too heavy to be hoisted atop any of the team's pyramids. And one look at her untoned arms was proof enough that she couldn't hold up a pencil let alone a hundred-and-ten-pound buxom teammate.

No, Hayley just didn't have what it took to even be an alternate member. And it was all cloaked in an earnest concern for her fellow cheerleaders, whose livelihood could be endangered by someone like Hayley, who might drop them, or at the very least, make them look bad during one of their award-winning routines.

Hayley wasn't that gung ho about being a cheerleader anyway, so she took the rejection in stride. But Sabrina Merryweather wasn't through playing with her. Hayley felt like a ball of yarn to Sabrina's cat, completely at her mercy and an amusement to be batted around and toyed with.

When Hayley met a boy she liked in social studies, and he asked her out, she had no idea he had already been targeted to go steady with one of Sabrina's BFFs. Sabrina was incensed that Hayley would interfere with the natural order of things, namely, her decisions on who should be dating whom, so an all-out assault was launched on Hayley's reputation. By the end of the school day, Hayley was suspected of cheating on her history test, battling an infectious venereal disease, and was seen kicking a defenseless dog in the school parking lot. Her budding romance with her new admirer was suddenly a nonstarter, and the next thing she knew Sabrina had brokered a date between him and her gal pal for the upcoming Homecoming Dance.

When Hayley finally got sprung from high school, she thought she was free of Sabrina Merryweather forever.

No such luck.

Sabrina went on to become a respected doctor

and was interviewed for the paper's health column
all the time. Her fake plastic smile was constantly
plastered all over the paper. Sabrina also busted
up her best friend's marriage to the president of
one of the local banks. The friend had stuck with
him through a financial scandal involving bad
loans that nearly brought them to ruin, only to
have him leave her for Sabrina after one particu-
larly rowdy couples retreat to a Mexican resort one
winter a few years ago. They got hitched the same
day the divorce was final.

Hayley wasn't the only one who despised Sabrina Merryweather.

Liddy refused to allow the name Sabrina Merryweather to even be mentioned in her presence.
Not because she had a history with her like Hayley
did, but out of pure jealousy. Sabrina dressed just
as stylishly as Liddy, who did not appreciate the
competition when it came to being the best
dressed in Bar Harbor, a title not a whole lot of
people spent time vying for. It was basically a two-
horse race, and Liddy was determined to remain
in first place and not let Sabrina come up from
behind.

Hayley had run into Sabrina on several occasions over the years, mostly at social events, and
chose to keep a healthy distance. Sabrina did call
the paper once to complain that the caption underneath a photo of her at a local charity event did not
include the word "Doctor," and that she had spent
far too much money going to medical school, and
worked very hard for years to earn that title, for it
to not be used. Sabrina didn't seem to recognize
Hayley's voice when she called, so Hayley didn't

jump at the chance to alert Sabrina that it was she who was on the other end of the line.

But now, with Hayley's column a local hit, it was impossible for Sabrina to ignore her any longer. She had to pretend to be chummy with Hayley, since her own mother was a fan.

But Hayley had no idea that Sabrina would rewrite history, and cast them as close friends since those memorable high school years. Now the story from Sabrina's point of view was that she valiantly fought to get Hayley on the cheerleading squad and was shot down by darker forces who for some reason had it out for poor Hayley. It had been such an injustice. And if Sabrina hadn't been so dependent on a cheerleading scholarship for college, she would have quit the squad in solidarity.

Honest.

Hayley would have loved to have told Sabrina to go to hell. Bar Harbor was a small town, but not too small. There was plenty of room for two people to avoid each other. But she needed her. And she was resigned to play along with Sabrina's new game.

"I've been thinking of you, sweetie," Sabrina cooed. "I've been so meaning to call you."

"You have?"

"I miss you!"

"Miss you, too," Hayley said into the phone as she stuck a finger in her mouth and pretended to gag.

"Where does the time ago? Why haven't Matt and I had you over for dinner?"

"It's been a busy time for both of us, I guess."

"Well, you certainly have been busy," Sabrina

said, giggling. "Who knew you would be the talk of the town?"

"I have to say I'm surprised the column has gotten such a positive reaction."

"I'm not talking about that cute tiny recipe thing you do in the back section of the paper," Sabrina said, effortlessly finding a way to belittle Hayley's new job. "I'm talking about your reputation as a badass."

"Sabrina, you've known me since high school. You don't think I had anything to do with—?"

"Oh, of course not, Hayley. A crime like that takes careful planning, and we all know how scatterbrained you are. Ever since high school! Did you ever get your diploma?"

"Yes, Sabrina. I sat next to you at the graduation ceremony."

"Really? I could've sworn you flunked out."

"No," Hayley said, gritting her teeth.

"I know you flunked out of something. Was it college?"

"I didn't flunk out. I dropped out."

Sabrina decided to let it just lay there so the silent point could be made that Sabrina was a success, and, in her eyes, Hayley was a big fat failure.

"Right. That's when we lost touch, I think. I went off to college and then medical school and then did that stint with Doctors Without Borders where I gave free medical care to those poor African villagers who have no running water. Thank God I had a driver to get me to the nearest Marriott at the end of the day."

Hayley desperately wanted to hang up. But she knew she needed Sabrina's help, so she kept her lips sealed and took whatever Sabrina wanted to dish out.

"When I moved back to Bar Harbor and found true love with Matt . . ."

After stealing him from her best friend.

"I was certain we would pick right up where we left off."

Yeah, right.

"But I guess we both let life get in the way. Matt has the travel bug, so when I do get a vacation, we're usually off to some exotic destination like Bali or Tuscany. And you, well, I'm sure being a single mother with no man around to help can keep you extremely busy."

"Oh, I get by."

"Well, we shouldn't let our harried lives keep us from staying friends. And I'm determined not to let this new job as county coroner completely get in the way of my having an active social life. We need to have a girls' night out one of these days. Maybe invite Liddy and Mona."

Liddy and Mona would rather eat a bowl of Karen Applebaum's New England clam chowder than spend an evening with Sabrina Merryweather, but Hayley wasn't about to let Sabrina know that.

At least not right now.

"I'm so proud of all you've accomplished, Sabrina, really I am," Hayley said, laying it on thick because she was so anxious to find out what she needed to know and get the hell off the phone.

Hayley was going to indulge Sabrina as much as it took, since she knew this would be the absolute last time she would ever have to speak to her.

I mean, really. What were the odds that Hayley would be investigating the facts surrounding a mysterious death ever again in her lifetime?

Pretty high, as it would turn out.

"So, is there any chance you could give me a little insight into the circumstances of Karen's death?" Hayley asked cautiously.

"Oh, sweetie, you know I would love to, but it's against policy for me to share anything with a journalist before the police receive my final report."

"Don't think of me as a journalist. Think of me as a friend."

"I am so touched by that. Really, I am."

"I look up to you, Sabrina, and everything you've accomplished, and, frankly, I find it awe-inspiring . . ."

Hayley stopped.

Had she gone too far? Was Sabrina on to her sycophantic assault?

Then she heard Sabrina sniffling.

"Sabrina?"

"No one's ever said anything that nice to me before."

Hayley was almost there. She swallowed hard and trotted out her biggest gun. "My daughter tells me all the time she wants to be as pretty and successful as you."

Using Gemma was low. The girl didn't even know who Sabrina Merryweather was. But desperate situations sometimes required desperate measures.

That was all Sabrina needed to hear. "What do you need to know? Hurry. Matt's going to be home any minute and he can't know I told you anything.

He's always telling me I don't act professional enough."

"Time of death. Just give me a ballpark."

"Given the amount of cyanide in her system and the condition of her body, the time of death had to be between eight and ten o'clock that night."

"Give or take a few minutes?"

"No. According to my findings, she had to have died within that time frame. Not before. Not after."

Hayley was floored.

"Anything else? I think Matt's pulling into the driveway."

"That's all I need. Thanks, Sabrina."

"So when are we getting together for cocktails?"

"I'll call you."

Sure. And Dustin would have his homework done when she checked on him.

Hayley hung up.

She just stood there, her mind racing. This was a huge development. Because even though Sabrina Merryweather was a bragging blowhard, she was good at her job. Her report would undoubtedly be accurate. That would mean Karen Applebaum was already dead at ten o'clock. But Hayley's e-mail from Karen was time-stamped 10:15. Karen was already dead by then!

That could only mean one thing. Karen didn't send Hayley the e-mail.

Someone else did.

Someone bent on setting Hayley up for murder.

Chapter 25

Hayley paced back and forth in her kitchen, debating with herself over what to do with this crucial new piece of information. There was a small part of her that wanted to call Bruce and let him in on Sabrina's findings. He could write about it in the paper and she would essentially be cleared of all charges.

Or so she hoped.

But Hayley still didn't trust Bruce. She knew he didn't mean her any harm. But he was first and foremost a reporter and her precarious predicament wasn't exactly his top priority. He just wanted the scoop.

Hayley had just slipped into some sweats and began washing the makeup off her face in the upstairs bathroom when her phone rang.

It was her brother, Randy.

"Hayley, I need you come to over to the house," he said, an ominous tone in his voice.

"Why? What's wrong?"

"I'll explain when you get here."

"Tell me now. You're making me nervous."

"I can't," Randy said, lowering his voice. "He's standing right here."

"Did you and Sergio have a fight?"

"You might say that."

"It's getting late. Can't we deal with this tomorrow?"

"No. You need to get over here now."

Hayley sighed, resigned. Randy was like a hound with a steak bone. He would just never let it go. "Fine. Give me fifteen minutes."

Hayley could've walked to her brother's house, but it was late and she was tired, so she fired up her Subaru wagon, and drove over.

The wheels crunched on the gravel driveway as she steered down the path to the two-story colonial house on the Shore Path set back a mere two hundred feet from the Atlantic Ocean.

Hayley breathed in the salty air and heard the waves clapping hard against the rocks as she walked across the lawn to the back porch and knocked on the door leading into the kitchen.

She could see Randy bent over in the refrigerator, scarfing down some leftover corn on the cob from a barbecue last weekend.

Uh oh.

Randy's food binges were almost always brought on by stress. This must have been some fight.

Randy opened the back door and ushered Hayley inside. Bits of corn and a little butter grease were sprinkled across Randy's concerned face.

"You have me so worried," Hayley said, grabbing a dishrag off the counter and wiping off her brother's face.

"You should be."

"This sounds really bad."

"It is."

Hayley's stomach began to churn. Randy and Sergio rarely fought. She just hoped whatever set them off could be fixed.

"Where is Sergio?"

"In the living room. Waiting for you."

"You told him I was coming over?"

"He insisted."

At least Sergio was open to a mediator.

Hayley took a deep breath, and then followed Randy into the main living room.

The area was expansive, decorated with plush antique furniture, and the walls were adorned with tasteful paintings by various New England artists. The picture windows looked out on the breathtaking Maine coast. But now, it was dark, and you could barely make out the ocean and surrounding islands nestled throughout the bay.

So Hayley had no choice but to focus on the scenery inside the house. And her heart sunk as her eyes came to rest on her brother's boyfriend, Sergio, sitting on the couch, stone-faced, his hands folded on his lap.

"Hi, Sergio!" Hayley said, a bit too upbeat and perky.

Sergio met Hayley's gaze and for the first time ever, Hayley saw anger in his eyes. He was usually so good-natured, so easygoing, so sweet and lovable. This was a whole new side of him.

And it scared the hell out of her.

"Whatever is upsetting you, Sergio, I am confident

you and Randy can work through it, and I will stay for however long it takes to help you."

"This isn't just about Randy," Sergio said, calmly and evenly.

"Oh?"

"No."

"Did I do something?"

Sergio stood up.

Hayley instinctively backed away.

Sergio was a puppy dog. But he was also a hot-blooded Brazilian, and she wasn't exactly sure what might happen if he lost his temper. She never thought she would live to see the day he actually got mad over something.

"Yes, Hayley. This is as much about you as it is about Randy."

At this point, Hayley was pretty sure this was not going to end well. "Okay. I'm listening."

Randy stepped between Hayley and Sergio as if to shield his sister from his boyfriend's wrath.

"You know what a busy schedule Karen had when she was alive. Well, it turns out she was paying the teenage boy next door, Bennie Taylor, to look after her cat, Puff, when she wasn't home," Randy said.

Sergio gripped Randy's bicep with his large hand and moved him aside so he could confront Hayley face to face. "Bennie came over twice a day to check on him and feed him."

"So do you think Bennie might have seen something, like the killer fleeing from the scene?" Hayley asked.

"No," Sergio said, shaking his head. "Karen suspected that Bennie was ignoring her expletive instructions on how much cat food he should give Puff."

"Explicit," Randy offered, gently squeezing Sergio's shoulder from behind.

"What?"

"Explicit instructions. Not expletive instructions. Expletive means a swear word."

Sergio just stared at Randy. "Do you really think it's a good idea to be correcting my English right now?"

Randy quickly took two steps back. "Sorry."

Sergio turned back to Hayley. "Puff was growing morally obese."

"I'm sorry, what?" Hayley asked.

"Morally obese!" Sergio said, losing patience.

Morbidly obese.

Hayley was about to correct him when she saw Randy standing behind Sergio, waving his arms frantically and mouthing the words "Let it go!"

Hayley remained silent.

Sergio continued. "Bennie denied overfeeding Puff, but Karen refused to believe him."

"Puff was tipping the scales at a whopping twenty-five pounds. That's like Rosie O'Donnell in cat weight!" Randy piped in before retreating again.

"Anyway, to prove the kid was lying, Karen installed a hidden camera to catch him in the act of giving Puff too much cat food."

"A Kitty Cam!" Randy said.

Hayley couldn't help but laugh.

Sergio didn't crack a smile. "She set it up over the fireplace where it had a clear view of the room where she kept Puff's food bowl."

"Too bad she didn't put it in the kitchen. It would've caught the murderer on tape and cleared my name."

"Yeah, too bad," Sergio said.

"So don't keep me in suspense," Hayley said. "Was Bennie guilty or not?"

"Oh, yes. He wasn't carefully measuring out the food as Karen instructed. He was just filling the bowl to the rim and Puff was woofing it down twice a day and packing on the pounds," Randy said.

"Case closed," Hayley said, still a little confused as to why she was hearing this story.

"Yes, the Kitty Cam did its job. It caught Bennie in the act. But that's not all it caught. After Karen's death, I intentionally left it on so I could monitor the crime scene and see if there was any suspicious activity that might pop up."

Suddenly Hayley had a sinking feeling as Sergio walked over and picked up the DVD remote and pressed the PLAY button. On the television, there in plain view, recorded by Karen Applebaum's Kitty Cam, was Hayley and Randy casing her house and searching for clues.

"Sergio, I can explain," Hayley said softly.

"Don't bother," Randy said. "I already tried."

As Hayley watched herself pounding up the stairs to search Karen's bedroom and Randy going through the drawers in her parlor, she couldn't believe how stupid she had been.

She finally had to turn away.

"I can't watch anymore."

Sergio turned off the DVD player.

"Breaking and entering is a violation of your bail, Hayley," Sergio said solemnly.

Hayley felt sick to her stomach. She braced herself, prepared to have her butt tossed back behind bars.

Chapter 26

There was an uneasy silence. Hayley waited for Sergio to slap his cuffs on her and drive her directly back to the jail cell. Do not pass Go.

If only she had implemented her better food for inmates plan before getting thrown back in the slammer.

Oh well.

Randy cleared his throat to break the tension. Both he and Hayley kept their eyes focused on Sergio, who stood in front of them, contemplating his next move.

Finally, he sighed deeply. "I might let you stay out of jail . . ."

"Oh, thank God!" Randy cried.

"If . . . ," Sergio said, folding his arms. "You tell me everything you know."

Hayley wasted no time bringing Sergio up to speed. She shared everything she and Randy had found at Karen's house that Sergio's officers missed. The life insurance policy that still listed her ex-husband, Martin, as the beneficiary. Karen's secret lover whose identity still remained a mystery. Sabrina Merryweather's timeline that basically cleared Hayley as a suspect.

Sergio was especially surprised by that one. He didn't think Sabrina had even concluded her autopsy as of this evening. He was duly impressed with Hayley's findings, but made sure not to show a hint of admiration. He didn't want Hayley believing he was condoning her playing Nancy Drew.

"Okay," Sergio said. "Anything else?"

"No. I think that's it."

Satisfied, Sergio nodded.

"So you're not going to arrest her?" Randy asked.

"No. She can remain out on bail. But this doesn't mean you're off the list of suspects, Hayley."

"What do you mean? You can check my computer. Karen e-mailed me at 10:15. She was already dead. I couldn't have killed her."

"Yes. It makes perfect sense. But how do I know you didn't go over to Karen's house and poison her clam chowder, and then send that e-mail to yourself to cover your tracks?"

Hayley hadn't thought of that.

"Oh, Sergio, now that's just ridiculous," Randy scoffed.

"Is it? Do you have any witnesses to corroborate your claim that you were home the whole time?"

"Yes, my kids were there."

"So they saw you?"

"Of course. It was after the bake sale and I made them macaroni and cheese for dinner. Then they went upstairs to their rooms to watch TV and play video games."

"Were you upstairs with them?"

"No. I went out on the deck and had a cocktail and . . ."

"And what?"

"I fell asleep."

"For how long?"

"I don't know. Twenty or thirty minutes. When I woke up, I went inside to check my e-mail and that's when I got the message from Karen and decided to drive over to her house."

"So you went upstairs and told the kids you were leaving?"

"Um, no. I thought I would only be gone a few minutes."

"You mean they never actually saw you from the time they finished dinner, which was what time?"

Hayley's face flushed.

She was suddenly nervous again. "I think it was around eight-thirty."

"So no one saw you between eight-thirty and the time you called 9-1-1, which was approximately ten forty-five."

"I did! I saw her!" Randy cried.

Sergio gave him a questioning look.

"I dropped by to catch up, remember?"

Hayley knew her brother was just covering for her, and she loved him for it. But she couldn't let him lie. "No, Randy. You didn't."

"Yes, of course I did! I had read your column about the clam chowder and was dying to try some so I came over and we hung out for an hour or so and we made some."

"Randy, that's impossible," Sergio said calmly.

"How do you know?"

"Because you were with me. Here. And I don't have to remind you what we were doing," Sergio said.

"Oh, right," Randy said, blushing. "Sorry, Hayley."

"Well, I know I'm innocent even if nobody else does."

"Then let me do my job and find the real killer, okay?" Sergio said.

Hayley nodded.

Sergio walked over and hugged Hayley tight. He whispered in her ear, "Don't worry. We'll find who did this."

Sergio turned and gave Randy a peck on the cheek. "It's late. I'm going to bed. Don't be too long."

Sergio smiled one more time at Hayley, and trudged up the stairs.

Hayley wanted to believe him. She really did. But leaving her fate in someone else's hands made her extremely uncomfortable.

She still felt the urge to clear her name.

"You need to just put all this out of your mind. Why don't we go on a shopping trip to Boston this weekend?" Randy asked.

"Maybe. Let me think about it," Hayley said, kissing her brother and heading for the door. "I'll call you tomorrow."

"Sergio may have trouble with certain words in the English language, but he's a damn good cop," Randy said. "You can trust him."

"I know," Hayley said. "Good night."

When Hayley got in her car to drive home, she remembered one clue she forgot to mention to Sergio. The threatening Mother's Day card from Karen's son Bradley. She was about to go back inside when she stopped herself. Bradley was a walking freak show. Kind of wild eyed and crazy. A big-time conspiracy theorist. He was a natural suspect. But was he capable of murdering his own mother?

Hayley knew she should march right back inside and tell Sergio all about the card. But Sergio was probably already asleep, and it would be a shame to wake him. Besides, Bradley despised cops. He'd never tell Sergio anything.

No, this needed a lighter, more delicate touch, and Hayley convinced herself she was the woman for the job.

Chapter 27

If Hayley had truly thought about it, driving out to a remote cabin in the woods on the far side of the island without telling anyone where she was going might not have been the brightest idea.

Especially since she was paying a visit to one of the more famous nut jobs on the entire island.

But as the sun rose above the crest of Cadillac Mountain and the early morning dew on her windshield slowly began to melt away, Hayley felt confident she had made the right decision. She had to know if Bradley Applebaum had any motive to see his own mother dead.

Hayley pulled onto a dirt road and the car rumbled along, the wheels spitting small pebbles in all directions. Hayley knew she was on the right path. Part of her job at the paper was printing out the police reports, and the cops had been called out to this location on numerous occasions, not to mention a few feds as well when Bradley's ire got up and he wrote threatening letters to the

U.S. Congress. He was a rock star to the anti-government survivalist establishment, almost as popular as the Unabomber.

Just beyond a thicket of trees, Hayley spotted a dilapidated one-story cabin, like something out of *Little House on the Prairie,* with a tarp thrown over a leaky roof, some cracked windows, and a pile of garbage obstructing access to the front door.

This showpiece was never going to make the cover of *Better Homes and Gardens.*

Hayley rolled to a stop several hundred feet from the cabin, and contemplated how she should proceed. Getting out and just knocking on the front door might spook him. And she really didn't want to get a bullet between the eyes. But she also didn't want to just sit in her car until Bradley spotted her, because that could take awhile.

As far as she knew, Bradley was still sound asleep. It was only a little after six o'clock in the morning. Or worse, he might not even be home. He could be out hunting his next meal or something. Most of Bradley's criminal record on file had to do with offenses related to hunting deer out of season.

Hayley got out of the car and slammed the door hard, hoping the noise might alert Bradley. It didn't.

"Bradley?" she called out, a little crack in her voice betraying her nerves.

She tried again. "Bradley?"

Nothing.

She slowly began walking toward the cabin, not

sure what to expect. That's when she heard a voice behind her.

"Who's there?"

Hayley spun around and peered into the woods. At first she didn't see anything. But then she spotted a shotgun propped up against a spruce tree. Followed by a flash of red. It was Bradley, clad only in a pair of red underwear, his skinny pale body standing near that same spruce tree.

He was taking a leak.

Hayley covered her eyes. There was no way she was going to lose that bagel she'd eaten on the way over because Bradley Applebaum flashed her.

"Hello, Bradley, I was hoping I could ask you a few questions."

There was a long silence as Bradley finished his business, a small trickle wetting the leaves, before he readjusted himself, grabbed his shotgun, and marched back toward the cabin where Hayley waited for him.

His hair was curly and sprouted in all directions. He had a long beard that rivaled some members of ZZ Top. And his lanky body was covered with dirt smudges.

Bradley eyed her warily, and Hayley wasn't sure if he recognized her or not. He had been quite a few years younger than her in school, but she had heard stories. His erratic behavior was legendary.

Hayley realized the cabin probably had no bathroom or outhouse, which would explain Bradley relieving himself on a spruce tree.

She decided to carefully watch her step since it

was likely she could come in contact with some of Bradley's other undesirable deposits.

Bradley eyed her up and down suspiciously.

She chose to plow ahead.

"First of all, I'm sorry about your mother's passing."

"You mean her murder."

"Right. Terrible. Just terrible."

"I know who did it."

"You do?"

"Come inside and we can talk."

Bradley pushed past her, gripping his twelve gauge shotgun, and disappeared inside the cabin.

Hayley hesitated. A little voice inside her was screaming at her to jump in her car and just haul ass out of there. But her interest was peaked. And maybe Bradley could help clear her name.

She took a deep breath and followed him inside.

The stench in the cabin was stifling. Like rotted eggs mixed with choking body odor. Hayley suddenly felt nauseated.

She looked around. Piles of garbage were everywhere. She squinted to see if the furry brown object in one empty corner was a dead squirrel, but she quickly averted her eyes, deciding she didn't really want to know.

"Can I offer you something to drink?" Bradley said, still clutching his gun and scratching himself as Hayley glanced away to avoid having to see his red underwear riding up in the front.

"No, thank you, I'm fine," Hayley said. "So you say you know who poisoned your mother's clam chowder?"

Bradley nodded. "Of course. It was the president."

Hayley rolled this one over in her mind for a moment.

"The president of the bank?"

"No," Bradley sighed, a bit irritated. "The president of the United States."

"I see. You think the president had your mother killed?"

"Yes. He dispatched some government spooks to get rid of her. Just like Kennedy did with Marilyn Monroe."

"Okay. So you think your mother was sleeping with the president?"

"No! I'm not some idiot. I know my mother wasn't having sex with the president."

Finally. A modicum of sanity.

"He did it to get to me. I'm the real threat," Bradley said.

"Oh."

"They're everywhere. They're watching us right now."

Hayley looked around before she realized that there was a small part of her that was actually taking this guy seriously.

She laughed to herself.

"But your mother *was* seeing someone. You did know that, right?"

Bradley nodded.

"Do you have any idea who it was?"

Bradley nodded again.

Finally. They were getting somewhere.

"Can you tell me?"

Bradley rushed over to the window and peered

outside to make sure no one was out there. Then he turned around and surged forward fast, surprising Hayley when he grabbed her by the arm and got up close in her face. The smell wafted up into her nostrils and she again felt like she was going to be sick.

"The vice president."

"I'm assuming you're not talking about the vice president of the bank."

Bradley shook his head wildly.

"No, I didn't think so," Hayley said.

It was time to go.

"Well, Bradley, thank you for your time."

She turned to go, but he gripped her arm tighter.

"Wait," he said. "Join us."

"Who?" Hayley said, glancing around. Was he talking about the dead squirrel decomposing in the corner?

"I have friends. We're building underground bunkers. Taking up arms. We're going to be ready when the army comes to take our freedom."

Hayley couldn't quite imagine herself as a part of some survivalist militia movement. They might not have TV inside the bunker and she couldn't possibly live without *NCIS* and her Lifetime movies.

She tried to shake off Bradley's grip.

But he refused to let go.

"I really need to get to work." Hayley was now desperate to get the hell out of there.

He gripped her even tighter. "I can't let you go now. You could lead the National Guard back here and ruin everything. We still have work to do building our stronghold."

"I won't say a word. I promise. Pinky swear."

She tried again to free herself from Bradley. She felt the bile rising up in her throat as he pulled her closer to him, staring directly into her face with his darting, crazy, almost–coal black eyes.

This was feeling way too dangerous now. What had she gotten herself into?

"Bradley, please, I really have to get to the paper. I'm going to be late."

Bradley eased up for a moment, a curious look on his face. "Paper? Are you a journalist?"

"You might say that. I work at the *Times*. Don't you remember who I am? Hayley Powell. We've both lived here all our lives."

Bradley gasped and completely released his grip. "Hayley? I remember you from when I was just a little kid. I had no idea that was you. You look so different. You're pretty now."

Okay. He wasn't so crazy that he didn't remember Hayley's frizzy hair, severe acne, and metal braces when she was twelve.

"I love you, Hayley!"

"Excuse me?"

"I'm a huge fan of your column!"

Okay, now this was just getting surreal.

"Wait! Hold on!" he yelled, beaming from ear to ear.

Bradley scampered over to the counter and cleared some dirty pots and pans away. There was a paper plate with some cookies on it. He proudly picked it up and carried it back over to Hayley. "Here. I made these applesauce oatmeal cookies, which was a big challenge, believe me, with no electricity, and not buying the ingredients at the store. I need your professional opinion."

The last thing Hayley wanted to do was eat anything in this disgusting dump that belonged on a very special episode of *Hoarders*.

But it could be her only escape.

Bradley gently removed the plastic wrap covering the cookies. Hayley picked one up, studied it carefully to make sure there was nothing crawling on top of it, and then took a teeny tiny bite.

It tasted like cardboard.

"Delicious," she said, in an effort to get out of there alive.

"Not too much nutmeg?"

"No. Perfection," Hayley said, chewing.

Bradley sighed, relieved. "I trust your opinion. You're my idol. I can't believe Hayley Powell is standing here in my house eating one of my cookies!"

Hayley desperately wanted to spit it out, but she was in self-preservation mode and swallowed the bit of cookie whole.

"I'm such a huge fan!" he screamed.

"Thank you," Hayley said, eyeing the door, waiting for the right opportunity to bolt.

"Why don't you come and visit me again and we can enjoy one of your mouthwatering cocktail recipes?" Bradley said, winking at her.

Oh, no.

He was turning amorous. She had to find some means of escape.

"You can meet some of the other cool dudes who are stockpiling for the war with the fascist government pigs. We're a tight-knit group."

"Of that, I have no doubt. Sounds delightful, Bradley. But if I don't get back to the office, I'm not going to get the next column in on time so you won't have anything to read when the next paper comes out."

"Well, we can't have that. Your columns are the highlight of my week!"

"You're too kind."

"And you're too beautiful," Bradley said.

Then he scratched himself again.

Hayley forced a smile, and backed away toward the door.

"We're going to need a lot of women who are still in their childbearing years joining us so we can repopulate after the revolution."

"Smooth talker."

"There's something about you. You remind me of my mother."

Hayley stopped in her tracks.

Karen Applebaum? Really?

Besides the disturbing oedipal undertones that were obviously going on here, the fact that she reminded anyone of Karen, especially her wacky son, sent shivers down Hayley's spine.

"I miss her," Bradley said softly.

Hayley saw the pain in Bradley's eyes. "You really did love her, didn't you?"

"Of course. She was my mother."

"Then why didn't you attend her funeral?"

"I was banned."

"By the government?"

Bradley looked at her as if she were out of her mind.

"No. Of course not. My father. He told me I wasn't welcome."

"But your parents were divorced. How could he have any say in the matter?"

"Because he's working with the president. He's a key player in the plot to subjugate the citizens of this country. I tried to warn my mother but she wouldn't listen. She always saw the best in people. She thought I was looney tunes."

The Mother's Day card that Bradley sent Karen. *Get out of town now or you're going to die.*

Of course.

It wasn't a threat. It was a warning.

Hayley suddenly felt confident that Bradley had nothing to do with his mother's murder. But her ex-husband, Martin, well that was a different matter altogether.

Chapter 28

After leaving Bradley, Hayley drove back across the island at lightning speed hoping to make another stop before she was due at the office. She knew Martin Applebaum ate breakfast every morning at Jordan's coffee shop on Cottage Street. That's where he met his latest girlfriend, one of the waitresses, who took his usual order of scrambled eggs and sausage links and a cup of black coffee.

Hayley pulled up in front of the restaurant, and almost forgot to put the car in PARK as she leaped out in a race to get to Martin before he finished eating.

Once inside, Hayley was greeted by the hefty blond hostess, an Eastern European immigrant with a gruff exterior who rarely cracked a smile. But Hayley knew she was a sweet girl who just hadn't quite learned the requirements yet for the position of perky hostess. The girl had a giant chest so a lot of the local lobstermen and electricians were quick to cut her some slack.

"Good morning, Hayley," the girl said flatly.

"Hi, Tatiana, I was wondering if you have seen . . ."

She didn't have to finish her sentence. As she glanced around the restaurant, she was suddenly blinded by bright turquoise. It was Martin Applebaum's shirt for the day, and it was just as loud and obnoxious as the man who wore it.

"Never mind."

"You want the blueberry stuffed pancakes today?"

Hayley stopped. She hadn't eaten breakfast. Well, she did have a bagel earlier, but that didn't really count as breakfast. And their pancakes were, after all, a signature dish.

"Sure. Just bring them on over to Martin's table."

Tatiana nodded, and went into the kitchen to place the order.

Hayley crossed to the corner booth, waving to a few people she knew seated around the main room before sliding into the booth, opposite Martin, who was intently scraping the last remnants of scrambled egg into a little pile with his fork. Then, using his thumb, he pushed the egg onto his fork and shoveled the remaining bits into his mouth.

He finally noticed Hayley sitting across from him. His look of surprise would've been comical if she hadn't found him so repulsive.

"Good morning, Martin," Hayley chirped.

"Morning," he said, chewing his eggs and looking a bit uneasy.

"I was just over at your son Bradley's house. You should see what he's done with the place. A decorator's dream!"

Martin didn't respond. He swallowed his eggs

and slurped the last of his coffee. Then he put down his ceramic cup and stared at Hayley.

"What on earth possessed you to go all the way over there?"

"I wanted to find out why he didn't attend his mother's funeral."

"And what did he tell you?"

"That you forbade him to go."

"Bradley's a big boy. He's long stopped listening to me."

"Why didn't you want him there?"

"Is it really necessary for me to answer that? He's unstable. His brain is out of whack. I didn't want him there causing a ruckus and maybe hurting someone."

"You're right. He does need help. But you don't seem all that interested."

Martin raised his cup and shook it, signaling his waitress—who also happened to be his lover—to scoot over with a fresh pot of coffee. She was startled to see Hayley sitting in the booth with her boyfriend.

A suspicious frown formed on her face. Was Hayley moving in on her man?

Hayley laughed to herself at such a ridiculous notion.

"Coffee, Hayley?" she said, squeezing the handle of the pot so hard her knuckles were white.

"Just some orange juice, thanks. I'm waiting for pancakes."

The waitress—Hayley couldn't remember her name, Jenny maybe—nodded and marched off to check on her other tables, never taking one eye off Hayley.

Martin was still giving Hayley the cold dead stare.

He had obviously been mulling over her last words.

"Of course I'm interested. He's my son. But Karen coddled him and indulged him and ignored the signs for years that something wasn't quite right with him. No matter how hard I tried to get him in to see a psychiatrist, Karen blocked me at every turn. She couldn't accept the fact that he had psychiatric problems."

"Bradley thinks you had something to do with Karen's murder."

"Of course he does. He's certifiable."

"You do have a motive."

"Enlighten me."

"The life insurance policy."

"What life insurance policy?"

"The one where you're named as beneficiary."

"We both changed all our policies once we got divorced."

"She forgot one."

Martin raised an eyebrow. "Really?"

"So you had no idea."

"No. Not a clue."

Hayley studied him. He looked totally surprised and suddenly over the moon.

"How much am I going to get?"

"Close to a million."

Martin dropped his coffee cup on the table, drawing some looks from the other diners.

"Are you serious?"

He was almost giddy, but at the same time desperately trying to control himself.

"That's probably just a drop in the bucket for a man of your means," Hayley said.

Martin caught himself. "Yes, yes, you're right. So you see? It really makes no difference and blows my so-called motive to get rid of her right out of the water."

But Hayley knew from what Randy'd heard from Martin's blabbermouth waitress girlfriend that he was indeed suffering from poor investments.

But she wasn't quite ready to play that hand yet.

The waitress brought Hayley's pancakes and slammed the plate down in front of her to make a point that she was doing so under protest.

She was gone in an instant.

Hayley knew Martin wasn't that good of an actor. She had seen him play Tevye in a community theater production of *Fiddler on the Roof*. DeNiro and Pacino had nothing to worry about in the twilight years of their careers.

No, it was obvious Martin really had no idea about the policy.

But maybe someone close to him did.

"Where were you the night Karen ate that poisoned clam chowder?" Hayley asked before taking a bite of her blueberry pancakes.

"Well, I certainly wasn't at the scene of the crime like you were," Martin said huffily.

Touché.

"Were you home?"

"No. I was out of town. In Portland. For a Toby Keith concert. I already explained all that to the chief."

"You could have had someone do the deed for you," Hayley said, pointing at Jenny the waitress, who was nervously glancing over at them as she scribbled down an order at another table.

"Janice was with me at the concert," Martin said.

Janice. Not Jenny.

Oh well. Close enough. And pretty soon she would be out of the picture and Martin would move on to the next girl. So why get attached to her actual name?

"We were on a date," Martin said. "She's a huge country music fan so I surprised her with tickets for her birthday. I can be very romantic."

That's when Hayley felt Martin's pudgy sausage-like fingers grip her knee.

She sat back, appalled, and just looked at him.

There was a slimy, salacious smile on his face, and it made Hayley's skin crawl. She tried to yank her leg away, but he held it firm.

"You could do worse," he said. "The way you're aggressively going after me, accusing me, it's like foreplay. Honestly, Hayley, it's making me hot."

"Snap out of it," Hayley said, taking another bite of her pancakes before wiping the fork off with her napkin, and then reaching under the table and jamming it down on Martin's hand.

Martin's face went beet red and he retracted his hand, howling in pain.

More looks from the other diners.

"You're disgusting," Hayley said.

"And you're fishing," Martin said. "I didn't kill Karen and you know it."

In a way, Hayley wished he had. Then he would be locked up and she would never have to be blinded by another one of his fluorescent shirts again.

But if Janice was with him on the night of the

murder, there wasn't anybody else she could think of who might commit murder for Martin. And a paid professional just seemed so unlikely, even if Martin could afford it.

Which if Janice was right, he couldn't.

Martin rubbed his hand, his eyes watery with tears from the pain.

Janice noticed and rushed over to see what was the matter.

"What happened?" Janice squealed.

Martin gave Hayley a pleading look.

He almost lost a hand. He didn't want to lose his girlfriend, too.

"He tried to eat my pancakes. And everybody knows I don't like sharing," Hayley said, waving her fork menacingly.

She turned to Janice. "Could you wrap the rest up for me to go? I've lost my appetite."

Janice nodded, and scurried off to find a plastic container as Hayley smiled at Martin, confident he wouldn't try to make another pass at her anytime soon.

Chapter 29

Once Hayley finally arrived at the office—only ten minutes late, to her surprise—it was business as usual with Hayley fielding calls and stealing a few moments throughout the day to work on her next column.

She worked through lunch, attended an editorial meeting mid-afternoon, and without even a coffee break, found herself lagging behind, trying to catch up with all the classified ads, subscriptions, obituaries, and press releases piled high in her inbox.

By the time she had a moment to catch her breath and look at the clock, it was going on six.

Hayley hadn't thought about the Karen Applebaum murder all day, and it made her nervous. The longer it took her to figure out what really happened, the more time the police had to build their case against her.

Not that Sergio reveled in her going down for the murder, but there were literally no other suspects.

And now that Hayley had ruled out Karen's ex-husband and only child, she was left with pretty much nothing.

She needed to clear her head and think about everyone remotely connected to Karen, anyone besides her who might have had a grudge. She needed to look at the other columnists and reporters at the *Herald*. Maybe Karen had crossed one of them.

And who was this mysterious boyfriend and why had she kept his name such a big secret?

Hayley drove home and prepared a lasagna. She popped it in the oven for the kids, who weren't even home yet. She then tossed a salad and slid the bowl in the fridge. She knew she had a good hour before the lasagna would be baked and the kids would be pounding their forks on the table, demanding to be fed, so she changed into some gray sweats and Nike running shoes, pulled her hair back in a ponytail, clipped the leash on Leroy's collar, and flew out the door for a quick run.

Leroy padded along the pavement, excited to be out in the fresh evening air. The sun had already set and darkness was falling over the island as Hayley picked up her pace, veering off the main road, through a cemetery, and into the heart of one of Acadia National Park's scenic trails, this one passing through the Kebo Valley Golf Course, and through the woods toward the park road that would eventually lead to the rocky cliffs of the Maine coast and scenic Sand Beach.

Hayley never bothered with an iPod and ear buds because she didn't want music obstructing the sounds of nature. The chirping birds, the cool night breeze, the crashing waves against the rocks.

When Hayley reached the ocean, with Sand Beach just ahead, she turned around to double back. She had already gone two miles. She stopped for a quick break, panting, wiping the sweat off her forehead and checking on Leroy. He had plopped down on his hind legs, his little tongue snaking out over his overbite, panting almost as loudly as Hayley.

"How're you holding up, Leroy? You ready to head home?"

Leroy was distracted by something.

When Hayley turned around to see what he was staring at, she saw a pair of headlights approaching. She instinctively scooped up Leroy and stepped to the side of the road, concerned the driver might not see her.

The car slowed down and stopped a few hundred feet away, the engine running, the driver's face shadowed and unrecognizable. It was too dark to even make out what kind of car he was driving.

Hayley waved at the driver and smiled. The car just sat there in the middle of the road, not moving.

What was he doing? He had to see her. Why didn't he just drive forward and pass her by.

The headlights shut off.

Hayley was enveloped in darkness.

Hayley's heart raced now. This was getting weird. She could hear the car idling. Why did the driver shut the lights off?

Hayley clasped Leroy to her chest and jogged

down a dark dirt trail leading away from the car and back toward home.

She heard the car turning around. It began following her along a paved road. She knew the road would eventually wind around. If the driver drove fast enough, he could cut her off as she came out of the trail back onto the main road. She could hide in the woods and wait for the car to give up and drive away. But she wasn't quite sure what was going on yet and didn't want to panic.

The car rolled slowly along and was now ahead of her. The driver clearly knew the dirt path Hayley had taken would end soon and lead her right out in front of him.

Hayley slowed her pace, deciding what she should do. She was ready to bolt into a thicket of trees and muzzle Leroy until the driver was gone, when suddenly the car's lights came back on and the man drove away.

She kept an eye on the red taillights until they turned a corner and disappeared.

Hayley felt an overwhelming sense of relief.

She'd probably overreacted. It could have just been a teenager out joyriding alone with only his permit and no adult supervision, afraid someone might see him and report him. Or it could have been a lost tourist.

Nothing to worry about. Leroy was getting heavy in Hayley's arms so she finally set him down.

"You can make it the rest of the way on foot, lazy butt," Hayley said, patting Leroy's head. And then she took off again, pulling Leroy's leash as he scampered to keep pace, now satisfied she wasn't in any kind of danger.

As she crested a hill, she stopped suddenly. Just ahead, she spotted the red taillights of the car. It had been pulled over to the side of the road. The driver's side door was open, and the engine was still on.

The surprise of seeing the car caused her to loosen her grip on Leroy's leash, and before she had a chance to react, Leroy sprung forward, dragging his leash as he ran toward the car.

"Leroy, come back here!" Hayley cried, chasing after him.

When she caught up to her dog, Leroy was sniffing the ground around the car, obviously picking up some kind of scent.

The car was empty.

Who would leave his car on the side of the road with the keys in the ignition and the engine still running?

Hayley looked around.

Something just didn't feel right. Her gut told her to get the hell out of there. She bent down to pick up Leroy's leash when she heard a sharp cracking sound and felt a whoosh just above her head.

Hayley stood upright.

What was that?

Leroy started barking wildly.

She leaned down and pointed her finger admonishingly. "Stop it, Leroy! Hush!"

Another crack.

Another whoosh.

This time past her right ear.

Dear God.

There was no mistaking what was happening.

Someone was shooting at her.

Hayley dropped to her knees, and yanked at the leash. The force choked Leroy's barking off for a few seconds as he flew toward her. She grabbed him in her arms and held him tight to her bosom, burying his face in her sweatshirt to muffle his incessant yapping.

Another shot rang out.

And the glass of the rearview mirror shattered to pieces, just inches from her head.

She was a sitting duck.

He would certainly get her with the next one.

Springing to her feet, Hayley plunged into the woods, carrying Leroy, running as fast and hard as she could, through tree branches that snapped back and lashed at her face. She kicked up some leaves, cranking her head around a few times to see if the shooter was pursuing her.

She couldn't make out much in the darkness. And she didn't see the thick fallen birch tree branch in her path.

Her Nike running shoe got caught underneath it.

Hayley lost her balance and went sprawling facedown in the muddy dirt. She lost her grip on Leroy and he sailed a few feet ahead of her, landing on his butt with a shocked yelp.

She lay on the ground, as still as can be.

The only sound was Leroy struggling to his feet. Did he see the shooter approaching? Her biggest fear was Leroy barking again and drawing the shooter directly to their location. But the little dog was still in a bit of shock, the air knocked out of him. He just sat there, not sure what had just happened.

Hayley didn't make a move.

Leaves blew past her. The trees swayed back and forth in the night breeze.

She heard a distinct clicking sound. Like someone cocking a gun.

And then footsteps. Not close. But close enough. If she stood up, she surely would be spotted.

Leroy began to growl softly, like he was warning her about approaching danger. She put a finger to her lips to shush him before realizing how foolish it was to expect a dog, especially her tiny slow-witted monster, to pick up on her hand signals.

She reached out and slowly, methodically began pulling Leroy's leash toward her. He kept up his low gutteral growling, and resisted being gently forced back in Hayley's direction. But she knew if she didn't shut him up, they would be easy targets for the shooter.

Leroy was now only a few inches from her.

She almost had him in her grasp. She couldn't tell where the shooter was, or if the crinkling leaves and twigs were from his approaching footsteps or the gusts of wind.

Then she heard a car door shut in the distance.

She raised her head just enough to see the car pulling away through a thicket of trees, rounding a bend and leaving for good.

By now, Leroy was too spent to even keep up his

growling. He looked exhausted, and welcomed the warm inviting arms of his master.

Hayley crawled to her feet, stroking his curly white hair, whispering in his ear that everything was fine, as she slowly hiked home, not quite ready to accept the fact that she was now in the crosshairs of a real killer.

Chapter 30

"Was it a man or a woman?"

"Man. Definitely a man."

Sergio began jotting down some notes on a pad of paper.

Hayley thought about it and then raised her hand.

"At least I think it was a man. It might have been a woman in bulky clothing. I'm not really sure."

Sergio stopped writing and looked up at Hayley.

Hayley shrugged. "It was dark. It all happened so fast."

Sergio nodded and scribbled over what he had written down.

"I'm so sorry, Sergio," Hayley said, reaching over and touching his hand. "I know this isn't really helping."

Sergio smiled and took Hayley's hand in his big bronze paw and squeezed it. "As long as you're safe. That's the main thing."

"At first I thought it might just be a deer hunter sneaking around illegally in the park when the first shot whizzed past me. But by the second and third one, I knew I was the target. And the whole thing of him driving ahead and waiting for me. Like he was setting a trap. It was terrifying," Hayley said, shivering as she relived the events.

Hayley had wasted no time driving over to Randy and Sergio's house the moment she dropped Leroy off with the kids and instructed Gemma to take the lasagna out of the oven at the top of the hour. She didn't mention her ordeal to them. Why scare them? But Gemma did notice that Leroy was out of sorts, racing around, a bundle of nerves, barking at the slightest movement.

Even more than usual.

"Let's move on to the car," Sergio said gently, poised to finally write some pertinent information down.

Hayley wracked her brain, desperately trying to come up with something useful. She was determined to help Sergio out somehow.

"I think it was a four-door sedan," she said confidently.

"Good. That's good," Sergio said, writing on his pad. "Color?"

"It was too dark."

"Could you tell if it was a light or dark color?"

"No."

"I don't suppose you saw the license plate number?"

"No."

Sergio nodded, trying not to give away his

disappointment. "Did you happen to notice if it was an out of state car?"

"I don't know," Hayley said, feeling awful.

Here she was running around the island like some amateur sleuth, gathering up clues in a murder mystery, but when it came to offering insight into her own attack, she was completely useless.

Sergio sighed, put down his pen and paper. "Well, if you do remember anything, Hayley, be sure to call me."

"There is one thing I definitely remember. One of the bullets shattered the rearview mirror on the driver's side."

"That's good!"

"It is?"

"Yes," Sergio said, relieved. "I can call all the auto shops in the area to be on the lookout for anyone who brings in a car with a busted mirror. It's a long shot, but it's a start."

The front door burst open, and Randy stormed dramatically into the living room interrupting the calm discussion between his sister and his boyfriend, who were sitting in front of a crackling fire with two glasses of wine.

"Are you okay?" Randy wailed as he shot over to Hayley, hauled her to her feet, and enveloped her in a tight bear hug.

Hayley could barely breathe.

"I'm fine, really, Randy, not a scratch on me," Hayley said, trying to calm him down while simultaneously squirming out of his firm grip.

Randy spun around to Sergio.

"I have to hear what happened to my sister

from Doofus Donnie who came into the bar to get hammered once he was off-duty?"

"I wanted to question Hayley while the details were still fresh in her mind," Sergio said, a defensive tone in his voice.

"So do we know who it is?" Randy asked.

"I'm a washout as a witness," Hayley said. "I totally choked when it came to noticing anything that might help identify the shooter."

"Don't blame yourself," Randy said. "The guy was shooting at you. Not the most opportune time to study his face."

"I do know one thing. This was no random shooting. Whomever it was who took those potshots at me wanted to see me dead. Which is why it has to be someone related to the Karen Applebaum case."

"How do you know that?" Randy asked, shoving Hayley down on the couch and then sitting next to her, wrapping his arm around her shoulder and pulling her so close to him; it was as if he were afraid to let her go.

"The people at work, the people who read my column, everybody knows I'm the number one suspect in Karen's murder. And it's no secret I've been running around town questioning people and trying to find the real killer. Maybe someone's afraid I'm getting too close to finding out the truth."

"That makes sense," Randy said, nodding vigorously at Sergio. "Doesn't it?"

Sergio half shrugged, not entirely convinced.

"Why aren't you agreeing with me?" Randy

asked, his voice betraying a slight irritation with his boyfriend.

"Because the whole town is related to the Karen Applebaum case. Everybody knew her. And those people we thought could have done it have airtight alibis."

"There's still one mystery person out there we haven't found yet," Hayley said.

"Who?" Randy asked.

"The man Karen was dating. The one who sent those flowers to her funeral. Find him. And I'll bet anything we find Karen's killer."

"How can you be sure?" Sergio asked.

"Call it a hunch," Hayley said, her mind racing.

"A hunch won't help me build a case against anyone," Sergio said softly.

"Would you please stop being such a Debbie Downer?" Randy scolded as he squeezed his sister tighter. "I swear, Sergio, if you let anything happen to my beloved older sister I'll never forgive you."

"Younger sister," Hayley said, making another futile attempt to wiggle out of her brother's grasp.

"What are you talking about? You're two and a half years older than me."

"But I stopped celebrating my birthday three years ago, so now you've gone past me and you're officially my older brother. At least that's what I tell everyone who didn't go to school with us."

They both laughed.

"I'm not worried about anything happening to me," Hayley said. "I'm more scared of you suffocating me to death if you don't let go."

Randy loosened his grip and Hayley was finally free.

She stood up and gave Sergio a hug.

"Thank you, Sergio. For everything."

"Don't worry, Hayley. You just go home and rest and don't think about it anymore. I'll find who did this."

Hayley smiled, and gave him a quick peck on the cheek.

Poor Sergio.

Not only was he going to have Randy riding him every second to clear Hayley's name and keep her safe, but he also believed that Hayley was actually going to go home and not think about this anymore.

But the truth was, it was all she could think about.

And now that she was both a murder suspect and a potential murder victim, she wasn't going to rest until she found all the answers.

Chapter 31

Sergio had no choice but to write a police report about the attempt on Hayley's life. So by the following morning, the entire staff of the *Island Times* was aware that someone had used Hayley for target practice the night before.

Sal asked if Hayley wanted to take the day off. She didn't.

The upside was nobody wanted to ask her to do any menial tasks for them because of the trauma she had just gone through.

And that suited Hayley just fine.

She basically just wanted to put her time in at the office, get her work done, and resume investigating the case.

On the down low of course.

The only person not around to talk about the incident was Bruce Linney. Hayley presumed he was out covering some local crime story, but she couldn't imagine it was more dramatic than an attempted murder. She was surprised he wasn't hounding her for details, or spitballing suspects, and generally just hanging around annoying her.

Hayley checked the clock on the wall. Four-thirty.

Another half hour and she would be set free. She began answering the last of her e-mails, one from Liddy about a new house listing on School Street, a fan letter for her strawberry and spinach salad recipe, and one of her mother's mass mailings to friends and family regarding another conspiracy theory involving Elvis still being alive and hiding out on an Indian reservation outside Santa Fe, New Mexico. She deleted that one without reading it.

Hayley was just about to shut down her computer and sneak out a few minutes early when Bruce threw open the door to the front office, and a gust of wind rushed through, blowing papers out of Hayley's inbox. He just as quickly slammed it shut while using a briefcase he was carrying to block out the wind.

He approached Hayley's desk.

Hayley gave him a sweet smile.

Bruce didn't smile back.

In fact, he had a very serious, very grave look on his face. He just kept staring at Hayley, but didn't say a word.

She shifted in her seat. He was making her uncomfortable.

"Everything all right, Bruce?"

"We need to talk."

"Okay, what's on your mind?"

Bruce looked around to see if anyone was listening to their conversation.

"We better do this privately. In my office. Now."

"You don't have an office. You have a cubicle. And everybody can hear you because you're always using your outside voice no matter where you are."

Bruce tapped his foot impatiently.

He was obviously in no mood for one of Hayley's playful insults.

"Then let's go get a drink or a cup of coffee. This is important."

"Is this about what happened to me last night?"

"It very well could be."

He had succeeded in stirring up Hayley's curiosity, and she quickly grabbed her bag and followed Bruce out the door, calling back on her way out, "'Night, Sal!"

She thought she heard Sal grunt a reply, but she wasn't sure, as Bruce gripped her by the arm and hurried her out and up the street. She had no idea where they were going, but she decided to allow Bruce to be in charge since he had such a grim look of determination on his face.

He steered her up a side street called Firefly Lane and past Mount Desert Island Ice Cream where Hayley shook him off.

She turned back and pulled open the door to the shop.

"Forget coffee. I want some salt caramel ice cream!"

Bruce sighed in frustration as he watched Hayley excitedly order from Linda, the pretty blond owner, who was wearing a white T-shirt stained with various flavors, and a blue bandanna tied around her head.

Bruce gave up and followed her inside, ordering a pralines and cream.

After Linda served them both, Bruce and Hayley sat at a small round table outside so no one in the shop could hear them talking.

"So I'm sorry to spring this on you. I know you've had quite a day, but . . . ," Bruce began.

"Oh, God, this is so good," Hayley said, shoveling the ice cream into her mouth with a white plastic spoon. "Did you know the president had the coconut when he was here with his family on vacation a couple of years ago?"

"Yes, I know," Bruce said. "Hayley, focus, please. This is important."

He reached out and grabbed Hayley's hand, preventing her from finishing her ice cream, which Hayley likened to sticking your hand into a lion's cage after poking him with a stick. The end result would be the same.

But she could see Bruce was agonizing over something, and since it obviously concerned her, she decided to sit back and let him talk.

"How much do you know about Lex?"

This caught Hayley off guard.

"Lex Bansfield?"

"How many men named Lex do you know?"

"Don't be smart, Bruce. It's just that you said what you wanted to discuss might be connected to the person who shot at me last night, so you can appreciate the fact that I wasn't expecting to hear Lex's name."

"No, I suppose not."

"You're not suggesting that Lex was the one

who shot at me last night, are you? Because if you are, we're done talking."

Bruce lifted up the briefcase he had been carrying, placed it down on the table, and snapped it open. He pulled out a folder, then closed the briefcase, and handed the folder to Hayley.

"What's this?"

"Police reports."

"I already have these. I downloaded them this morning for the next issue."

"These aren't from Bar Harbor. They're from Burlington, Vermont."

"I'm not following you, Bruce."

"Burlington. Where Lex lived before he moved here."

Hayley studied Bruce for a moment, and then opened the folder and began flipping through the pages.

"Aggravated assault. Illegal weapons possession," Bruce said grimly.

"I don't believe this."

She skimmed through the reports.

Sure enough, Lex's name was all over them. A bar fight. Failure to register a handgun.

And most troubling, a domestic dispute.

She poured over that one to see if Lex had threatened or harmed a woman he was dating, but the details in the report were vague.

"Obviously there is a pattern of violent behavior," Bruce said.

"Okay, so he's been in trouble with the law. Big deal. I remember you spent a night in jail after getting so drunk watching a Patriots game, you busted a pool table at my brother's bar."

"Ancient history. And I didn't hurt anyone."

"How do you connect a few incidents in Vermont to whomever it was who shot at me last night in the park?"

"I can't. But I think you should stay away from him until we find out more about why you were targeted."

"What possible motive would Lex have to hurt me?"

"You tell me."

"Why are you even checking into his background? What business is it of yours?"

"I told you, I just don't trust the guy."

Hayley felt her face flush. She was getting angry.

She polished off the last of her salt caramel ice cream and crushed the empty paper cup in her bare hands.

She stared daggers at Bruce.

"You know, Bruce, you make a very convincing argument. This certainly doesn't make me feel good about Lex. And I probably need to talk to him about this. But I also don't feel good about you and what you're doing."

"Trying to protect you."

"Is that what you're doing? Or is this some ploy born out of jealousy to keep me from finding someone who can make me happy?"

"Did you look at these papers? How can a guy like this make you happy? Are you that deluded?"

Bruce was only half-finished with his cup of pralines and cream when Hayley snatched it from his grasp and upended it in his face.

Bruce howled, surprised, as the store owner

popped her head up from behind the counter to see what the commotion was about.

Hayley stood up, grabbed her bag, and said, "Stay out of my business, Bruce."

And then she stalked off, as Linda came running out of the shop with a fistful of napkins to help Bruce clean the sweet praline bits and sticky cream off his face.

Hayley's head was spinning as she charged down the paved sidewalk to her car, which was parked back at the office. She was furious with Bruce and his obvious attempts to scare her away from Lex.

But there was also a small feeling in the pit of her stomach that she was trying to ignore.

One she knew she would have to confront eventually.

Maybe Lex Bansfield wasn't the all-around great guy she had thought or hoped he would be.

Maybe he was, as the police reports from Burlington suggested, a very dangerous man.

Chapter 32

Hayley had barely pulled into the driveway when she received an urgent text from Liddy demanding she join her and Mona at Randy's bar, Drinks Like A Fish, ASAP.

But all Hayley wanted to do was make sure Gemma and Dustin did their homework, pour herself a nice glass of Pinot Noir, settle on the couch, and nod off to sleep with Leroy nestled in her arms while watching an old cheesy Lifetime movie.

Unfortunately, the follow-up text from Liddy pretty much ensured that Hayley's well-laid plans were kaput.

I have juicy gossip. And it has to do with Karen Applebaum.

There was no way Hayley would ever be able to focus on Heather Locklear running away from a homicidal Harry Hamlin in the woods of Vancouver, Canada, in some fabulously awful nineties woman-in-jeopardy thriller with a text like Liddy's staring up at her all night from her cell phone.

No, Liddy knew exactly what she was doing, and Hayley knew it would be pointless to fight it.

She and Mona were probably propped up on stools right now waiting for her while Randy tended bar. And she was sure Liddy was teasing the two of them with tantalizing hints as to what her big bombshell was, but refusing to divulge any significant details until Hayley showed up.

Hayley went inside to check on the kids. She gave them money for pizza, and apologized once again for depriving them of a home-cooked meal. She was worried this was becoming a habit, but knew she could resume being a responsible mother once she cleared her name of murder.

Gemma and Dustin didn't seem all that heartbroken that they wouldn't be having dinner with their mother. In fact, they barely acknowledged her until she put her hand out holding a twenty dollar bill. Gemma got to it first and snatched it out of Hayley's fingers, and told her brother in no uncertain terms they would be getting pepperoni and mushroom, whether he liked it or not. Then, she dashed into the kitchen to call Little Anthony's on the landline. They were pretty much the only place in town that delivered.

Once Hayley inspected their homework to make sure it was done, she told the kids she wouldn't be gone long, and was back behind the wheel of her car within minutes, heading to her brother's bar.

Just as Hayley suspected, Liddy and Mona were

at the bar, sitting atop their usual stools. But Randy wasn't there.

Michelle, a tall statuesque goddess with bronze skin and long, jet-black hair—a mix of Native American and Greek blood—was filling in. Michelle went to school with Randy, and had served as his beard for every prom that popped up. They remained close after Randy came out, and when she divorced her husband after he emptied their joint checking account and skipped town, Randy hired her as a bartender. She hadn't known a Greyhound from a Sea Breeze, but Randy schooled her himself and now she was the most popular server in town, especially given her exotic beauty and winning smile.

"What can I get you, Hayley?" Michelle said, waving to Hayley as she scurried in and headed to the long oak bar.

"Glass of Pinot Noir," Hayley said, not wanting all her plans for the night to go out the window.

Michelle nodded, and reached for an open bottle of wine and a clean glass.

Liddy was sipping a Cosmo and Mona stirred a straw in what looked like a nearly empty glass of Diet Coke, and she didn't look happy about it. She kept throwing resentful glances at Liddy's cocktail.

"It's about time you got here," Liddy said. "I called and e-mailed you at work but got no answer."

"I left a few minutes early. Bruce wanted to talk to me about something."

"His undying love for you?"

"Not exactly."

"It's only a matter of time," Liddy said.

"Hayley, get your ass up on this stool so we can finally hear what kind of dirt Liddy dug up before my water breaks," Mona said, sighing.

Michelle busted up laughing behind the bar as she poured Hayley's wine and delivered it to her.

"Thanks, Michelle," Hayley said, smiling.

Michelle winked at her, and then went to refill Mona's soda.

"Okay, I've been a basket case ever since I heard what happened to you last night in the park," Liddy said breathlessly, clutching her heart.

Mona was a little more subdued in her concern, but did reach out and give Hayley a gentle pat on the shoulder. "You okay?"

"I'm fine. He missed completely. He might have just been trying to scare me. If it was a him. I couldn't really tell."

"Well, the last thing I want is to see my best friend riddled with bullets, so quite frankly, this latest drama spurred me into action," Liddy said.

Hayley wasn't sure if this was a good thing or a bad thing.

"What did you do?"

"You're not the only one who can play detective. I went to the *Bar Harbor Herald* and conducted my own investigation."

"This should be good," Mona said, chuckling.

"It is. You're not going to believe what I found out," Liddy said, a knowing grin on her face.

This was pure heaven for Liddy—knowing something everyone else in the room did not. She adored being in any kind of power position.

"What, Liddy? What? I have to be at work in the

morning," Hayley said before taking a generous sip of her wine.

"Well," Liddy said, drawing out the suspense as long as she could, "I wanted to know if anything unusual might have happened on the day before the bake sale. Karen's last day in the office before she was murdered."

"So what did you find out?" Mona asked.

"Well, Carol Pinkerton, who does the society column, had a desk next to Karen's at the *Herald*, and she told me—after I promised to lower the asking price on that quaint little three-bedroom fixer-upper I listed out on Route Three—that after the police returned Karen's computer it's just been sitting there. No one's tried to log on or erase the hard drive or anything. So I went over during my lunch hour today when almost everybody was gone, and I had Carol serve as my lookout while I went through her files."

"Wait. You broke into Karen's office computer with Carol Pinkerton as your accomplice?" Hayley asked incredulously.

"Yes. She really wants to put a bid in on that house. But without my help bringing down the price, she'll never qualify for the loan. So you can thank me when I'm finished with my story."

"Go on," Hayley said, taking another sip of wine, her curiosity peaked.

"There wasn't much, believe me. I can see why the cops came up empty. But then I noticed on the day before she died, which was a Friday, Karen went home for lunch," Liddy said, slapping a hand down on the bar for emphasis. "It was right there plain as day, typed into the calendar on her computer!"

Hayley and Mona waited for more.

But there wasn't any more.

Even Michelle, who had stopped washing glasses at the other end of the bar to eavesdrop, had a confused look on her face.

"Is that it?" Hayley asked.

"Ladies, according to Carol, Karen Applebaum never, ever went home for lunch. She ate out every day, like clockwork. I used to see her at all the different restaurants in town."

"Because you also eat lunch out every day since you make more money than all of us and can afford it," Hayley said.

"Precisely. So why on this particular day did Karen break her routine and go home? I asked Carol that question, and she told me she remembered specifically on that day that Karen took a phone call around ten-thirty, and told someone she would meet them at one-fifteen. Well, Karen took her lunch hour from one to two. And it's about a ten-minute drive from her office to her house."

"Liddy, maybe she was just meeting a contractor to have some work done on her house or something completely innocent," Hayley said.

"That's what I thought at first. But then Carol told me that when Karen noticed that she was listening to the conversation, she quickly turned away and started whispering, like she didn't want Carol to know who she was talking to."

"So you think it might have been the man she

was secretly seeing, the mysterious man who sent flowers to her funeral service," Hayley said.

"Yes, and if she rendezvoused with him the day before she died, it would not be a stretch to think that maybe they had some kind of big fight and he got enraged. He would have had motive and opportunity. The chowder could've been simmering on the stove in a Crock-Pot all day Saturday. He may have had a key to her house and came back the next day to add the cyanide while she was at the bake sale. She got home from the library, had some chowder for dinner, and it killed her."

Hayley turned to Mona. "You know, she does make sense."

Mona nodded. "I'm shocked."

"So who do you think it is?" Hayley asked, spinning back around to Liddy.

"You can't expect me to know everything," Liddy said. "I thought I did a pretty good job coming up with all that. Now it's your turn."

Hayley's mind raced.

How could they uncover the identity of this mystery man?

And then it hit her.

The answer was right in front of her.

"The Kitty Cam."

Liddy turned to Mona. "What's she talking about?"

Mona shrugged, completely in the dark.

"When Randy and I broke into Karen's house to poke around for clues . . ."

Mona interrupted her. "She says it like it's something she does every day."

Hayley playfully slapped her arm.

"Anyway, the only reason we got caught was because Karen had a Kitty Cam recording everything, and it was still running after she died. That's how Sergio found out about us breaking and entering. If Karen was meeting someone at her house the day before she died, wouldn't the camera have recorded it?"

"Genius!" Liddy squealed. "Oh my God, we're so good at this!"

"Wait just a minute," Mona said. "If Sergio saw you and Randy, wouldn't he have seen whomever visited Karen that day, too?"

"Not necessarily. The Kitty Cam was set up in the living room. Sergio never saw the killer poisoning the chowder or me discovering Karen's body because it all happened in the kitchen. But it's worth checking out! Maybe he missed something!" Hayley said, signaling to Michelle at the opposite end of the bar. "Michelle, where's Randy tonight?"

"At home. Date night with Sergio," Michelle said, wiping a beer mug dry with a blue rag.

"Perfect! Let's go!" Hayley said, downing the rest of her Pinot Noir and leaping off the bar stool.

"We're going to crash their date night?" Mona asked, eyebrows raised.

"Please. They just got home from a Mexican cruise a month ago. They've had plenty of alone time together," Hayley insisted as she waved good-bye to Michelle and scurried out the door.

Mona followed after her, as Liddy paid the tab,

grabbed her bag off the bar, and followed them out the door.

When the three women arrived at Randy and Sergio's house on the shore, Hayley was starting to have second thoughts about barging in on their evening alone together.

In fact, she wasn't even sure Sergio would allow them to review the tape.

But she had to try. This was too important.

She hurried up the steps of the front porch just as the headlights from Mona's truck rounded the corner with the lights from Liddy's Mercedes close behind.

Hayley rapped on the door, and within a few seconds, Randy answered, wearing a plush beige robe and dark brown slippers.

"Hayley, what's wrong?" Randy said, concerned that his sister had shown up on his doorstep so late.

He saw Liddy and Mona get out of their respective vehicles and race across the expansive lawn toward the house. "Is this some kind of intervention? My only addiction is *American Idol.*"

"This isn't an intervention. Where's Sergio?"

"Upstairs running the bath. I'm supposed to join him in five minutes."

Hayley perked up.

Maybe they could get away with scanning the tapes without Sergio ever knowing. Why get him angry and spoil date night?

Liddy and Mona pounded up the porch steps, shoving each other, trying to be the first one to reach the door. Liddy finally gave up, allowing Mona to go first.

"Honestly, Mona, it's like we're back in the third grade with you cutting in front of me to get your cup of green Jell-O first," Liddy said.

"Did you tell him?" Mona asked.

"Tell me what?" Randy said.

Mona studied Randy in his robe. "Are you naked underneath there?"

Randy peeked inside his robe to double check. "Uh, yeah, Mona, I am."

Mona covered her eyes.

"You gays, always flaunting your gayness and naked bodies."

"That would be true, Mona, if I had invited you here and greeted you at the door like this. But you just showed up here unannounced."

Mona thought about this. "I guess he has a point."

Hayley shushed Mona and then quickly explained to Randy the situation and how important it was for them to review the Kitty Cam recordings from the day before Karen Applebaum died.

"I'm sure if Sergio had seen anything, we would know about it," Randy said.

Hayley nodded. "I know. But I won't rest until I see for myself. Do you know where he has the tapes? Are they at the station?"

"No. He was watching them here when he saw the one of us inside Karen's house. I don't think he ever took them back, because he didn't want anyone to see us breaking into Karen's house."

"So they're still here?"

Hayley felt a surge of excitement.

"Yes. He keeps all of his work-related files and tapes in the top drawer of that wonderful zebra desk I bought in Africa when we went on that safari last year."

"Oh, I love that desk," Liddy cooed. "I have been searching the Internet for months to find one just like it for my home office."

Hayley whirled around and glared at Liddy.

"Let's try and stay on topic, shall we?"

"Right," Liddy nodded.

Randy turned to go inside. "Let me just make sure. Although I'm not sure Sergio is going to be comfortable letting us all watch it."

Hayley grabbed Randy by the arm.

"Does he have to know?"

"Hayley, he's right upstairs," Randy said.

"I know. In the bathroom. With the bath water running real loud. Probably can't hear a thing."

Randy hesitated, but then ushered the lot of them inside. "Okay, we'd better make this quick. I was downstairs looking for matches for the scented candles when you showed up. He's up there waiting, so we don't have much time."

Mona clomped inside, the floor creaking underneath her weight.

Hayley waved frantically at her to restrict her movements.

Mona plopped down on the couch and rolled her eyes.

Randy disappeared into the den and within seconds reappeared with a compact disc. "Jackpot! He even labeled it with the date."

Hayley mimed clapping her hands but didn't really clap so as not to make too much noise and alert Sergio.

Randy went over and loaded the disc into a

DVD player and then picked up a remote and snapped on the large screen TV that was mounted on the wall adjacent to the fireplace. When the scratchy image of Karen's empty living room appeared on the screen, Randy fast forwarded looking for some kind of action.

"This reminds me of those movie nights we used to do. Should we pop corn and open a bottle of wine?" Liddy asked.

Hayley just threw her a look.

Finally, an image of Karen arriving at the house came on, and Randy slowed down the disc to normal speed. Karen looked radiant and happy and was checking herself out in the mirror. She seemed anxious and excited about her impending visitor. The doorbell rang, and she jumped a bit, startled. She turned and headed for the door, but then stopped and came back. She walked right up to the camera, her face filling the whole screen, and shut it off.

The image turned to snow.

"Oh, no!" Hayley cried.

When she turned the camera back on, Karen was alone again. Her visitor was clearly long gone by this point.

"Well, that's why Sergio didn't say anything. Karen didn't want anyone finding out who it was that stopped by her house."

"Back to square one," Hayley said, disappointed and frustrated.

"No, we're not," Liddy said, staring at the screen. "I know who it is."

They all looked at Liddy as she stood up and grabbed the remote out of Randy's hand. She reversed the recording back to where Karen was primping, before the doorbell rang.

"Look, there!" Liddy screamed, freezing the image and pointing at the screen.

Suddenly they heard footsteps from upstairs followed by Sergio's booming voice.

"Randy, is someone here?"

They all froze.

"No, baby! I'm just still looking for the matches!"

"Did you look in the Yosemite Sam cookie jar in the kitchen? I remember putting some in there when we went on a diet and threw out all the cookies, but still wanted to fill the jar with something."

"Good idea. I'll look, and be right up!"

They listened quietly as Sergio walked back to the bathroom, turned the faucet on again, and resumed filling the tub.

Hayley shot Liddy an admonishing stare, and whispered urgently, "Keep it down."

Liddy whispered back, "I'm sorry, but I got a little excited because I've solved the case!"

She pointed at the screen again.

They all studied it.

"I don't see anything," Mona said.

"There! Behind Karen. Outside the living room window."

Hayley moved closer to the screen and stared up at it. "I don't see anything."

"On the far left side."

Hayley got even closer.

"What is that?"

Randy joined her. "It looks like some kind of tiny statue."

"It's silver," Liddy added, waiting for them to catch up.

"Is that a tiger?" Hayley asked, scrunching her face up.

"No it's a Jaguar. I saw it come into view a few seconds before the doorbell rang. It's the ornament on the hood of a car."

"You know, I think she may be right," Hayley said, turning to the others.

"And there is only one person in town who drives a Jaguar," Liddy said confidently.

"How do you know that?" Mona asked.

"She knows what everybody drives," Hayley said.

"Ted Rivers," Liddy said. "Karen was having an affair with Ted Rivers."

"The lawyer with the office upstairs from your real estate firm?" Randy asked.

"Yes. The *married* lawyer with the office upstairs from my real estate firm," Liddy said emphatically. "I just had lunch with his wife, Sissy, last week. She was cool as a cucumber, that one, she didn't give anything away."

"Maybe she doesn't know," Hayley said.

"Which is why Ted and Karen had to skulk around in secret, and why Karen was so careful not to leave any evidence around that would expose their affair," Randy said, getting excited.

"And why he didn't sign the card on the flowers he sent to the funeral. He couldn't risk anyone finding out they were involved," Hayley said.

"Exactly! He loves that car more than anything. What if Sissy found out he was screwing Karen? She'd have the upper hand in the divorce proceedings and could wind up with his beloved Jaguar," Liddy said.

"And maybe Karen decided to go public with their affair! And he couldn't let that happen! Not if he didn't want to lose everything. That would give him a motive to get rid of her! Ted Rivers poisoned Karen's clam chowder!"

It all made sense. Hayley just needed proof.

Chapter 33

After leaving Randy to hop in the tub with Sergio—who was none the wiser—Hayley, Liddy, and Mona hurried excitedly back to their parked cars. At least Hayley and Liddy were excited. Mona was just sticking around because it was a better alternative than going home and watching TV with her husband and five screaming kids. Hayley suggested they continue this impromptu girls' night out by driving over and staking out Ted Rivers's house.

"Why?" Mona asked.

"Because we might get lucky and find out more about the state of his marriage," Hayley said. "Maybe we'll catch him sneaking out to see another woman, who knows how many he could be cheating with, or maybe we just might stumble across some hard evidence we can take to Sergio that will be enough to get him booked for Karen's murder."

"Okay. Sounds better than spending time at home," Mona said. "But there's no sense in all of us driving. Why don't we just take my truck?"

Liddy laughed. "Oh, Mona, please. We can't take your truck."

"Why not?" Mona asked.

"Because, honey, we're going to a high-end neighborhood and your dilapidated rusty truck that smells like—and I mean no offense by this—a stinky lobster boat, will get more attention than a virgin at a prison rodeo."

"Did she really just say that?" Mona said, turning to Hayley.

"I think so," Hayley said. "But sometimes it takes a few seconds for the words to sink in before my mouth drops open in shock."

"This is a stakeout," Liddy said. "So obviously we need to blend in."

"Fine then," Mona said, shaking her head. "We'll take your Mercedes."

They all piled into Liddy's car and within five minutes were parked outside the Rivers' house on West Street. Ted Rivers, a successful attorney who had bought one of the old majestic waterfront mansions just off the town pier, was indeed home as they pulled up; they could see him through the kitchen window.

Rivers was around fifty-five with silver hair and horn-rim glasses, a long handsome face, a few inches north of six feet. He was at the sink, and it looked like he was drying dishes. He was talking to someone but they couldn't see who it was. Presumably it was his wife, Sissy.

Liddy, her eyes fixed on the Rivers' house, slowed the car down but didn't stop, and it rolled right into the back of a parked pickup truck. Hayley grabbed the dashboard while Mona was tossed around in the back.

"Liddy, watch where you're going!"

Liddy spun her head around to see if Ted Rivers had heard the crash, but he was too engaged in his conversation inside the house and wasn't even looking in their direction.

"What's a ratty old pickup truck like that doing in this neighborhood?" Mona asked with a big smile.

"Sarcasm noted, thank you, Mona," Liddy said, throwing her an annoyed glance through the rearview mirror.

"Are you going to get out and check for any damage?" Hayley asked.

"No, I can't risk being spotted," Liddy said.

"Well, are you going to leave a note on the windshield?"

"What for? That truck's got to be twenty years old. Look at all the dents it has already. Who is going to notice one more? If anything sustained serious damage, it's my Mercedes. I'll take it in tomorrow and have my mechanic look at it."

Mona swiveled around and was looking out the back window. "I think there's an old lady in the house across the street watching us. I saw her part the curtain and she was putting her glasses on."

"She'll go back to watching Bill O'Reilly in a minute. Don't worry about her," Liddy said, rolling down the window and sticking her head out to get a good clear view of what Ted Rivers was doing in his kitchen.

Suddenly, Rivers ducked his head as a coffee mug sailed through the air past him.

Liddy gasped. "Somebody just threw a coffee cup at him!"

Rivers's wife, Sissy, was now visible. She was a bottle blonde with sunken cheeks, tired eyes, and a few too many wrinkles from stress, and she was wearing a low-cut white negligee that sadly didn't do much to enhance her cleavage, which was generally lacking. She was yelling at her husband, pointing a finger at him with one hand, while holding a dish in the other.

"What great timing," Hayley said. "They're having a huge fight!"

"I just wish we could hear what they're saying. I bet it has to do with his affair with Karen Applebaum!"

Mona popped her head in front from the backseat. "That old woman is looking right at us."

"Would you relax, Mona?" Liddy said, pushing her face away.

And then Liddy opened the door and started to get out.

"Where are you going?" Hayley asked.

"I'm going to move in closer so I can try and hear what they're fighting about."

"Liddy, I'm not sure that's such a good idea. What if . . . ?"

But before Hayley could get any further, Liddy was already out of the car, crouching down like some U.S. Marine Commando, sprinting across the front yard of the Rivers' house, and then dropping down just underneath the windowsill.

She slowly raised her head just as Sissy Rivers threw that dish that was in her hand. Ted Rivers raised his arm, and the dish hit his elbow. They could hear him howl in pain as the dish hit the floor and shattered. Liddy dropped back down, pressing her back against the brick wall exterior of the house.

Inside the car, Mona was now rocking back and forth, nervous and jumpy. "Oh, I don't like this. I don't like this at all."

"What is it?" Hayley asked.

"The old woman is now at her front door, looking right over at Liddy, and she's talking on the phone."

Hayley looked at the house across the street and, sure enough, an old woman with gray hair and granny glasses in a powder-pink-colored robe was talking on her cordless phone.

"I better warn Liddy. That lady might be calling the cops," Hayley said, opening the door and slipping out. She kept low as she circled around the front of the parked Mercedes, where she noticed a giant gash in the bumper where Liddy had collided with the truck in front of her.

Hayley called out to Liddy in an urgent whisper. "Liddy, I think we need to get out of here! Now!"

Liddy waved her away. And then she turned back around, took a deep breath, and prepared to take another look inside the kitchen window to see if Ted and Sissy Rivers were still fighting.

Hayley knew she had to get Liddy out of there. She sprinted across the yard, hunched over, and joined Liddy underneath the windowsill.

"I'm serious, Liddy, that old woman across the street just called the cops."

"How do you know? She might have just been talking to her grandkids or something."

And at that moment, Hayley saw the flashing blue lights of a police cruiser turn the corner heading straight toward the Rivers' house.

Liddy didn't notice at first because she had already raised her head high enough to get a peek inside the house, and was staring right into the face of Ted Rivers, who at that exact moment was looking out the window to see why the cops were pulling up in front of his house.

Ted Rivers jumped back and screamed. Liddy screamed. Sissy Rivers dropped the ceramic bowl she was about to hurl at her husband and screamed. Everybody was screaming. Except Mona, who Hayley caught a glimpse of looking out the open backseat window of Liddy's Mercedes, with the biggest "I told you so" expression on her face that she could muster.

Donnie and Earl got out of the cruiser and ambled over to where Hayley and Liddy were crouched down together underneath the window.

"Evening, Hayley," Donnie said, tipping his hat.

"Evening, Earl, Donnie, how are you boys doing tonight?"

"Just fine. No complaints."

There was an uncomfortable silence.

"Only one complaining tonight is Mrs. Wentworth, who lives across the street," Earl said. "Said she spotted some prowlers casing the neighborhood. Said one of them looked a whole lot like Liddy Crawford and the other one resembled that nice lady who writes the food and wine column at the *Island Times.*"

Another uncomfortable silence.

Ted and Sissy Rivers raced out their front door.

Whatever conflict had been brewing between them was momentarily sidelined while they investigated who was outside their house stalking them.

"Liddy Crawford, what are you doing skulking around my house at this time of night?" Ted demanded to know.

"I'm not skulking," Liddy said, climbing to her feet and brushing off the twigs and dirt from her blouse. "It just so happens I had an out-of-town buyer inquire about your house today and I was just stopping by to see if you might be interested in selling."

Nobody said a word. They didn't have to. Liddy's on-the-spot excuse wasn't going to fly with any of them.

Earl stepped forward. "Maybe we should discuss this further over at the station."

"I'll radio the chief and have him meet us all over there," Donnie said.

Hayley went to stop him. "Now, Donnie, I don't think we have to bother Sergio about this." She went to grab his arm, but her hand ended up pulling at his gun holster, which snapped open. Donnie jumped back in surprise and stumbled, before drawing his weapon from the holster and pointing it at Hayley.

"She just went for my gun!" he wailed in a high-pitched voice.

"I did not!" Hayley said.

"Earl, you better cuff her," Donnie said, eyeing Hayley warily.

"Cuff me? Why, that's the most ridiculous thing I've ever heard," Hayley said, laughing.

But Earl was already behind her pulling her wrists together and snapping handcuffs on her.

Liddy charged forward. "Let her go!"

Donnie intercepted Liddy, yanking her arms behind her and holding her tight. She struggled, trying to shake his grip, but he was too strong for her.

"Ma'am, please don't resist arrest," Donnie said softly.

"If you don't want me to resist, don't call me ma'am. I'm not old enough to be a ma'am, Donnie."

"Yes, Ms. Crawford, now hold still while I snap these on you."

"You're arresting me, too? I didn't go for anybody's gun!" Liddy cried.

"I didn't either! It was an accident!" Hayley yelled.

Donnie turned to Ted and Sissy Rivers. "Would you folks mind getting dressed and meeting us over at the station?"

"Not at all, Officer," Ted Rivers said, eyeing Hayley and Liddy suspiciously.

Then he and his wife went back inside the house as Donnie and Earl escorted Hayley and Liddy to their cruiser.

Mona was already out of the back and getting into the driver's seat of Liddy's Mercedes. "I'll follow behind you and meet you there."

Mona got behind the wheel, turned the ignition, and the Mercedes roared to life.

"I'm really not comfortable with her driving my car," Liddy said as Donnie put a hand on top of her head and lowered her into the backseat of the squad car.

"That's really not our biggest problem right now, Liddy," Hayley said as Earl did the same to her from the other side.

Luckily when they all arrived at the station, Sergio was already there and intervened just in time to stop Donnie and Earl from booking Hayley and Liddy on a number of charges. Liddy was quickly dismissed and sent home, and Donnie ushered Hayley into Sergio's office, where she was brought a cup of coffee and told to sit tight until Sergio was finished interviewing Ted and Sissy Rivers.

The wait was interminable. But maybe her misguided attempt to expose Ted Rivers's affair with Karen Applebaum would somehow lead to the truth of what really happened. If anybody could grill a suspect, it was Sergio. He came off at first as this naive foreigner who hadn't quite mastered the English language, and gave the impression he could easily be manipulated, but before you knew it he was backing you into a corner with the facts. He was a master of getting you so scared and off-kilter, a full confession would just fall right off your tongue. There was a reason he was made chief at such a young age.

Hayley gulped down the last of her coffee and was peeling away the Styrofoam from her cup out of boredom when the door to the office finally opened and Sergio walked inside.

"Did you get him to confess about his affair with Karen?" Hayley asked, sitting up in her chair.

"No," Sergio said. "He very emphatically said he didn't have that kind of relationship with her."

"He's lying," Hayley said.

"I honestly don't think he is."

"Well, then what were he and his wife fighting about tonight?"

"She was angry because he wasn't drying the dinner dishes properly."

"What? Now that's a whole lot of crazy! She was throwing dishes at his head! Over something silly like that? And they live in a mansion! They don't have a dishwasher?"

"It's on the fin," Sergio said, a serious look on his face.

"What fin? How did we get onto the topic of fish? Oh, you mean *fritz*. It's on the fritz. The dishwasher is broken."

"Yes, that's what I said. According to Mr. and Mrs. Rivers, they have a very voluptuous and passionate relationship and sometimes fighting is an afro conditioner."

Okay. Hayley didn't need a translator for this one. Sergio meant the Rivers have a volatile and passionate relationship. And sometimes fighting is an aphrodisiac. She wasn't about to correct him. She was in enough hot water as it was.

"Okay, Sergio, suppose they're telling the truth. Suppose Ted Rivers wasn't sleeping with Karen. And he's completely faithful to Sissy. If all that's true, then what was he doing at Karen's house on the day before she was murdered?"

"It was a business meeting."

"What kind of business meeting?"

"She wanted legal advice."

"About what?"

"Karen was going to get married and she wanted to discuss the ins and outs of a pre-natal agreement."

Pre-nup agreement.

"I don't believe this," Hayley said, slack-jawed. "Karen was going to tie the knot? To whom?"

"She didn't mention a name to Ted and he didn't ask. He said it wasn't any of his business. He just gave her information on what kind of financial considerations there should be."

This floored Hayley. Karen Applebaum was by no means a rich woman, but she was certainly comfortable. Her father had left her a nice chunk of change when he died, and she certainly made out well in her divorce settlement with Martin. She probably had a nice little nest egg collecting interest at the First National Bank. So whomever she had fallen in love with might have been of lesser means, and she wanted to protect her portfolio if the marriage went south. If the mystery man wasn't Ted Rivers, then who was it?

Chapter 34

As Hayley drove home from the police station—luckily for her, a free woman—she thought about the facts and was certain of only one thing. The man who sent that big bouquet of flowers to Karen's funeral most definitely had to be the man she was planning to marry. But, according to Sergio, he had already spoken to the owner of the local florist, and the flowers were not from her shop. And there was no company logo on the card. It was plain white. All she had to go on was the handwritten inscription on the card.

Hayley blew through the back door of the house to find Gemma and Dustin polishing off the last remnants of a macaroni and cheese casserole, left-overs from a few days ago, having already polished off the pizza they ordered earlier. Hayley suddenly felt like a bad mother. Her kids were eating scraps, while she was out tracking down a killer.

Gemma reassured her. "If you made us a home-made meal every night the way you'd like to do, we'd just be another statistic for the childhood obesity epidemic."

This made Hayley feel a bit better.

"Where have you been all night?" Dustin asked.

"At the station. Visiting with Sergio. We never get any one-on-one time anymore, what with Randy always around, so I thought I'd go hang with him for a bit tonight."

Gemma and Dustin exchanged dubious looks.

"What?"

Gemma pointed to the police scanner Hayley kept plugged in on top of a shelf above her stove-top to keep abreast of all the goings-on in town. "We heard everything. Two women prowlers on West Street. One wearing a lavender blouse. I said to Dustin, didn't we give Mom a lavender blouse for Christmas last year? And wasn't she wearing it when she went out tonight?"

Dustin laughed. "And the other woman with auburn hair? That has to be Aunt Liddy!"

"Where was Aunt Mona?"

"In the car," Hayley said, giving up. "She was the lookout."

Hayley wasn't the only amateur sleuth living at this address.

"I'm not even going to ask what you were doing," Gemma said. "Are you going to be in the Police Beat? Is the whole school going to know you were arrested for trespassing?"

"Nobody got arrested. Okay, I was in handcuffs, but only for fifteen minutes. They took them off as soon as Sergio saw me."

"Our mother, the role model," Gemma said, cracking up.

"You're right. I screwed up. Again. I never said my strong suit was leading by example. But you know why I'm doing this. If they arrest me . . ."

"We'll have to go live with Dad," Dustin said. "Believe me, none of us wants that!"

"So did you find any helpful clues on your little adventure tonight?" Gemma asked.

"Not really," Hayley said, sighing. "Well, we did learn that Karen was planning to get married."

"Who would marry that old hag?" Dustin asked, scrunching up his face and looking disgusted.

"Dustin, please, we've already talked about this," Hayley said, folding her arms. "The poor woman has died. Show some respect."

"You hated her!" Dustin cried.

"You're right. I did. When she was alive. But now she's dead. So I can't anymore. I think it's a sin or something. We have to be nice."

"Fine," Dustin said. "I'll start over. Who was the fine upstanding gentleman who was going to carry Karen off into the sunset to live happily ever after?"

"Well, don't overdo it," Hayley said, grabbing a can of Diet Coke from the fridge and popping it open. "We actually don't know."

"Do you at least have any idea?" Gemma asked.

"I thought I did, but I was wrong. Dead wrong. The only thing I have to go on is an unsigned card that came with a bouquet of flowers sent to Karen's funeral. It said, *I will miss you forever. Today.*

Tomorrow. And always. With all my heart. Oh, and whoever it was dotted their 'i's' with little hearts."

"Kendra Mitchell," Gemma said, not even blinking.

"Excuse me?" Hayley asked, confused.

"That's Kendra Mitchell. She's in my class at school. Her parents own Mitchell Florists in Ellsworth. She works there on weekends taking orders over the phone and she always dots her i's with little hearts. It's, like, her signature."

Hayley couldn't believe what she was hearing. Her daughter had just produced the most solid lead yet. She reached out and grabbed Gemma by the cheeks and planted a big wet kiss on her. "I don't tell you how much I love you nearly enough!"

"It's okay, really," Gemma said, wiping her mother's spittle off her cheek.

"Will Kendra be there tomorrow?"

"Yes. She's there every weekend."

Hayley's mind was racing. "How about we go shopping in Ellsworth tomorrow, Gemma, and I'll buy you that new Land's End jacket you've been squawking about for weeks?"

Gemma was onboard immediately.

"We can have lunch, buy your jacket, and, if we have time, we can pop in and say hello to your friend Kendra," Hayley said, grinning.

"Like I'm dumb enough not to know this is all a bribe to pump Kendra for information. But who cares? I'm getting a new jacket!"

Gemma began dancing around the kitchen.

"What do I get?" Dustin said.

"A mother's undying love," Hayley said.

"I'd rather have my Xbox 360 back," he said, wandering out of the room.

"Once you're caught up with your schoolwork, you'll get your wish," Hayley said before ushering the kids to their rooms for the night, as it was getting late.

She then crawled into her own bed with Leroy snuggled into her side. Finally, she thought as she drifted off to sleep, she could see a little progress just off in the distance.

The following morning, Hayley roused Gemma out of bed shortly before eight, and gently pushed her to take her shower and eat some breakfast as she wanted to hit the road to Ellsworth. By the time Gemma dragged herself downstairs, rubbing the sleepy seeds out of her eyes, it was going on nine. After throwing some frozen waffles in the microwave for Dustin (she wouldn't mention that in her next column), she steered Gemma toward the car and they were finally on their way.

Hayley and Gemma arrived fifteen minutes before the shop opened, so Hayley parked the car across the street. She saw some movement inside, but wasn't about to arouse suspicion by forcing her way in before store hours and hammering Kendra with a barrage of questions. This situation demanded diplomacy and a light touch. Hayley thought she and Gemma could enjoy some mother–daughter quality time while they waited, but Gemma was too busy texting her friends. So Hayley turned on the radio, a soft-rock station, featuring a classic from Air Supply.

Gemma groaned. "Really, Mother? Must we?"

Hayley shut off the radio. Normally, she would have told her daughter to just deal with it, but she needed her help when the store opened and couldn't risk starting an argument.

Hayley checked her watch. Two minutes after ten. She tapped her right index finger on the steering wheel impatiently.

Gemma looked up from her cell phone. "Relax, Mother. It means Kendra is the only one working today. She's always late for school and getting written up. She has no sense of time."

Good sign. It was better if Kendra was alone.

Finally, at ten after ten, Hayley spotted a young girl around Gemma's age, with long stringy brown hair, spindly arms and legs, and an expressionless, can't-be-bothered face, unlocking the front door of the shop and flipping the CLOSED sign over so it read OPEN.

Hayley was out of the car in a flash and raced into the store. Gemma had to run to catch up. Inside, Kendra had already moved back behind the counter and was immersed in one of the *Twilight* novels.

"Gemma, look who it is!" Hayley said in a booming voice that startled Kendra, who jumped back slightly on the stool where she was sitting.

"Dial it down a notch, would you, Mom? You're going to scare her," Gemma said under her breath. And then she turned to the still somewhat shaken girl. "Hey, Kendra, how's it going?"

"Oh, hi, Gemma," she said, eyeing Gemma's hyperactive mother warily.

"We're here because my mother's birthday is

next week, that's Gemma's grandmother . . . ," Hayley said with a big smile.

"Yeah, I kind of got that," Kendra said, glancing at Gemma as if to say, "Your mother's weird."

Hayley had a single focus. She knew she was close to finding out who sent the flowers. She had to calm down. Take things slow. She was happy Gemma was there with her to help. She decided to pull back and allow Gemma to take the lead.

"We were thinking a spring bouquet, lots of different colors. You have anything like that?" Gemma asked.

"Oh, yeah, we'll put together something real nice," Kendra said. "What do you want the card to say?"

Gemma turned to Hayley. "What do you think, Mom? Something like 'Happy Birthday, Gram! Have a wonderful day and we wish we were there to help you celebrate. Love, Hayley, Gemma, and Dustin'?"

"That sounds very nice," Hayley said.

They both watched as Kendra grabbed a card and started writing it all down. Sure enough, Kendra dotted all her "i's" with little hearts.

"What a nice touch, drawing those little hearts," Hayley said.

Kendra stopped and looked at the card. "What? Oh. Right. I've been doing that for so long, like since the third grade. I've stopped thinking about it."

"Well, it's very sweet," Hayley said.

"My mom told me about the flowers at Karen Applebaum's funeral and I knew it had to be you who had written the note," Gemma said.

Kendra looked up at Gemma, a bit confused. "Who?"

"You know, that lady who died from eating the poisoned clam chowder?" Gemma said.

"Oh, her! Yeah, what a way to go. And I read they think your mom . . ." Kendra caught herself.

"For the record, dear, I'm one hundred percent innocent," Hayley said.

"Of course," Kendra said. "Now will that be cash or charge?"

Hayley slapped down her credit card. "Those were lovely flowers at Mrs. Applebaum's funeral. Did you put together that bouquet?"

"No, my mom did. I just took down the order and ran the credit card."

"I see," Hayley said. "Everyone at the service wanted to know who sent such a beautiful arrangement, but unfortunately there was no name on the card."

"That's because the guy didn't want us to put his name on it," Kendra said.

"Why not?" Hayley asked.

But Kendra just shrugged. "I don't know."

"Well, who was it?" Hayley pressed.

"My parents told me never to share customer information with anyone," she said.

"Good rule. Completely understandable. Your parents are absolutely right," Hayley said, giving Gemma a quick nudge.

Gemma looked at her mother, not sure what she wanted her to do.

With a quick move of her head, Hayley tried to indicate to Gemma that she should try to keep Kendra distracted.

Gemma knew what her mother planned to do and shook her head vigorously.

Unfortunately, Kendra was watching the whole scene. "Is something wrong?"

"No, everything's fine. We're just having a little disagreement. Gemma really wants a brand new Land's End jacket, but I told her she should get a job after school and pay for it herself because in the end, it will mean so much more."

Gemma sighed. Checkmate. Her mother just scored big-time. And Gemma knew what she had to do if she was going to get that jacket.

"Kendra, have you done your trigonometry homework yet?"

"Yeah, I finished yesterday."

"I'm stuck on question ten. Can I see how you did it?"

"Sure. But I left my laptop at home."

"Mine's in the car. Can you come outside and I'll show you where I got hung up?"

"My parents said never to leave the store," Kendra said.

This kid was so responsible, Hayley thought. It was starting to get annoying.

"Well, I'll go get it and you can help me in here," Gemma said.

And then Gemma bounded out the door. Hayley offered up a fake smile, which Kendra ignored. In a few seconds, Gemma was back in the shop with her knapsack. She pulled out her laptop and fired it up on the counter. She positioned herself between Kendra and her mother, and kept Kendra focused on the computer screen.

"I'll just browse and enjoy all these beautiful flowers," Hayley said, casually walking away, disappearing into the forest of plants and roses and daffodils and lady's slippers, before reemerging from the other side and slipping around behind Kendra and into the back office of the shop.

She knew she only had a couple of minutes, as Kendra was already rattling off how Gemma could reach the right answer to the problem. Hayley went behind the desk and quietly opened a few drawers, rifling through the hanging file folders until she came to one labeled RECEIPTS. She pulled it out and opened it on the desk, flipping through the stack of credit card receipts at a clip, hoping a name would pop out at her.

She was almost through the entire stack when she stopped cold. She picked up one receipt and studied it. It was dated the day before Karen's funeral. And it was for a flower arrangement to be delivered to the church for Karen's service.

The name on the receipt was Lex Bansfield.

Hayley blanched. She felt sick to her stomach. She stuffed the receipt in her pants pocket, returned the file to the drawer, and tiptoed out of the back office just as Gemma closed up her laptop.

"Thanks, Kendra, you're a lifesaver," Gemma said.

"Yes, Kendra," Hayley said. "You most certainly are."

Hayley and Gemma said their good-byes and left the shop. As they reached the car, Gemma said, "You better call Gram and say she's getting a bouquet of flowers for her birthday seven months early."

Hayley nodded, but didn't say a word.

Gemma looked at her. "Is everything okay, Mom?"

Hayley nodded again. She hated fibbing to her kids. But she wasn't ready to talk about this. She was still in a state of shock. The closer she got to the truth, the less safe she felt. How could she have been so wrong?

Lex Bansfield, the man with a troubled, violent past in Vermont, who perhaps moved to Bar Harbor to escape his demons—or worse—the law, was the man Karen Applebaum was going to marry before her murder.

Chapter 35

Hayley found Lex raking leaves with a couple of his workers, two teenage boys working part time to make some extra pocket change, on the expansive, sprawling Hollingsworth estate nestled against the rocky coastline. It was a crisp September day, with a light breeze and a nip in the air, as Hayley made her way down the gravel path in her car.

Lex heard the vehicle approaching and shielded his eyes from the sun with one hand to see who it was.

He broke into a smile and waved as Hayley got out of the car. She slowly walked over to him.

"Hey you," Lex said, genuinely happy to see her. "You here to steal me away for some lunch?"

"I was hoping we might have a talk," Hayley said, not cracking a smile.

"Uh oh, I'm not sure I like the sound of that," Lex said, and then turned to the two teens, who were now listening intently. "Boys, why don't you take five?"

They both really wanted to hear what Hayley

had to say, but a break from raking leaves trumped their curiosity and they strolled off toward the shore path to catch some sun and the spray of the ocean waves collapsing against the jagged rocks.

Lex looked at Hayley tentatively. "So what's on your mind?"

"I know about your brush with the law in Vermont."

Lex laughed. "Oh, it was more than one brush. I think they named the local jail cell after me once I left."

"What about the assault charge?"

"Look, it was a long time ago. I was a heavy drinker. I'm not anymore."

"You were also involved in a domestic disturbance."

"Overblown. And I was on the receiving end of that one. I'm not making any excuses about my past, Hayley, but I have never physically harmed a woman when I was angry, drunk, or otherwise. You might get one or two to say I hurt them emotionally, but everybody's had relationship struggles in their past, and I never said I was perfect."

"Okay, I believe you," Hayley said, not one hundred percent confident.

Lex noted her hesitation. "Why the third degree all of a sudden? What's changed?"

"I know you sent a bouquet of flowers to Karen Applebaum's funeral. I saw the card and read what it said."

"Those weren't from me."

"Lex, I also saw the credit card receipt. It was you."

"Have you been investigating me?"

"No. I'm trying to find out who killed Karen Applebaum so they don't name a jail cell after *me*!"

"And you think I did it?"

"I don't know. Did you send those flowers?"

Lex just stood there, his face betraying nothing. She stared at him long enough until he averted his eyes, not wanting to look directly at Hayley. He then shoved his hands in his pants pocket and, looking down at the leaves blowing across the front lawn, said, "Yes."

It was like a kick in the stomach.

Hayley thought she was going to pass out. Lex Bansfield. The town's most eligible bachelor. In love with Karen Applebaum.

"So you loved her?" Hayley asked.

"It's not what you think," Lex said, stepping forward.

Hayley backed away, her head spinning.

Lex's cell phone chirped. He checked the screen. "It's the boss. He's been to some board meetings in New York. His private jet just landed, and he's twenty minutes early. I have to get to Trenton and pick him up. Can we talk about this later?"

Hayley didn't answer. She just stared at him, still processing all of it, feeling completely duped, like a fool.

"Please, Hayley, give me a chance to explain. I'll come clean about everything, but if I don't pick up Mr. Hollingsworth right now, my ass is going to be on the line."

"Go. I'm not stopping you."

Lex gave her one last pleading look as if to beg her to trust him.

But Hayley didn't know what to believe.

Lex checked his watch. "Do me a favor?"

Hayley arched an eyebrow. Really? A favor?

"Go tell the boys I'm coming back with the boss, so if they're sneaking cigarettes down by the shore, they better not toss their butts in the garden. Mr. Hollingsworth is a stickler about that."

Hayley nodded.

Lex gave her one last look. He leaned in to try and kiss her on the cheek, but she tensed up, and folded her arms tightly around her chest, sending him a clear signal she did not want to be touched.

He quickly retreated and then jumped in his jeep and drove off.

Hayley turned and saw Lex's workers sitting on some rocks, and they were indeed puffing and exhaling and chattering away. They were so engrossed in their conversation, they didn't even see her, so Hayley made a beeline to the small gray house with white shutters perched on a small hill a few hundred feet from the main mansion. This was the caretaker's cottage where Lex lived year-round whether the Hollingsworth family was in town or not. He was in charge of the property full time.

Hayley kept an eye on the two boys, making sure they didn't see her, and then she hurried up the steps onto the front porch, opened the front door, which was unlocked, and slipped inside.

She didn't really know what she was looking for. But she was determined to find out exactly what Lex was hiding from her. She tried a few drawers in the kitchen, then made her way into the living room. The cottage was sparsely furnished. Lex didn't do much in the way of interior decorating. There was the distinct lack of a woman's touch. She saw an antique wood desk in desperate need of some refinishing in the corner. There were old newspapers and magazines, a few bills, and some clippings stapled together. Hayley thumbed through them. They were all her "Island Food & Spirits" columns to date. Lex had saved them all.

Hayley was touched. Maybe this was all just a big misunderstanding. But then again, he didn't deny sending the flowers with the romantic note to Karen's service. In fact, he admitted it. How many different ways could she interpret that? She put down the clippings and kept searching through the piles of paper.

She tried the desk drawer. It was locked. She tugged at the metal handle, but the drawer was secure. Hayley was about to leave, but something drew her back to that locked drawer. She had a feeling in the pit of her stomach. She had to see what was in there. She looked around and found a gold letter opener with a brown wooden handle. She stuck the end of it through the small crack of the drawer and started pumping the tip up and down. Finally, she heard a crack and then a pop. She knew she had not only busted the lock, but the whole drawer. She'd write a check for the repairs. She yanked it open.

Inside was a stack of letters bound together by two thick elastic rubber bands. She fanned through the letters. They were all addressed to Lex and they were all from Karen Applebaum. Only the first few letters had been opened. The rest were still sealed. Hayley pulled the letters out of the open envelopes and began reading them. Her heart sank. They were love letters.

Karen's writing was like poetry. Passionate. Dramatic. Romantic. And now one thing was crystal clear. Karen Applebaum had been hopelessly in love with Lex Bansfield.

It only confirmed Hayley's worst fear. Lex Bansfield was Karen's secret boyfriend. And the fact that he was still trying to hide it to the extent that he had tried to date Hayley behind Karen's back only highlighted the possibility that he had something to do with her murder.

Island Food & Spirits

by
Hayley Powell

What a week. Eye-opening to say the least. Sometimes I wonder why I even leave the house. So tonight was all about staying home for some much-needed rest and opening a bottle of Pinot Noir that has been sitting on my kitchen counter all week. Tonight seemed like the perfect time to finally pop it open and just sit back, relax, and reflect on the recent events in my life.

I must have done a lot of reflecting because when I went to fill another glass the bottle was empty. So I decided to finally get something done and make a nice dinner for the kids, because with me so distracted this week they had been fending for themselves with leftovers, not to mention supporting our local pizza joint. I had also been mulling over the recipe for our sixth course and was torn between a nice broiled beef or homemade pasta raviolis stuffed with cheese, ground pork, and spinach.

Feeling somewhat rejuvenated from my wine, I decided on the homemade pasta raviolis for the sixth course and I was going to surprise the kids by making some for when they got home. So I gathered all of the ingredients to make the pasta dough and, of course, had to move the large stack of papers the kids left all over the counter to another area of the room. I swear I don't know why anyone in my house can't just put things where they belong. Is it really such an inconvenience for the kids to put things away? Am I right, mothers?

Once I had the ingredients lined up in front of me for the filling, I began the process of grating, chopping, shredding, dicing, mixing, and rolling. I had forgotten what a long and involved process making homemade pasta with fresh ingredients could be, but I knew this meal would be well received and it made me feel good that I was preparing a home-cooked meal for my family.

After finally finishing the raviolis, I looked at the clock and was surprised to see that a whole hour had already passed. I knew the kids would be home soon and ready to eat so I tossed a salad, sliced a loaf of Italian bread and placed butter on the slices, wrapped that up, and put it in the oven to warm. I even made a homemade marinara sauce to have on top of the pasta.

Feeling exhausted and quite pleased with myself for preparing this delicious-looking feast, I decided to have another glass of wine (luckily there was an extra Malbec in the cupboard) and turn on *NCIS* while I waited for the kids to come home.

I became so engrossed in the show, and, honestly, who wouldn't with that hunk of a man Mark Harmon staring at you with those bedroom eyes? Have I mentioned my Mark Harmon crush before?

Anyway, I didn't even realize another forty-five minutes had gone by and still no kids. Now I was starting to get a little worried because if you know my kids, you know they love their mealtimes, and they always call and let me know if they are going to be late.

My raviolis were getting cold, the bread was already hard, and I was wondering where they could be when at that moment, the front door flew open and my daughter marched in, announcing loudly and dramatically that she would never, ever eat another thing again as long as she lived. Her brother was right on her heels, nodding in full agreement.

I couldn't believe my ears! Where did they eat? Who paid for it? Why didn't they tell me? My daughter, in her most exasperated teen voice, answered, "We ate at the italian restaurant on Main Street with Uncle Randy and Uncle Sergio. They came by earlier and said you were having a rough week and it would be nice if you could just relax when you got home and not worry about making us dinner. Didn't you find the note we left you?"

I just sighed and realized I'd never looked at the clutter of papers when I moved them to make dinner and failed to notice their note on the top of the pile. My son then noticed my delicious-looking raviolis and remarked how my pasta dish couldn't possibly compare to the fabulous ones they'd had at the restaurant. Well, I guess both kids will find out for sure tomorrow night when they have leftovers again.

For our sixth course, I'll be making the raviolis stuffed with sausage, cheese, and spinach! The first ingredient I suggest is a good bottle of Pinot Noir to calm the chef. And make sure to check and see if anyone else will be eating before you start cooking.

Sausage, Spinach, and Cheese Ravioli with Creamy Tomato Sauce

Make your favorite pasta dough, then follow the recipe below.

Roll your pasta out into sheets, cut each sheet into squares (for tops and bottoms). Using a teaspoon, fill the center of half the squares with the filling. Brush around the filling with the egg wash and place the remaining squares on top. Press down around the seal to push out any air bubbles.

Filling

8 cups fresh spinach, cleaned and coarsely
   chopped
4 large italian sausage links, removed
   from casings
1 medium onion, chopped
2 cloves garlic, peeled and minced
3 Tablespoons olive oil
½ cup grated Parmesan cheese
1 egg
salt and pepper to taste
fresh Parmesan to serve on top

Sauce

> 2 Tablespoons olive oil
> 2 cloves garlic, minced
> ½ teaspoon crushed red pepper flakes
> 1 (28 ounce) can crushed tomatoes
> salt and pepper to taste
> ½ cup heavy whipping cream
> ¼ cup chopped fresh parsley

To prepare the filling, steam the spinach and drain well. Press the spinach to remove any excess water. In a frying pan, heat the olive oil and sauté the onions with the sausage meat until the onion is tender and the meat lightly browned. Add the garlic and season with salt and pepper. Put the sausage mixture, spinach, egg, and cheese in a food processor and pulse until the mixture is combined. Make sure you don't over-process the mixture.

To prepare the sauce, heat the two tablespoons of oil in a heavy pot and cook the garlic for two minutes, being careful not to burn it. Add the tomatoes, salt, pepper, and pepper flakes and cook over medium low heat for 10 minutes. Add the cream and fresh parsley, and mix well. Cook over low heat an additional 10 minutes. Leave on low while you cook your pasta.

Cook the ravioli in boiling salted water until tender. They will float to the top when ready. Drain your ravioli and return to the pot. Carefully pour half of the sauce mixture into the pot and gently stir until the ravioli is lightly coated. Serve the ravioli with additional sauce and fresh grated cheese.

You might as well be dining in Naples!

Chapter 36

"So you think Karen was going to marry Lex Bansfield?" Sergio asked, more than a bit surprised.

"Yes," Hayley said, sipping an iced tea on the front porch of Randy and Sergio's house just a few minutes from the Hollingsworth estate. She had rushed right over after finding the love letters, and sat down with her brother and his boyfriend to discuss her theory.

"I think Karen had a little money stashed away after her divorce from Martin and she didn't want Lex getting half of it if the marriage went bust. That's why she met with Ted Rivers. To discuss putting together a prenup."

Randy sat forward, completely engrossed in the story. "Maybe Lex found out about her fear that he was a gold digger and went berserk!"

"Absolutely," Hayley said, "Given his violent history, it all makes sense."

"Wait just a second," Sergio said, swaying back and forth next to Randy in a wicker love seat rocker with plush orange cushions, his arm draped around Randy's shoulder, while sipping his own iced tea. "Karen's murder was carefully planned and executed. A drop of poison in a pot of clam chowder does not point to a crime of passion."

"He's right," Randy said. "I read those reports from Vermont you gave Sergio."

"You did?" Sergio said, turning toward him, a scolding look on his face.

"Yes, and nothing suggests Lex has a calculating mind. All of those arrests were alcohol related. Disturbing the peace, that kind of thing. He always wound up in the drunk tank and was released the next morning on his own recognizance when he had sobered up."

"But just because he only broke the law when he was drunk doesn't mean he isn't capable of plotting a murder," Hayley said.

"Yes, and there is only one way we are going to find out for sure," Sergio said. "I'm going to bring him in for questioning and get to the bottom of this." Sergio stood up from the love seat. "Any idea where I can find him?"

"He drove to the Bar Harbor Airport to pick up his boss," Hayley offered.

"I guess I'll be waiting for them when they get back," Sergio said, pounding down the porch steps and striding toward his car.

Hayley turned to Randy. "If we're wrong, Lex is never going to speak to me again."

"And if we're right," Randy said, "you may have just dodged a bullet. Literally."

"Should we wait here until Sergio questions him?"

"Hell, no," Randy said, jumping to his feet. "The file room is right next to Sergio's office. The walls are so thin we'll hear everything!"

"Won't Sergio be mad if he finds out we're eavesdropping?"

"Honey, we've already been busted for breaking into the house of the murder victim. This is nothing compared to that."

"I like your logic," Hayley said, setting her glass down on the glass-top wicker table and following her brother, who was already halfway to her car.

Hayley and Randy even had time to pick up some coffee before heading to the station and positioning themselves in the file room.

They sat there for about a half hour until they heard the front door of the station opening. There were some low voices and scuffling of feet before the volume of the voices got louder and they could tell Sergio and Lex had entered the office and were sitting down to have a talk.

Sergio put Lex at ease with some small talk, apologizing for taking him away from his work on the estate, hoping there wouldn't be a problem with his boss, Edgar Hollingsworth. Lex replied pleasantly that there would be no issue, and he was due for a short break anyway now that the elder Hollingsworth was at home resting after his long trip back from Manhattan.

Randy yawned and gave Hayley a look that said, "Get to the good stuff already!" And right on cue, Sergio cut to the chase.

"Lex, I've been going over the facts of the Karen Applebaum case, and a few things have come to light involving your relationship with the murder victim."

"From your boyfriend's sister, I suspect," Lex said, a cool even tone to his voice.

Hayley cringed.

"I can't tell you how these things came to my attention," Sergio said.

"Fine," Lex said. "Go ahead. Hit me with what you've got."

"I believe you are in possession of some love letters. From Karen Applebaum."

There was a long pause.

Hayley, her ear pressed to the wall, could picture the stunned expression on Lex's face.

"How . . . How . . . ?" Lex stammered.

"Were you two involved intimidatingly?"

"Intimidatingly?"

Both Hayley and Randy wanted to scream "Intimately! He means intimately!" But neither was willing to give themselves away and lose out on hearing the entire conversation.

Lex did it for them. "Do you mean intimately?"

"Yes," Sergio said, losing patience. "That's what I said."

Lex paused again. And obviously decided to let it go. "No."

"I saw the letters."

"Yes, she sent me those letters. She was in love with me. But I'm telling you, chief, it was not mutual. I had no feelings for her whatsoever. I didn't even like her that much. Most of those letters I didn't even open. I couldn't stand reading them anymore. I tried to get her to stop but she refused. She just kept trying to convince me we were meant to be together. After a while, I stopped contact with her altogether and just let the letters pile up."

Hayley listened intently to every inflection of Lex's voice, and in her mind and to her utter surprise, he sounded very convincing.

Lex continued, "The whole thing was one big mess. I didn't want to lose my job over it."

"How would you lose your job?" Sergio asked.

"Because it was a very sticky situation and it involved someone I'm close to who did love Karen."

"Who?"

"My boss. Edgar Hollingsworth."

Hayley and Randy audibly gasped and both instinctively slapped their hands over their mouths.

This was a shocker.

"They spent a lot of time together on the estate, sneaking around, secretly dating. All of us who worked for the old man knew exactly what was going on, but we were never going to say anything. We didn't want to get fired. But Mr. Hollingsworth flew to New York a lot for board meetings, and Karen kept hanging around when he wasn't there, strolling through the gardens, watching us tend to the property, and somehow she got fixated on me and started following me around and asking me personal questions. Because she was the boss's girlfriend, I tried to be polite, but then it got out of hand and she tried to kiss me. I pushed her away, but she was relentless. She kept calling me at home and saying she loved me. When I stopped answering, she began writing letters. Jesus, she was stalking me and it scared the hell out of me, because I

love working for Mr. Hollingsworth and I didn't
want her to ruin that."

"So you decided to take matters into your own
hands?" Sergio said.

"No!" Lex screamed. "I didn't touch a hair on
her head! Why does everybody think I'm some
kind of monster?"

"I think you know why, Lex," Sergio said. "Take
a look at this arrest record I have from Burlington, Vermont!"

There was silence for a moment and then Sergio
spoke again.

"What about the flowers?"

"Yes. I ordered the flowers and used my credit
card."

"And you wrote, and I quote, *I will miss you
forever. Today. Tomorrow. And always. With all my heart.*
I'm about to swoon, that sounds so romantic."

"Yes, I told the girl who took the order to write
that on the card. But those weren't my words. Mr.
Hollingsworth asked me to place the order. He
didn't want everybody knowing his personal business, that he was involved with Karen Applebaum,
that they were going to elope. There was enough
gossip and rumors about him already, given how
rich the guy is and how famous he is in town. But
he was heartbroken over Karen's death and wanted
some symbol of his devotion to her at the service.
So he had me do it, and reimbursed me for the
expense and for my trouble."

Hayley looked at Randy.

It made sense. It all made sense.

"I was just doing my job," Lex said, sighing.

Hayley actually felt sorry for him. He had won her over. She was completely on Lex's side now. And she felt awful for doubting him.

Lex Bansfield was innocent of Karen Applebaum's murder.

She was elated and wanted to burst into Sergio's office and give Lex a big hug. But she knew that would probably be a bad idea. For both her and Randy. She restrained herself, but her mind was all over the place.

This meant the real killer was still out there. And she was dying to know if the key to the mystery was with the man who loved Karen deeply with all his heart.

Edgar Hollingsworth.

Chapter 37

Sergio continued interrogating Lex, and Hayley knew his questions would probably go on for another hour, and, frankly, she just didn't want to wait. She knew Lex had just picked his boss Edgar Hollingsworth up at the airport, so chances were he was at the estate right now.

She squeezed her brother's arm and he turned to her.

"Keep listening," Hayley whispered. "I'll be right back."

"Where are you going?" he said, a bit too loudly. "This is getting so good."

"I have to take care of something."

And she slipped out the door of the file room, ducked her head down so Sergio didn't see her sneaking past his office, and headed out the door.

Outside, she texted Liddy and Mona with the news that Karen Applebaum's secret lover was none other than Edgar Hollingsworth, and that she was driving over to his house right now to ask him a few questions.

And then she got in her car, and drove straight back over to the estate. The grounds were deserted when she pulled through the front gate. She appreciated the fact that the super rich who owned mansions and estates on the island rarely had security or guards or gates that were locked up tight to prevent trespassers. No, on this sleepy island, locals didn't much care about the comings and goings of the top one percent.

Hayley parked her car in front of Lex's cottage, and walked down the dirt path to the main house. She rang the bell but didn't get an answer. She looked around. The wind was picking up, there was a chill in the air, and the waves pounded against the rocks with a restless vengeance. She heard a banging sound and circled around the house toward the back to check it out. She spotted an expensive sport fishing boat, a Sea Ray 280 Sundancer, which rocked furiously in the water, slamming against the wooden dock, just east of the house, and was the source of the banging.

She decided to try the back door and headed up the lawn to the enclosed porch—with spectacular views of the ocean and surrounding islands—when she spotted Edgar Hollingsworth sitting in a rocker, reading the paper. The windows were open, so the noise of the surf and wind had drowned out her knocking on the front door.

She made her way to the screen door of the porch. She didn't want to give the old man a heart attack by rapping on it, so she cleared her throat and said, "Mr. Hollingsworth?"

She had to repeat it a few times before Edgar,

who was obviously hard of hearing, lowered his paper and looked around curiously.

"Over here, Mr. Hollingsworth," she said, waving and smiling.

"Who's there?"

"It's me. Hayley Powell. I'm a friend of Lex's."

He squinted his eyes, trying to focus, and then, finally, a look of recognition crossed his face, and the tension melted away. "Oh, yes, the pretty young woman who ran him over."

At least there was nothing wrong with his memory.

"You've made quite an impression on dear old Lex," the old man said, chuckling. "I'm afraid he's not here. He had to go run an errand."

She didn't expect Lex to have told his boss he was being hauled in for questioning about a murder case.

"Actually, I came to talk to you, if you're not busy," Hayley said.

Edgar looked at her, somewhat surprised, but then put down his cocktail and made an attempt to stand up from the rocker. "Yes, of course. Come in."

"Don't get up," Hayley said as she pulled open the screen door and entered the back porch.

Edgar looked relieved, and fell back in his rocker. He just wasn't as spry as he used to be. Although if she were alive, Karen Applebaum might dispute that assessment.

"Come. Sit down," Edgar said cheerily. "Can I make you a drink? I've got some really good gin. We could make those Orange Blossoms you wrote about in your column."

"No, thank you," Hayley said, for two reasons. One, she didn't want the poor man to have to try and get up again and shuffle into the house to make a cocktail. And two, if he was the one who poisoned Karen's clam chowder, she didn't want him putting the same cyanide in her drink.

"How can I help you?" he asked, looking like a sweet doddering grandfather in an oversized gray wool sweater, rather than a millionaire businessman who had just returned from big-time board meetings in New York.

He winked at her. "You want me to give Lex some time off so you two love birds can plan a romantic getaway?"

"Actually, we're not the couple I've come to discuss with you. This is about you. And Karen."

His sweet smile froze on his face. Hayley could tell he was contemplating whether or not he should deny his relationship with Karen, but Edgar was a smart man, and he knew he had been caught.

"I see," he said, clearing his throat. "So what do you want to know?"

"I'm sure you're aware that a lot of people in town think I had something to do with Karen's death, since we had a nasty dispute over a recipe, and then she died. Eating a bowl of clam chowder laced with cyanide."

"Yes, and I never took any of that idle gossip seriously," Edgar said. "I'm confident the police will find the real culprit. And when they do, I'm going to do everything in my power to make sure he or she pays."

Hayley noticed a tear fall down the side of

Edgar's wrinkled face. He reached into his sweater and pulled out a handkerchief and wiped it away.

He really did love her.

"Why did you keep your relationship a secret?"

"Because it's nobody's damn business, and I didn't want people chattering about it, and saying nasty things about Karen because of our age difference, and the fact that I have money."

More tears welled up in Edgar's eyes. He raised the handkerchief again and blew his nose. The honking sound startled Hayley momentarily.

"So you weren't hiding it because you were afraid the police might suspect you?"

Edgar laughed. "Of course not. I could never have touched a hair on Karen's pretty head. She meant the world to me. We were going to be married. How could I possibly harm her in any way?"

Hayley listened to Edgar, the tears now streaming down his cheeks, his voice cracking, stopping occasionally to fight back the sobs. She could almost hear his heart breaking as he spoke about believing he would never have a second chance at love after his beloved wife had died of cancer almost fifteen years ago. How he expected to live out his days surrounded by his only grandson and the people who worked for him, his life an empty void, a shell of the man he once was. Never again had he expected to be a man in love.

He thought that part of his life was over forever until he met Karen at a local charity function last year. He had been reading her column for years without ever having met her. He thought from her picture in the paper every week that she was attractive, but never in his wildest imagination did he think that when the two of them would finally come together it would be electric. And he knew deep down he had the opportunity for happiness once again. But then, just as cruelly, Karen was taken away from him, too.

Hayley knew he was speaking from the heart. Edgar broke down and lowered his face into the crook of his arm, crying into his thick bulky gray sweater, and Hayley felt awkward just sitting there next to him.

So she stood up and put a hand on his shoulder to comfort him.

"Please, I'd like to be alone now, if you don't mind," he choked out, waving her away with his free hand.

"I understand," Hayley said. "I am so, so sorry."

She quietly slipped back out the screen door, feeling awful that she had dredged up his wrenching pain all over again. She knew Edgar Hollingsworth was telling the truth. He couldn't have touched a hair on Karen's head. So who did?

Hayley walked to her car, going over all the facts in her mind. Karen didn't meet with Ted Rivers to discuss a prenup to protect her own money. She wanted to know about a prenup because Edgar's lawyers were probably insisting upon one, and maybe she was trying to find a way to get around it. Because one thing was clear—although Edgar was deeply in love with Karen, she was marrying him for his money. The love notes to Lex proved that. She was holding out hope that Lex would come around, and in the meantime, why not marry a millionaire and be set for life? Especially since, if Edgar died—and he was already in his eighties—if she found a way to circumvent a prenuptial agreement, she would get it all. And perhaps she cynically thought that if she had all that money, Lex might change his mind.

Hayley knew that would never have happened, because she was now convinced Lex was a stand-up guy.

One to whom she owed a huge apology.

So if Karen were planning to end up with the bulk of the Hollingsworth estate, then there was only one person who stood to lose if that happened. Of course!

That's when Hayley noticed that one of the doors to the four-car garage adjacent to the main house was open and inside was a parked car. It looked similar to the one that stalked her in the park a few nights earlier. She walked over to the garage and looked at it.

It could be the one. She had been so frightened and confused by the attack, she never really registered any pertinent information that would help track it down. But then she noticed the side mirror.

The glass was missing.

One of the bullets from her assailant's gun had smashed out the mirror.

It was the same car!

She sensed someone behind her. Before she could react, there was a cracking sound as something hit her in the back of the head and everything went dark.

Chapter 38

The throbbing in her head made Hayley want to slip back into unconsciousness, but there was an imminent sense of danger, and she forced herself to open her eyes.

Everything was blurry, and it was hard for her to focus, and she felt nauseous, almost as if she were seasick.

There was an incessant chugging sound and the smell of gasoline.

Her head was resting against what she thought was an orange pillow, but as she tried to sit up, she realized it was a life jacket.

She was on the floor of a boat.

It was the Sundancer, which had been tied to the dock back at the Hollingsworth estate.

Hayley lifted her head. She was out at sea, Mount Desert Island a tiny speck in the distance fading away to nothing as they continued their journey. When she turned around to see who was driving the boat, she shuddered.

There he was. A sick, satisfied smile on his face.

Travis Hollingsworth. Edgar's grandson.

"Time to get up, sleepy head," he said, smirking.

Hayley rubbed her head. She was in a lot of pain. She noticed next to her feet a tire iron. It didn't belong on a boat, so she surmised that was probably what he'd used to knock her out.

She tried to stand up but it was impossible. Her feet were tied to sandbags.

Hayley looked ahead at the dark and foreboding vast ocean. The boat kept cutting through the choppy waves, heading farther and farther out. Travis's plan was suddenly clear. He had no intention of ever letting her see shore again. He was going to dump her overboard, the bags dragging her down, and she would never be heard from again.

"Got it all figured out finally?"

"Yes," Hayley said, practically spitting out the word. She was kicking herself for not putting all the pieces together earlier. She might have saved herself from this fate. "Your parents died in a plane crash years ago. I remember reading about it when I was in high school."

"I was a little kid. I don't even remember them."

"It made you Edgar's sole heir. He's been spoiling you for years. You've never even had a real job. Basically you've just been biding your time waiting for him to die. Because when he does, you will become one of the richest men in Bar Harbor overnight. For doing nothing."

"That's right. And everything was going according to plan until Granddaddy started sneaking around seeing that ridiculous Anna Nicole Smith–wannabe, Karen Applebaum! I couldn't believe it!

I mean, what did he see in her? She wasn't even a stripper with platinum dyed hair and silicone enhancements! She was a mousy nothing with a stupid cooking column!"

"Some men look a little deeper," Hayley said. "But not you. Your grandfather falling in love wasn't something you had counted on. Your entire future was in jeopardy. You were scared as hell you would lose everything, so you had to act," Hayley said.

"That's right. And then you came along. Perfect timing," he said.

"You knew Karen and I were feuding. It was all over town. So you showed up at Karen's house, I'm guessing on the pretense of making peace with her and to toast her upcoming nuptials to Edgar."

"Good guess."

"Karen's Kitty Cam was set up in the living room so it didn't catch you two in the kitchen where you spiked her clam chowder with cyanide."

"She was so happy for me to try it. I pretended to have a spoonful when her back was turned. I raved about it. In her mind we were suddenly allies. She had no idea. And then she dove into her own bowl, gulping it down while I watched. And after a few minutes, she started having convulsions and her face turned white, and she clawed at her throat, and I'd be lying if I didn't say I enjoyed watching every damn minute of it, watching as she sank to the floor and stopped breathing. I felt so relieved she was finally out of the picture."

"And then you sent me an e-mail, presumably from Karen, asking me to come over," Hayley said.

"That was your way to get me to the crime scene so I would automatically fall under suspicion."

Travis smiled. "Worked like a charm."

"You wiped your prints off Karen's computer to cover your tracks. And later, you managed to quietly slip a vial of the poison in my bag to further implicate me. It was at the funeral! You bumped into me on purpose! It gave you the opportunity to plant the cyanide on me!"

"All the fingers were pointing at you. Nobody knew Granddaddy and Karen were dating except for a few of the employees at the estate, Lex included, but they weren't going to talk if they wanted to keep their jobs. The cops would never make any kind of connection."

"But then Edgar got sentimental and sent flowers to Karen's funeral, and he had Lex place the order," Hayley said.

"Yes," Travis said, clenching his fists angrily. "Stupid, stupid, stupid! I knew you were hell-bent on clearing your name and that you were running all over town asking questions and it made me nervous. I was afraid you would trace those flowers back to Lex and then to Granddaddy and then to me and I couldn't let that happen."

"So you followed me into the park that night when I was jogging with my dog and took a few potshots at me hoping to scare me off," Hayley said.

"Yeah, I wasn't really trying to kill you. Honestly, I didn't think you would put it all together. But now you have. And so it's time for you to disappear."

Travis cut the engine. The boat floated aimlessly in the water, bobbing up and down.

Hayley's stomach was doing flip-flops.

She was dizzy. Her head still ached. Her throat was dry and she felt weak.

She didn't have a lot of fight left in her.

Travis stepped away from the wheel and stomped over to her, towering over her, staring down, his smile gone, his face now a reflection of brutal determination. He reached down and grabbed Hayley.

She screamed.

Chapter 39

Travis was young and muscled and strong. Hayley was no match for him. She went to scratch at his eyes, but he anticipated the move and grabbed her by the wrists. Then he spun her around, and locked his arms around her, pinning her. He dragged her closer to the edge of the boat. Hayley leaned forward and then threw her head back as hard as she could.

The back of her head slammed into Travis's face. She heard a crunching sound like Travis's nose breaking and he growled in pain. He was sniffling, like his nose was bleeding, but Hayley couldn't be sure.

Then she heard his low scratchy voice whispering in her ear.

"Don't fight it. You're already dead."

This only made Hayley fight harder. She kicked up her feet and pressed them against the side of the boat as he tried to get her close enough to hurl her body overboard. He gripped her tighter, like a sack of potatoes, and leaned his weight forward, trying to force her legs to give out so he could manage her more easily.

But this proved impossible, and finally he released her.

Hayley stumbled, and fell back down to the deck. She got on her hands and knees and scurried away from him, trying to drag the sandbags along behind her.

When she spun around to see where Travis was, he was fast approaching, the tire iron clenched in his fist. He had decided she would be easier to dispose of if she was unconscious. Or already dead.

He raised the iron, ready to crash it down upon *her* head.

Hayley covered the top of her head with her arms in a desperate attempt to protect herself.

Suddenly she heard the sound of an engine. It was faint at first, but with each passing second it got louder and louder.

Travis heard it, too. He lowered the tire iron and strained to hear where it was coming from.

Hayley pushed away from Travis, and scrambled to her feet in time to see a lobster boat cut through the thick fog. She recognized it immediately.

It was Mona's boat!

And she could make out Captain Mona, behind the wheel, with one of her kids strapped to her chest in a moss-colored baby carrier. Liddy was onboard, too, hunched over the side, throwing up, horribly seasick.

Travis wasn't about to give up. He raised the

tire iron again, in one last attempt to crush Hayley's skull.

Mona saw what was happening and threw forward the throttle, and her lobster boat barreled into the side of Travis's Sundancer.

Both he and Hayley lost their balance and toppled over from the impact.

Travis still held onto the tire iron, and wasn't about to be stopped by a couple of soccer moms. He crawled back to his feet, trying to get a solid foothold, brandishing his weapon, his eyes filled with fury, ready to cause some serious damage.

But Mona was having none of it. By now, she had unstrapped her kid and handed him off to Liddy, and was leaping onto the Sundancer with a lobster buoy. Before Travis had a chance to turn his head to face her, she brought the buoy down on his skull so hard, he dropped the tire iron and it clanged to the deck of the boat.

Before Hayley had a chance to take a breath, Travis Hollingsworth pitched forward and collapsed facedown, unconscious.

"You all right?" Mona asked, dropping the buoy and helping Hayley back to her feet.

"Yes. Am I glad to see you guys."

Liddy was still in the midst of projectile vomiting into the sea while holding Mona's kid under one arm.

"I told her to stay ashore but you know how she is," Mona said, smiling. "Can't miss anything."

"How did you find me?"

"We got worried after you sent that text and we didn't want you going over to the Hollingsworth estate alone," Mona said. "So we drove over in my truck just in time to see Travis pulling away from the dock in his boat. Mr. Hollingsworth told us you had left, but your car was still there, so we put two and two together. The only way we could have missed you leaving was if you left by boat, so we figured you were with Travis. So we drove over to the town pier where my boat was anchored and set out to cut him off."

"You were just in time, believe me," Hayley said, hugging her.

More boats approached. Coast Guard boats. Sergio stood at the bow of one of them, clutching a bullhorn.

"Hayley, are you all right?" he called.

Hayley gave Sergio a thumbs-up.

"We called him, too, and he decided you were important enough to bring in his Coast Guard buddies," Mona said.

"Wow, I feel so special."

"It isn't every day a local celebrity gets kidnapped."

"I just have one question," Hayley said.

"Shoot," Mona said.

"Why on earth did you bring little Reese with you?" Hayley said, pointing to Mona's youngest— at least for another few months—boy.

"Do you know how hard it is getting a babysitter on such short notice? If I took the time to call around, you'd already be fish food."

"Can somebody please take him? I think he just took a dump in his diaper and I'm already sick enough," Liddy wailed as she held the crying baby out as far from her nose as she possibly could.

Hayley was more than happy to climb aboard

Mona's lobster boat and take Mona's youngest away from Liddy, who leaned over the side again to wretch some more.

Hayley watched as Sergio and a few Coast Guard officers boarded the Sundancer and handcuffed a still-unconscious Travis before carrying him to the side and handing him over to some sailors who hauled him aboard the Coast Guard vessel.

Hayley bounced baby Reese in her arms, relieved and happy, and secure in the knowledge that this whole nightmare was finally over.

Chapter 40

Hayley was front page news in the next issue of the *Island Times*. Actually, she was front page news in the *Bar Harbor Herald*, and in most of the state of Maine's other major newspapers as well. The sordid details of Karen Applebaum's murder and the fact that the perpetrator had such a famous last name as Hollingsworth drew a lot of attention to the case.

And Hayley's role in unmasking the killer was played up to the hilt.

Her phone rang off the hook with requests for interviews, but Hayley declined all of them, even her own paper's, which didn't quite sit well with Sal. But he understood she wanted to try and maintain as low a profile as she possibly could.

Gemma and Dustin, on the other hand, relished their roles as the offspring of such a famed kitchen-loving crime solver. Gemma made no secret of the fact that she had accompanied her mother to the flower shop and was instrumental in helping her crack the case, while Dustin had begun work on a

new comic book hero who was a mother by day and
caped crusader by night. His drawings of the fear-
less heroine bore an uncanny resemblance to
Hayley, who, according to the author, "Saved the
world to put food on the table!" He was counting
on his mother's newfound notoriety to help him
get his first comic book published. Hayley admired
her son's ingenuity.

Liddy was another one who played up her role
as part of the investigative team. Unlike Hayley,
she gave interview after interview, detailing her
suspicions about Travis Hollingsworth all along,
and how she was ever present and gently pushed
Hayley in the right direction.

Mona, on the other hand, had no use for public-
ity of any kind, and hung up the phone on anyone
who dared to call and interrupt her watching
repeats of Discovery Channel's *Deadliest Catch*.
She had no interest in the hysteria surrounding
the solution to Karen's murder and refused to
speak about her thrilling rescue of Hayley on the
high seas.

Sal was over the moon because thanks to Hayley's
connection to the murder and the fact that she
was a regular columnist, sales of the *Island Times*
shot through the roof. He was absolutely giddy
that he had lucked into such a coup, but that still
wasn't enough for him to cough up more money
for Hayley's extra workload and newfound star
status.

Like Mona, Bruce Linney chose to ignore all the
hullabaloo, but for an entirely different reason.
Everyone knew he was dying inside, being the town's
self-proclaimed "premier crime reporter" and not

having cracked the case himself. It was a blow to his reputation, though he tried to cover his devastation by trumpeting his latest scoop, snagging an interview with the juvenile delinquent who broke into Razor Rick's Barber Shop.

And then there was Lex Bansfield.

Poor Lex had vanished after all the speculation about his involvement in the Karen Applebaum case. He was extremely embarrassed about the details of his past criminal record in Vermont making the rounds in town, so he stuck to his chores on the Hollingsworth estate, and spent much of his free time comforting his boss, Edgar Hollingsworth, who was heartbroken over his grandson's betrayal, and whose poor health got even worse over the stress.

So that long talked-about date was probably out of the question.

But Hayley had been wrong about a lot of things during the course of her amateur investigation and, as it turned out, she was wrong about Lex, too.

Her heart skipped a beat when he strolled into the front office of the *Island Times* a few days later, and marched right up to Hayley's desk.

"So when are we finally going out?" he asked.

Hayley just sat there, trying to get over the shock of seeing him hover over her, his arms folded, waiting for her to answer him.

"You mean on a date?"

"Of course I mean on a date. Don't you think you've kept me waiting long enough?"

"Well, I . . . it's just that I thought . . ."

Hayley noticed Bruce standing in the doorway

to the back offices, watching her intently, waiting expectantly for her to turn Lex down flat.

She almost did, because she was still a little uncomfortable with his checkered past in Vermont.

But here was this guy, this handsome and low-key man, who was putting himself out there, taking the risk of getting shot down yet again, and she asked herself why.

Maybe it was because Lex Bansfield really did like her. Maybe he sensed something special could develop between them, which was why he was so persistent. And if she wasn't smart enough to see it herself, she might as well put her trust in him.

"You think you can get us a table at Havana tonight, say around seven?"

"Already done."

"My, you're awfully confident."

"That's because I figure what are the odds you'll get arrested again before we have a chance to drive to the restaurant?"

Touché.

Hayley glanced at Bruce, who glowered, as the blood drained from his face.

"Pick you up at six forty-five," Lex said, and then he bounded out the door.

"Please don't say a word, Bruce," Hayley said.

"I'm sorry, Hayley, but like I said, I don't trust the guy."

"I know. And I appreciate your concern. But after thinking it over, I believe everybody deserves a second chance."

"Fine. I get it. So when are you going to give me one?"

Before she could ask Bruce what he was talking

about, he was gone. He had disappeared into the back.

Hayley had no intention of getting involved in an office romance. She had just lived through enough drama for the entire year, what with being accused of murder and nearly being dumped into the ocean by a murderous heir.

No, she needed to indulge in her favorite pastime—lounging on the couch watching the Lifetime Movie Network, with Leroy snoring softly into her oversize sweatshirt as she taste-tested a variety of dessert recipes for the column's seventh course.

Oh, no. Her column.

She still hadn't written her column.

The Karen Applebaum tribute.

But now, with all the questions answered, it didn't seem so hard. It was true Karen had resented her for being fresh competition and had made her life miserable by accusing her of stealing recipes, but had Karen lived, Hayley was sure they would have settled into a healthy rivalry, all the brouhaha would have calmed down, and perhaps in time, the two of them might have even become friends.

Stranger things have happened.

Hayley began typing. And she was happy to be focusing on her column. Her days as an amateur sleuth were officially over.

Really.

What were the odds of her stumbling across another dead body?

Island Food & Spirits

by
Hayley Powell

Well, we've finally reached the last course of
our seven course meal, which, as I'm sure is no
surprise to you, dear reader, happens to be my absolute favorite. The dessert course. I am so grateful you have stayed with me through these rather
action packed weeks, and I appreciate your un-
wavering support during this very trying time.

This all began with a huge misunderstanding
between me and the late Karen Applebaum. It was
bound to happen with both of us being at different newspapers and thrown together as competi-
tors in a town where having two newspapers can
stir up quite a spirit of competition among folks.

But I know in my heart if Karen were still with
us, we would have eventually resolved our differences and coexisted with mutual admiration and
respect.

Because at the end of the day, we shared a
common passion.

Food.

It was what drove us apart, and it was what I am

convinced would have brought us together as friends. There are so many reasons we cook. To calm our nerves after a hectic day at the office. To serve our community, like with the recent library bake sale. But most importantly, and I think Karen would agree, we cook to show our love. To our family. To our loved ones. To our neighbors at a time of need. For those of us who love to cook, it's a bond we share forever.

Some may believe that since Karen is physically no longer with us, her voice has been silenced. Well, I couldn't disagree more. Karen will always be with us. And she will be speaking to us for generations through her recipes. The ones we all couldn't wait to read every time the *Bar Harbor Herald* hit the stands.

So for our final course, I would like to share one of Karen's favorites, her cherries jubilee pie. I'm sure her many loyal fans out there remember this one as a true Applebaum classic.

And speaking of loyal fans, I received a letter today from one of Karen's most devoted readers. He suggested this particular recipe close out our seven course meal. He didn't want his name mentioned, but you know me, I can't keep a secret. So I dedicate this column to Karen's ex-husband, Martin, who, despite what you may have heard, felt blessed to have known her. And I share with you his closing words about Karen, a fitting tribute if you ask me: "To know Karen was to love her, but to love her cooking was one step from worshipping something special from above."

Karen's Cherries Jubilee Pie

   1 9-inch baked pie crust (your favorite pie
      crust will do)
   1 quart pitted sweet cherries
   ½ cup white sugar
   3 teaspoons cornstarch
   dash of salt
   1 teaspoon fresh lemon juice

Place sweet cherries in medium-size bowl. With a
spoon, push at the cherries to extract the juice,
and drain juice into a saucepan.

Reserve your cherries. Add sugar, cornstarch, and
salt to the cherry juice in saucepan. Stir to blend.

Cook and stir over medium heat until clear and
thickened. Remove from heat and stir in lemon
juice. Cool to lukewarm.

Fold your cherries in to a cooled glaze. Chill to
rethicken mixture. Transfer to baked pie shell.

Chill until firm. Top with homemade whipped
cream.

Tonight's Menu

Appetizer
Maine Crab Stuffed Mushrooms

Soup
New England Clam Chowder

Salad
Strawberry and Spinach Salad

Sorbet
Mango Orange Sorbet

Entreé
Creamy Chicken Marsala

Pasta
Sausage, Spinach, and Cheese Ravioli

Dessert
Karen's Cherries Jubilee Pie

Hayley Powell Will Return In . . .
Death of a Country Fried Redneck

Coming in November 2012!

Chapter 1

Hayley Powell didn't think she was screaming that loud. But when her boss, Sal Moretti, came barreling out of his office, strawberry yogurt dripping down the front of his light blue short-sleeve dress shirt, angrily pointing a pudgy finger at her and blaming her for scaring him so badly he spilled his breakfast all over himself, she finally managed to shut her mouth and contain herself.

It was a natural reaction. This was huge news. Her all-time favorite singer—four-time Grammy winner and last year's Sexiest Man Alive, according to *People* magazine—country music hottie Wade Springer was coming to town to perform two charity concerts. How could she not be screaming?

However, if she'd had the slightest clue at the time that Wade's imminent arrival to her little hometown of Bar Harbor, Maine, would lead to murder, she definitely would not have been so excited.

But right now, without the power of hindsight,

Hayley was in a joyous and celebratory mood. Hayley jumped up from her desk, situated in the front office at the *Island Times* newspaper, scurried into the small bathroom in the back, and quickly returned with a paper towel. She began frantically dabbing at the bits of strawberry that rested in the crease of Sal's shirt just above his ample belly.

"I'm sorry, Sal, I'll go to the store and get you another yogurt," Hayley said apologetically.

"Forget the yogurt. I want another shirt," Sal bellowed. "My wife spent almost twenty dollars on this at Walmart."

Hayley suspected Sal would not be caught at New York's Fashion Week anytime soon.

"I don't get what's the big deal about some Nashville crooner coming to Bar Harbor," Sal grunted. "Big name celebrities come here every summer. We've had the president of the United States bring his family here. Martha Stewart owns a home on the other side of the island. I've never even heard of this guy!"

"You mean to tell me you've never listened to his number one hit, 'I'm Not a Wife Beater, I Just Wear One'?"

"I don't listen to much music. I'm a newsman. That's why I prefer NPR," Sal said, snorting. He grabbed at a tiny piece of strawberry that Hayley had missed and popped it in his mouth.

Sal snatched the paper towel out of Hayley's hand and continued to wipe the yogurt off his shirt himself.

Hayley smiled and dutifully scooted back behind her desk. She scrolled down the e-mail on her computer announcing Wade's upcoming Bar Harbor appearances.

"Wade has always been committed to the environment. He even wrote the theme song for that Oscar-winning documentary about the melting glacier ice, remember that? I loved that song. He sang about the planet being like a cocktail left on the bar too long and how the ice cubes have all melted away," Hayley said to her half-listening boss, who was now pouring himself a cup of coffee. "Anyway, when the College of the Atlantic heard he was going on tour in the Northeast, they wrote him a letter requesting he do a benefit concert to help raise funds for their ocean research department. My friend Jamie McGowan—he's a professor there—sent me an e-mail telling me Wade's people just confirmed the dates. You know Jamie. His wife owns the ice cream shop that has the pumpkin spice flavor you love so much . . ."

"Is there a point to this story?"

"Well, no, Jamie just wanted me to be the first to know about Wade Springer performing at the Criterion Theatre."

Sal perked up. "Wait, so we have a scoop?"

"I could go get us each one. You know how much I love the salt caramel."

Sal sighed. "No, Hayley. A news scoop! We've got the story that this singer is coming to town before the *Herald* does?"

"Yes, Jamie wanted me to be the first to know because he knows I'm such a fan."

"Have one of the reporters write something up so we can post it on our website before word gets out and the *Herald* beats us to the punch."

"All our reporters are out covering the city council meeting."

"Then you do it."

Hayley wasn't a reporter. She was just the office manager who wrote a regular cooking column called "Island Food & Spirits," where she shared anything on her mind along with a few tasty food and cocktail recipes.

Sal could read the doubt in her face.

"Just because you write about seafood casseroles and rhubarb pies doesn't make you any less of a journalist. And a journalist drops everything he or she is doing to alert the public to any breaking news."

"Got it!" Hayley said, as she began typing furiously. She noticed Sal heading for the door. "Where are you going?"

"I'm starving. I'm going to get some blueberry pancakes at Jordan's."

Hayley raised an eyebrow, amused.

"Don't give me that look. I didn't say I was the one who has to drop everything. I'm the editor. I delegate. I pay *you* to drop everything!"

Sal marched out of the office.

Hayley quickly typed a few sentences, quoting an unnamed source at the college, since she didn't want Jamie to get into trouble for talking out of school, literally, and then she posted the item on the paper's website.

Within seconds, the office phone rang and Hayley picked it up. "Island Times, this is Hayley."

There was loud screaming on the other end of the receiver. Even louder than her own high-pitched shrieking earlier.

Hayley knew exactly who it was.

"Hi, Liddy," she said, smiling.

"Is it true? Is he really coming?"

"Yes! Can you believe it?"

More screaming. From both of them. It was like when they were teenage girls and ran away from home together, taking a Greyhound bus to Boston to sneak into a Backstreet Boys concert. They made it as far as Bangor, just an hour outside of town, before their parents intercepted them.

Liddy was one of Hayley's closest friends. They had grown up together. Their lives diverged a bit when Hayley found herself divorced and struggling to raise two kids alone, while Liddy made a big splash in the local real estate market during the boom, and was now tooling around town in a Mercedes and flying off to Manhattan every month for retail therapy.

"We have to meet him!" Liddy squealed. "I'm on the board of directors of the Criterion Theatre so I'm sure I can arrange it."

"Liddy, are you serious? That would be like . . . a dream come true." Hayley couldn't allow herself to believe that it was even possible.

"Of course. And now that he's divorced from that hillbilly whore, the one who can barely carry a tune—what's her name?"

"Stacy Jo Stanton," Hayley offered.

Actually Stacy Jo was a successful country singer in her own right, but Liddy just couldn't bring herself to admit it.

"Right. Her. Well, now Wade's available again so he might be in the market for some female companionship while he's in town, and since you're dating Lex Bansfield and I'm one hundred percent single, that someone could be me!"

Liddy was right. Hayley was dating Lex Bansfield, the handsome caretaker of one of the multimillion dollar oceanfront estates, but she wasn't sure where that was going, or how serious it was, and she certainly didn't consider herself partnered at this point. But realistically, Hayley knew that neither she nor Liddy stood a chance in hell of ever dating someone like Wade Springer. Liddy loved to get carried away sometimes.

"I had a dream the other night when I fell asleep listening to one of Wade's CDs on my iPod," Liddy said, taking a long pause for dramatic effect. "I dreamed that someone was spooning me from behind and that when I opened my eyes, I was wearing one of Wade's signature ten-gallon white cowboy hats and he was snuggling me, one strong arm pulling me into his buffed, furry chest, and in this deep voice, he said, 'Mornin' sunshine' and I just . . . Oh God, it's so hot in my office! What's the weather like outside?"

"Forty-two degrees. It's not your office. It's you," Hayley said, laughing.

"Oh, before I forget, I read online that Wade just fired his personal chef who was cooking for him while he's on tour."

"What? Why?"

"The guy bought some bad shrimp and gave everybody food poisoning. Luckily, Wade was doing a sound check and didn't eat any, but four crew members were hospitalized. Isn't that good news?"

"I don't see how that's good news," Hayley said.

"He fired his chef! There's a rumor the tour organizers are planning to hire someone local to fill in while they're here on the island."

"I know where this is going. There's no way I'd ever get the job."

"Why not? You're an award-winning cooking columnist!"

"I got third place. And there were only five columns nominated."

"It's all about perception. You're still award winning! Now don't dismiss this opportunity like so many others."

Hayley chose not to press Liddy on what other opportunities Liddy believed she'd dismissed. That was another discussion. Right now the discussion was all about bringing Liddy back down to earth.

"Okay, let me think about it."

"There's no time to think. We both know Wade's favorite dish is country fried chicken. He's southern, after all. You need to write about that in your next column. Show these guys you've got what it takes to satisfy Wade's palette."

Hayley thought about it for a second and realized Liddy had a good point. Why not write about Wade's local concert and include a recipe for his favorite dish? Chances are he would probably never see it, but what would be the harm? And if someone close to him did read it, then maybe there was a slight possibility that she would be considered. It certainly was worth a shot.

"I'm hanging up now. Go write," Liddy said, and then there was a click.

Hayley was jammed with phone calls and managerial duties at the office until quitting time, so she didn't have time to write her column. It would just have to wait until she fed her kids dinner and took her dog, Leroy, for a walk.

When she arrived home, Leroy, her dirty white Shih Tzu, with a pronounced underbite, was running around in circles, bursting with excitement over her arrival. Much like Hayley's own reaction to the news that Wade Springer was coming to town.

Hayley's two kids, however, fifteen-year-old Gemma and thirteen-year-old Dustin, were nowhere to be seen. Neither had *ever* displayed even a fraction of the excitement over their mother coming home from work that Leroy did. Ever.

She assumed they were both out with friends.

Suddenly a screech came from upstairs.

Scratch that. Gemma was home.

Hayley grabbed her ears to cover them. Lord. Where did Gemma get that loud ear-splitting screaming from?

Gemma came pounding down the stairs, the phone pressed to her ear. Her face was beet red and Hayley noticed the hand holding the receiver was shaking.

"Honey, are you all right?" Hayley asked.

"Shhhh, Mom, please! This is important!"

She was all right.

Gemma turned her back to Hayley and whispered frantically into the phone, a few excited giggles escaping every few sentences.

After giving Leroy a doggie treat, Hayley filled a pot with water and placed it on the stove burner and turned the heat up to high. She had made some of her homemade spaghetti sauce the night before, so a quick pasta dinner would be easy to prepare and give her more time to get to work on her Wade Springer tribute column.

Gemma finally finished her call.

She screamed again.

Leroy, startled, dashed out of the room and hid behind the couch.

"Mom, Reid Jennings aked me out on a date! I can't believe it! Reid Jennings!"

"I'm so happy for you! Who's Reid Jennings?"

"He's a new kid. His parents just moved here this year. They bought that seafood restaurant on the pier after the last owner skipped town."

Hayley had heard of the family, but didn't know much about them.

"Anyway, Reid's an artist and a really, really talented one," Gemma gushed.

"He paints?"

"No. He's a singer–songwriter and he's playing at that new-agey coffeehouse next to the organic food market on Cottage Street, and he asked me to come tonight and hear him perform one of his original songs!"

"So it's not really a date. He just wants to fill the seats."

Gemma gave her mother a withering look.

"Way to pop my balloon," Gemma said, sighing. "Is it so hard for you to allow me this one ounce of happiness?"

"I'm sorry," Hayley said. "I didn't realize your life was so full of disappointments and despair."

"Don't count me in for dinner. I couldn't possibly eat now. Oh, and Dustin's at Cameron's house so he won't be eating either."

Hayley immediately shut off the burner and dumped the pot of water into the sink. She turned to see Gemma halfway up the stairs to her room.

"So how old is he?"

"I don't know. A little older than me."

"How much older?"

"He's a senior."

"Seventeen?"

"Eighteen, okay? Come on, Mom, enough with the third degree."

"I'm not convinced it's wise for you to be dating an older boy."

"Stop being so overprotective. I'm old enough to make my own decisions," Gemma said, continuing up the stairs to her room.

"So what time do we have to be there?" Hayley asked.

Gemma stopped cold. "Be where?"

"The coffeehouse. We're not staying late, because I have a column to write."

"Mom, you're not invited."

"It's a public event. And I'm sure Reid will appreciate an extra body there to help fill the house."

"Why are you doing this to me?"

"Because I don't like the idea of you dating someone I've never met, and since I know you—and that you will never bring him around to meet me—this is a nice alternative to me actually crashing one of your real dates."

Gemma opened her mouth to protest, but then thought better of it. Her mother was right. Her meeting Reid in a public place was much better than her "coincidentally" showing up at a restaurant where they were having dinner, or volunteering to chaperone a school dance and hovering too close to them while they slow-danced.

"Fine!" Gemma sighed. "But we have to be there by seven-thirty."

Hayley didn't like the fact that she would be out late. She just wanted to pour herself a glass of red wine and write her Wade Springer column. But her kids came first. She had to do this.

The coffeehouse was half-full when they arrived on time at seven-thirty. Lots of teenagers sipped lattes and flavored teas and were slouched over wooden tables talking. Hayley guessed she was the oldest one in the room.

Gemma had dressed to the nines and stood out from the others, who were in jeans and T-shirts. Hayley refused to sit alone at a table in the back, much to Gemma's chagrin, and joined her at a table up front directly in front of the microphone that had been set up.

The coffeehouse owner, a frizzy-haired woman in her late twenties wearing a bulky wool sweater and jeans skirt, stepped in front of the mic and gave a quick rundown of upcoming events before turning it over to Reid.

Hayley almost gasped out loud when Reid entered from the back, a guitar slung around his shoulder. No wonder Gemma was so googly-eyed and excited over the attention he had shown her. The kid was incredibly handsome with the face and body of a male model. His brown hair was scraggly and mussed and he wore thick glasses that hid his eyes, but otherwise he was perfect.

Hayley glanced over at Gemma, who was the only one wildly clapping. It took a moment for everyone else to catch up. After most people stopped applauding, Hayley had to physically restrain her daughter from clapping anymore, so Reid could start his song.

Reid launched into his number, and Hayley was surprised by what a soothing, melodic voice he possessed. He also played the guitar well, and Hayley noticed he quickly had the crowd in the palm of his hand.

When it was over, Gemma jumped to her feet, forcing everyone else to haul their butts up out of their chairs to give Reid a standing ovation. Reid looked over at Gemma and gave her a wink.

Yeah, the kid was cute. Probably a heartbreaker, too. But Gemma was right. Hayley had to let her make her own decisions and her own mistakes.

Hayley and Gemma hung around long enough for the crowd to thin out and Reid to finish accepting accolades for his performance from his friends.

Finally, when the coffeehouse was nearly emptied out, Reid ambled over and gave Gemma a warm hug.

"Thanks for coming," Reid said with a smile that lit up the room.

Hayley had to gently grab Gemma by the elbow to stop her from swooning.

"This must be your sister," Reid said with a straight face, nodding to Hayley.

The easiest line in the book to impress a girl's mother. But damned if it wasn't effective one hundred percent of the time.

"Oh, God, no! That's my mother!" Gemma screamed.

"I had her very young," Hayley said, but then caught herself. "But I'm not condoning motherhood at an early age whatsoever."

Reid laughed.

"You were very good," Hayley said, and meant it.

"Thank you, Mrs. Powell," Reid said. "That means a lot to me."

The kid had obvious talent and a laid-back charm. He was hard to resist.

"Can I buy you two some coffee or tea?" Reid asked, slipping an arm around Gemma. Her body jerked slightly from the thrill of his touch.

"No, we need to get home. I have some work to do before tomorrow," Hayley said.

"Yes, Mom's a columnist for the *Island Times* and has left things to the last minute as usual. I, however, have already finished all my homework and would love to join you for some tea."

Checkmate.

Hayley decided not to drag Gemma home with her. The coffeehouse owner was stationed behind the counter and could serve as a makeshift chaperone. And Reid seemed like a nice enough kid. So she told Gemma to be home by ten, and turned to leave. As she was heading out the door, she heard Gemma say breathlessly, "Your singing gave me goose pimples. Look, I still have them."

Hayley walked the short distance home and wondered why girls always fall so hard for a guy

with a handsome face and a nice singing voice.
She thought Gemma would go more for someone
with brains, a whip-smart college prep kid with
plans to be a doctor or lawyer. But no, she was
obsessed with the soft-spoken artist who had a way
with a guitar.

Where did she get that from?

Oh well. No time to ponder that question. Hayley
had to get home and write about her idol Wade
Springer.